Dearest

Dearest

Jacquie Walters

MULHOLLAND BOOKS

LITTLE, BROWN AND COMPANY

NEW YORK   BOSTON   LONDON

Mulholland Books / Little, Brown and Company
Hachette Book Group
1290 Avenue of the Americas, New York, NY 10104
mulhollandbooks.com

First Edition: September 2024

Mulholland Books is an imprint of Little, Brown and Company, a division of Hachette Book Group, Inc. The Mulholland Books name and logo are trademarks of Hachette Book Group, Inc.

The publisher is not responsible for websites (or their content) that are not owned by the publisher.

The Hachette Speakers Bureau provides a wide range of authors for speaking events. To find out more, go to hachettespeakersbureau.com or email hachettespeakers@hbgusa.com.

Little, Brown and Company books may be purchased in bulk for business, educational, or promotional use. For information, please contact your local bookseller or the Hachette Book Group Special Markets Department at special.markets@hbgusa.com.

ISBN 978-0-316-58029-8

Library of Congress Control Number: 2024941342

Printing 1, 2024

LSC-C

Printed in the United States of America

For my mother, who, mercifully, did not inspire this story.

Can you hear it?

Dearest

Prologue

When Flora wakes, her mouth is so dry that the inside of her cheeks are stuck to her teeth. She carefully opens her jaw—*POP!*—and the hinge releases with a jolt of pain to her left ear. Her legs and torso are heavy, weighed down.

blankets

these are blankets

Flora is in bed.

She lies still, eyes darting for answers on the ceiling, and wills her brain to catch up to the present moment. When she tries to sit, her left shoulder screams a pulsing protest. She rolls onto her right side and pushes herself up with her palms. The room spins, and she closes her eyes to avoid hurling, though it might be inevitable given the hangover-like headache that pounds at her temples and tugs at her raw throat.

How did she get in this bed? She tries to remember. Needs to remember.

It's there—the memory—surrounding Flora like a mist, escaping the fingers of her brain as they attempt to grasp it. A word traveling rapidly along synapses until it pops onto the tongue like a gumball landing in the cup of a machine.

water

so much water

She was in the bathroom. She had desperately needed a bath. Desperately needed to get clean. She was so dirty and so, so tired.

Crying. There was crying. She remembers pulling baby Iris into the bath with her.

Iris where is Iris

Flora jerks her head toward the other side of the bed and sees that the bassinet is empty. The house is quiet, the surrounding silence oppressive. This isn't right. She should hear her six-week-old baby crying or complaining or grunting. She should at least hear the whir of the sound machine from the nursery. But in the absence of all that, she is left with a silence that only gets louder and louder as the unspeakable truth finally wiggles its way out of hibernation and blasts like a severe weather alert.

oh God what have I done to my baby

PART

1

1

Flora's nipples are infected.

She didn't even know nipples could get infected, though she probably should have guessed it given the crusting skin and yellow discharge and sharp intake of breath that accompanies even the softest caress of her loose cotton T-shirt against her bare breasts. But everyone claims this is normal. They say to push through because the first couple of weeks are brutal but then it all "clicks." So that's what she's waiting for. The *click*.

This morning, after finally admitting that breastfeeding has only gotten harder in the first three weeks of Iris's life, Flora called the hospital and scheduled a meeting with the lactation consultant. They squeezed her in for noon, which gave her two and a half hours to map out the process of leaving the house. She needed the diaper bag: diapers, wipes, cream, pacifier, pacifier clip, burp cloth, extra outfit (in case of spit-up or blowout— terms for baby accidents tend to indicate a direction of projectile, she is learning), the stroller, the travel sound machine, a muslin blanket, the carrier. She made a checklist on her phone. This was the first time she was leaving the house with Iris alone.

Apparently, it was going to take more planning than a goddamn PhD dissertation.

Now, sitting in the lactation lounge, ten minutes into the appointment, Flora is exhausted. And that's when Genevieve, the sixty-something breastfeeding guru, looks at Flora's raw, scaly nipples and says, "Those are infected."

At first, Flora is horrified, but that feeling is quickly surpassed by relief—

does this mean I can stop breastfeeding

—and then that is triumphed by immeasurable guilt.

As if reading her mind, Genevieve coos, "But not to worry. It's perfectly safe to continue nursing. I'll put in a prescription for some all-purpose nipple ointment." She smiles, one front tooth shorter than the other, and latches the baby onto Flora's left breast. Flora braces herself for the pain, but it doesn't come. Not even a tugging. Genevieve is a wizard.

Flora's insides hollow out with the realization that she's even more of a failure than she thought. She assumed Genevieve would assess the situation, shake her head in sympathy, and admit, *Looks like it'll be formula for the two of you. Iris just won't take to the breast.* But instead, when someone *else* does it, the baby latches with ease, and Flora barely feels the tiny human sucking life-force from her chest.

When Genevieve weighs Iris after the first feed, she beams with satisfaction. "She took almost two ounces on that side! She's a great eater."

Iris has betrayed her—even if she is only a three-week-old baby, she has committed treason. Before, this was something they were having trouble figuring out *together.* Now it's very clearly a *Flora* problem. Iris's instincts have kicked in just fine. It's only Flora's that are still missing in action.

Genevieve explains that no amount of pain is normal, despite what people say. Flora thinks about all the mothers who insist it gets better after the initial weeks, after the nipples "toughen up." She wonders what other helpful motherhood tidbits are actually just lies.

"Anyone else at home? A partner?" Genevieve asks.

Flora shakes her head. "My husband is deployed. He'll be back in a couple of weeks."

"That must be tough."

Flora adopts a dismissive tone. "Oh, it's not so bad. I'm used to it," she says, which is half-true, since this is her husband, Connor's, third deployment. But she has to admit it's different this time. Before, she would miss Connor, of course, but it was more like a craving. Like being deprived of chocolate. But as a single parent, not having Connor is like being deprived of a limb. She's desperate for him to get home.

Genevieve cradles Iris and holds up her little fists. "See how her fingers are balled up? That means she's still hungry. Would you like to try latching her on the other side?"

It's a fair question, but Flora doesn't want to try. She wants to fold Genevieve up into the diaper bag and take her home.

"Sure," Flora says, awkwardly pulling Iris toward her chest.

Flora does exactly as Genevieve has instructed. Exactly as the dozens of YouTube videos have directed. Exactly as she learned in the online breastfeeding class she took before Iris was born.

And still, her toes curl in her worn tennis shoes the second Iris clamps on with her X-Acto knife lips.

"That looks great," Genevieve says. "Does that feel better?"

"Much better," Flora lies, because she refuses to confess that she is a total, utter failure at something that should come so naturally. And if *this* is a challenge, what else does motherhood have in store for her?

As Iris sleeps in the living room, Flora tries to decipher the smudged Sharpie written on the foil-wrapped chicken potpie she found in the freezer. Her stepmother, Esther, prepared some meals before she and Flora's father left last week. It has only been five days, but Flora has already worked her way through them all. This potpie is the last remaining semi-nutritious food item in the house.

She was thirty-eight weeks pregnant when she went to Labor and Delivery with a bad headache. Three hours later, they were prepping her for induction. Her blood pressure was elevated, and they didn't want to take any risks.

Her dad, Michael, and Esther arrived the next morning with gifts in tow for the nurses. That was classic Esther; they were beautiful woven baskets full of snacks and lip balms and comfy socks, with thick, delicate ribbon tied artfully around the handles. Esther is a Quintessential Mom. She's that woman in Hamburger Helper commercials who makes people think, *Nobody is that domestic.* But Esther is.

"You are just the bravest person I know, Flora," she said as the anesthesiologist poked Flora's back for the fourth time in an attempt to place the epidural. "If my husband hadn't been there when I gave birth—well, he might not have been around much after that, either! I might've had to kick him out!" She laughed, crinkles smiling at the corners of her eyes.

Flora knew her stepmother was trying to be playful, but Flora was twenty-nine hours into labor and hadn't slept in two days. The joke triggered a fierce protectiveness in her to defend her hardworking husband. Plus, someone was threading a small tube under her skin and up her spine and she thought she might puke.

"It's not like Connor has a choice," she said, wincing as the anesthesiologist pressed. Then, to the doctor: "I feel that on the right. On the *right*. Ouch!"

He pulled the tube out again. "Maybe we hold off on the conversation for now," he said, primarily to Esther.

"Oh, yes, sorry," she said, her thin fingers finding the ends of her long white hair and caressing them compulsively. Then, quickly, under her breath: "Of course Connor doesn't have a choice, sweetie. That's not what I meant. I know he'd be here if he weren't deployed." Flora responded with a half-hearted smile and felt guilty for sucking Esther into her sleep-deprived, crabby vortex.

Her father and Esther stayed at the house for two weeks after Iris's birth, cleaning dishes, prepping meals, and doing laundry. The real shock came after they left, when Flora was on her own. How could they possibly leave her with this perfect human specimen whose literal survival depended on her and her alone?

"We're just a phone call away," her dad said as they pulled out of the driveway on their last day.

yeah and a three-hour drive

Flora is now five days into her solo-parenting journey. The house feels hollow, like a termite-infested log. She has the sensation that if she screamed loud enough, the walls would collapse. Of course it is quieter without her father and Esther here. But it's something more than that. Flora spent nearly her entire pregnancy in this house alone, and it didn't feel as empty then as it does now.

When she was pregnant, the house was fattened up with hopes and plans and chores and preparations. Now that Iris has arrived and the anticipation has deflated, so, too, has the air that Flora breathes. Everything she waited for is here. And since she is no longer preoccupied with the promise of the future, she is highly attuned to the now, which feels somehow two-dimensional in comparison to the three-dimensional world she had imagined.

Flora preheats the oven for the chicken potpie and thinks about Connor. Between the two of them, he is the one with any semblance of talent in the kitchen. Yet another example of how things would be easier if he were here.

Something scuttles behind a half-filled bag of rice Flora has left on the counter. She moves the bag, and a fat black bug shimmies himself along the grout line to safety. This is the third beetle she has seen in as many days, but she punts any fears of an infestation to the back of her mind. Under normal circumstances, she'd have called the exterminator at the first sighting, but she does not have the mental capacity to deal with that right now.

Instead, she wraps a paper towel around her index finger and stalks the beetle as he pauses just beside the oven. If he disappears down the crack between the appliance and the counter, she'll lose him. She swoops in and almost misses—he reacts quickly—but she's faster. She presses her finger into his crunchy body, popping him like bubble wrapping. The sensation is satisfying.

She wipes away his splattered remains just as the oven beeps.

2

F lora sits in the home office for her regularly scheduled video visit with Connor. In another era, she would have gotten done up for the chat with her husband, or at least brushed her hair and rubbed on tinted lip balm. But today, she's rocking loose cheetah-print sweats with an oversized red cotton top. Spit-up and milk have stained both items of clothing—along with everything else she owns. In many cases, she doesn't know where the spit-up ends and the milk begins.

"I wish your dad could have stayed longer," Connor says, waving to a fellow soldier just offscreen. He is planted in front of a computer in the Morale, Welfare, and Recreation Tent. Flora doesn't know where in the world he is, and while that would normally bother her, she is so unmoored in her own body these days that it is oddly relatable. She's not the only buoy bobbing in the endless ocean.

"Well, he was here for two weeks…" she says.

"My mom feels so bad she can't be there," he continues, "but since Dad's knee surgery got bumped up, and she had to push the trip, she—"

"It's fine, really, she shouldn't feel bad. I'll send her a text."

The video feed skips, and she's not sure Connor has heard her. But then his voice comes through sharper than before. "Do you want to hire someone?"

"*He asked as if we had the money,*" Flora quips—then feels guilty for being dismissive. "It's fine, really. You're home in a couple of weeks. It would take me longer than that to find someone. Plus, I wouldn't even know where to start."

Connor nods and smiles, stretching the scar that runs from his upper lip to his nose. He was born with it: a result of something that happened in the womb. His dark brows are thick and harsh, a stark contrast to the still-boyish cheeks that redden the second he has a sip of alcohol.

He runs his hand through his hair, dipping his head forward and scratching at the crown. A uniquely Connor move. He did it the day they met at a hole-in-the-wall bar where they were gathered for their alma mater's basketball game. He did it the day they bought this house in Bennington, Vermont, knowing it was a stretch for their budget. And he did it the day she found out she was pregnant.

"Guess what, chicken butt?" she'd said as she flashed the tiny stick with two blue lines. She was using the tests that had come with the ovulation sticks, so they were much smaller than what she had seen in movies. This one was barely longer than a toothpick. And yet, it somehow seemed unwieldy, this tiny thing that held so much significance.

"So this is happening," he'd said, eyes wide. And she'd repeated the words as she climbed into bed next to him, where he had just woken up and was scrolling on his phone. She nuzzled her head in between his shoulder and neck: a spot that had been carved out especially for her, like stone weathered by rain and wind until smooth.

Their master bedroom had been largely unfurnished then; the purchase of the house had overshadowed their ability to buy things to fill it. This meant that the house often emitted an eerie feeling, like the space didn't yet know itself. But on this day, that unknowing presented hope. A new beginning. The space had not yet been defined because the life that was going to define it had only just sprung into existence.

"Flora?" Connor's voice from the computer pulls her back to the now. She sees him squint at the screen. "Can you hear me?" Flora fidgets in the old office chair, whose wheels catch as she tries to move it.

"Sorry, got a little lost there," she says to her husband. "I'm tired."

"Is Iris sleeping at all?"

Flora shrugs and sticks out her bottom lip. "I mean…yes? But I'm realizing even the best-sleeping newborn is still exhausting. I'm up every two or three hours at night. Oh, and the biggest news: my nipples are infected."

"Jesus."

"I picked up some cream. But that's probably the last time I'm leaving the house until you get home. I went to the hospital to meet with the lactation lady, and I forgot a diaper for Iris. I brought a diaper bag and *no diapers.*"

Connor shrugs slightly. "Yeah, but it's the hospital. They had diapers, right?"

He doesn't get it. He didn't feel the intense shame that Flora felt. Like she was outing herself on the spot: *I'm so ill prepared for motherhood, I can't even remember a diaper!* The very first thing on her apparently useless iPhone checklist.

Connor holds up his finger for Flora to wait a second. Someone offscreen has requested his attention. Flora stares at the space behind her husband, which offers few clues about his day-to-day life. The large white tent billows in and out to his right. It must be windy outside. Behind him, a natural wooden bookcase is stuffed with colorful worn paperbacks, and next to that is a cheap metal shelf holding a stack of board games. She wonders if he has played any of them. If any of their pieces are missing.

"Sorry about that," Connor says, returning to her. "There's a line, so I should probably let one of the other guys on here." He pauses and gives her a sincere look. "Are you sure you're okay?"

She could break down right now, she really could. She's on that edge of exhaustion, where tears come easily and it's hard to not see everything through a dark lens. But telling this to her husband, who is tens of thousands of miles away with no option to return home early, would only stress him out. And he has a job that requires him to be focused. So instead, she says, "I'm good. I promise."

"I wish I was there to help you," he replies, and she knows he means it; his fierce green eyes have a way of shining when he is earnest. "I feel useless over here."

"Well, you are"—she smiles—"but you'll make up for it when you're home."

He leans into the camera, largely blocking the shelves behind from view, and raises an eyebrow. "Oh, I will? Sounds like a plan."

Flora can't help but laugh. A deep belly laugh. "Just to be clear, you think I'm asking you to have *sex* with me? *That's* how you think I want to be repaid for a month of no sleep?"

"Oh, is that—I misread—is that just totally off the table?"

Flora tilts her head to the side. "I'm still in diapers, man. Literal *diapers*."

"Well, hey," he jokes, "next time lend Iris one when she needs it, will ya?"

This sends them both howling, and her heart feels full.

"Hold on a minute," Flora says when she has caught her breath, "you're not laughing at me wearing diapers, right? I *know* you don't find that funny."

Connor holds up his hands in innocence, but his eyes bulge wide. "Of course not." Then a sneaky smile sprouts on his face, and Flora explodes playfully.

"You dick! I spent thirty-six hours in labor with your child—"

"I said nothing!"

"—and am still bleeding three weeks later!"

She flicks him off as he succumbs to another fit of laughter. Flora smiles. She hasn't felt this light since Iris was born. And then, as if merely thinking about her daughter could wake her from sleep, Flora hears Iris cry in the other room. "I'm being summoned," she says, then points to her breasts, where two small blooms of milk are forming on her shirt. "Isn't that fun?"

"You're leaking? Damn. That baby's got a hold on you."

"She does," Flora says. "She really does."

3

The moment Iris emerged into this world and the closest nurse finagled the squealing baby onto Flora's chest, a thought grabbed Flora by the throat—

I would step in front of a train for this creature

—and squeezed. Flora didn't have words for the feeling. She might have said "love," but suddenly that word was meant for greeting cards or lazy afternoons in bed, legs tangled and plans forgotten. It didn't get close to *this*. What she had now, with this impossibly tiny human on her naked chest, was primal.

She remembered a day in her late teens when she joined her father by the chiminea on their deck. It must have been fall; she could just start to see her breath in the air. She was watching the flames overtake a thick log as her father talked about the book he was reading on quantum entanglement. The idea that a split atom's two parts could communicate through time and space. If one was affected, the other was, too, even miles away.

At the time, it was an anecdote. But now, it was her whole existence.

The cells of her body had formed another body that was now exposed to the world, and she knew that she would never stop fighting for that body as if it were still her own.

If those cells died, then her cells died.

Nothing had ever made more sense.

4

F lora is so in love—and also so, so tired.

She doesn't know the last time she slept for longer than a stretch of two hours. Iris disrupted her slumber long before she arrived three weeks ago. Insomnia was one of Flora's earliest symptoms.

no one should glamorize pregnancy

It's a goddamn miracle how the female body works, but it certainly doesn't *glow* while performing its magic. At least, not in Flora's experience.

The breast pump *suck suck sucks* while she sits stiffly, four pillows stacked behind her so that she cannot lean back and lose suction or, worse, leak milk. She is trying exclusive pumping, something she read about online that will allow Iris to get Flora's milk without shredding her nipples in the process. But Flora's lower back already aches from sitting stick straight on the too-soft cushion beneath her. She doesn't know where else in the house she could set up with the milk-extracting machine and all its accoutrements. Bottles, tops, tubing, back-flow protectors, connectors, flanges. *Flanges.* What a funny word. One that Flora didn't even know until a few days ago. But now that sterile plastic tool has become an essential part of her universe.

She looks around the living room, whose empty spaces echo the whining of the pump. It would be impossible to know the time of day without a clock. Outside, the sky is all clouds, dark blues and sad grays. Little light comes in through the windows, giving the furniture around her a dusty, muted quality. It's unnerving. Like a calm before the storm—which, rife with anxiety about the coming unknown, really isn't a calm at all.

Flora is no stranger to loneliness. In some ways, the feeling is so familiar that it could almost be mistaken for comfort. She was trained from her earliest days. But age has, ironically, deprived her of her strongest coping mechanisms. The last time she felt this alone, she was young enough to still have her imaginary friend, Zephie. It has been a long time since Flora even thought about her, but Zephie had kept Flora company from her toddler years into childhood. They would read books on the couch or cuddle in bed after a bad dream. Zephie had always been a kind of anchor for Flora.

Like one time, when Flora was four years old, she'd gotten separated from her mother in the mall. She'd stepped into the flow of foot traffic and become overwhelmed by shoes clacking on the shiny floor, voices echoing up to the high ceiling above, competing radio stations blasting from nearby stores. The world roared. Loud, so loud, just like it did on the nights she couldn't sleep, those late hours when the Night Hag came.

Standing in that mall, overstimulated and scared, she'd started to go under. And that's when she'd felt small fingers slip into her own. It was Zephie, her thin smile beaming right when Flora needed it most. As soon as her friend appeared, the world slowly came back into focus. And that's when Flora saw a blob of bright coral far ahead, just inside the doors of a department store. Her mother.

"Mamma!" Flora cried out, zigzagging with Zephie through the bustling crowd and finally lunging for her mom, who was spinning a glass case of silver earrings. "I was lost! You lost me!" Flora shouted.

Her mother looked around self-consciously before kneeling to Flora's level. "You don't look lost to me," she said, smiling and brushing a strand of Flora's hair behind her ear. "What could it have been, five minutes?"

Flora knew exactly how long it had been. She had just learned to tell time in school. She was without her mother for nearly half an hour.

Later, when Flora told her father what had happened, she saw something like anger or annoyance flicker in his eyes before he kneeled down next to her. "You know," he said, "I had an imaginary friend when I was your age, too. His name was Stinky. He always left dirty footprints behind him."

Flora laughed.

"What's your friend's name?" he asked.

"Zephie," she told him.

Her father's face scrunched up. "Well, that's an unusual name. How did you come up with it?"

Flora shrugged. "I don't know. That's just always been her name."

"I like it," he said at last, but his smile looked forced, so Flora could tell he probably thought it was weird. "Have you told your mom? About your friend?"

"No," Flora said quickly. Then she wondered if telling Dad about Zephie had been a mistake. "Don't tell Mom, please!"

"Oh, don't worry, bunny," he said, wrapping her in a giant bear hug. "I won't tell if you don't want me to."

Then he squeezed her and rocked back and forth for a long, long time. Flora liked it very much.

The timer on Flora's phone dings: pumping session over. She turns off the machine, unhooks her breasts, and dresses herself. If only Zephie could see her now. Flora chuckles, imagining what her friend would think about the nipple-sucking machine. The playfully horrified faces she would make in response to its mechanical wheezing.

The room is even darker now, long shadows stretching around her. As Flora walks toward the adjoining kitchen, she passes the armchair that has become a toy receptacle. Iris might not be old enough to enjoy toys, but that didn't stop Esther from sending them in numerous "predelivery deliveries." There are socks with tiny bells attached, wooden blocks, a squeaky giraffe. Most are still in the packaging. On top of the pile is the brightly colored plastic activity cube that she unwrapped earlier, each side boasting large buttons that light up and play music when pressed. The buttons feature animals' faces, every one of them plastered into a cheerful smile. Unmoving markers of forced joy.

In the kitchen, Flora gingerly places the extracted milk on the top shelf of the refrigerator. She read in some mom forum to never put it in the door.

Flora would be lost without the internet. She uses it for everything. She read up on wake windows and studied charts that compare the size of a newborn's stomach to various fruits (at one day, it's a cherry; at one week, it's an apricot). She double-checked that loud grunting at night is normal, and she even reverse-image-searched a rash on Iris's eyelids. How did mothers survive before the internet?

And then it hits her: before the internet, mothers had *mothers*. They had the older generation to show them how to burp the baby, how to get poop stains out of cotton, how to relieve newborn gas pains. They had helping hands to prep bottles and change diapers, cook meals and brew fresh coffee.

Flora's heart burns. She will never have that. Because she will never see her mother again. She remembers the day they stopped talking—a day impossible to forget, as it was also Flora's wedding day. She remembers her mother's heavy expression, her sulking form a shadow over the ceremony. And of course Flora remembers her own outburst that sealed the fate of their relationship, severing it forever. She can hardly believe it has been four years since she last heard her mother's voice.

Time has a habit of folding in on itself if not watched closely.

Flora positions a giant green plastic bowl in the sink and places the disassembled pump pieces inside: four squirts of the special nontoxic, all-organic-whatever soap and some hot water. Washing the parts every two hours takes its toll; her hands are already raw, her right middle knuckle cracked and bleeding.

Another beetle emerges from seemingly nowhere and glides across the white tile countertop. With little reaction, Flora cups her hand and sweeps the bug toward the sink. Then she turns on the faucet and chases the little guy around the porcelain with the detachable spout. When the blast of water upends him, he scurries helplessly, his legs scrambling furiously but getting him nowhere. She turns up the pressure and disappears him down the drain. Then—for good measure—she runs the garbage disposal, imagining his small body crunching swiftly in the sharpened blades.

Let that send a message to the rest of them, wherever they may be hiding.

5

Flora places the last pump piece on the spiky drying mat just as Iris wails from the nursery upstairs. She wipes her hands on her sweats and heads through the kitchen toward the staircase. Outside, there must be a break in the clouds; the sun shines brightly just beyond the front door but by some trick of the mind seems to be swallowed away before entering the house, rendering the tiny foyer dim. She grips the wooden railing with her right hand and traces her left fingertips on the wall as her feet carry her upward.

Iris's cries become more urgent, so Flora picks up the pace through the hallway, passing the small bathroom and old curio cabinet full of fragile trinkets she inherited from her mother. Two steps beyond that, and she pivots to the right, toward the nursery, whose windows face the front yard. But when she arrives, she finds that Iris is sleeping quietly in her crib.

of course

Flora approaches lightly and finds her sweet baby dozing calmly, her chest rising and falling beneath the teal fabric of the swaddle. Flora's teeth grind as she thinks about how cute Iris is

I could eat her I could literally eat her

and then she catches a whiff of something truly rank. She lifts her left arm and begrudgingly points her nose toward her armpit. Yep, it's her. This isn't the first time she has noticed her new body odor. She spent her last middle-of-the-night pump reading about it. Apparently, it's some evolutionary thing so the baby can smell its mother and find the breast to feed. Flora can't even describe the stench. Some combination of sweat, sulfur, and old cheese.

Since Iris is, in fact, sleeping and not crying, Flora makes her way farther down the hall to the master bathroom. She turns on the shower and picks at a fresh pimple on her chin while she waits for the water to get warm. Once inside, she carefully maneuvers her body so that her breasts stay clear of the pressurized water. In one instance, while reaching for the soap, her right breast grazes the stream, and she yelps in pain.

Just as she lathers some shampoo and begins to massage it into her scalp, she hears Iris wailing again. She curses herself for not bringing the monitor into the bathroom. Flora considers finishing her hair anyway, but the cries only get louder, and guilt pulls her out of the shower, only half-bathed, and hastily into a bathrobe. She pads down the hall, careful to walk on her tiptoes and not slip in her own wet wake.

And yet again, when she arrives, Iris is sleeping soundly in the crib.

Flora can feel the shampoo residue in her hair, which now seems dirtier than it did before. Her shoulders slump in defeat. The clock on Iris's sound machine tells her she has less than thirty minutes before her next pump.

That night, lying in bed, Flora wakes with an audible gasp. She feels the sensation of the *suck suck sucking* and is mortified to realize she has fallen asleep attached to the pump.

But no, that is just muscle memory, her body remembering, like how it sways after a day on a boat. The pump is stowed away downstairs by the couch, where it belongs.

And then a much more horrifying realization takes hold. Flora feels her baby's head pressed face down into her chest, mere inches from her own chin. Iris's impossibly tiny nose is blocked by Flora's disgusting melon breasts. It must be. She has done what they always warn new mothers about: she has fallen asleep with Iris in bed, and she has suffocated her baby.

Adrenaline lights up every lamp in the house. Terror ignites a flash sweat that soaks her shirt in an instant. She lifts her head, stray hairs stuck to her wet neck and pillow, heart echoing loudly through every limb of her body, and sees that Iris is not on her chest.

She is not in the bed at all.

She is three feet away, safely sleeping in her bassinet.

Suddenly, Flora gasps as familiar pinpricks stab her nipples from the inside: her milk is coming in. This always makes her think of those pin impression toys that save a handprint in the pins. Like her milk is marking its shape emphatically toward the exit. She has learned that this is called the "letdown."

Who knew that motherhood came with a whole new vocabulary? Her growing lexicon makes her feel increasingly lonely, as if the acquisition of each new word pulls her further from her old life.

letdown
noun [s]
1. the painful release of milk every two hours
2. life since Iris was born

6

The sun angles in through the nursery's window, dust dancing in its rays.

Flora sits in the rocking chair with Iris asleep in her arms. She watches as her daughter's beautifully long eyelashes flutter in slumber and her lips occasionally mimic a sucking motion, as if she has a pacifier in her mouth. Flora carefully reaches for her phone and discreetly takes a video of the sleeping baby for Connor. She hates that he is missing these moments.

She almost laughs when she realizes that just twenty minutes ago, Iris was screaming, resisting sleep, and driving Flora to her wits' end. And now, merely looking at her daughter melts Flora into a gooey mess. She is learning that parenthood means existing as a sine wave in constant oscillation.

this child is perfect

Flora admires the jet-black tuft of hair, the dip beneath her nose that leads to the top of her lip, the outline of her sweet chin. Her eyelids are still a purplish red, something the nurses said would subside with time. And even the blister on her upper lip, a result of nursing, makes Flora swoon. It is difficult to fathom

28

that just a few weeks ago, this creature was inside her. Not only difficult, in fact, but nearly impossible.

Flora cries. The tears come suddenly, and she watches as Iris moves up and down with the sobs. This baby is so vulnerable now. When she was inside, Flora could protect her. Now, she is completely exposed. A hostage to her environment.

Flora feels simultaneously helpless and omnipotent. Both make her equally uncomfortable. In one sense, without the safety of her womb, she cannot control what happens to her baby. In the other sense, her baby is completely dependent on her. Flora could do anything to this tiny human, who cannot fight back.

Bile burns her throat.

Iris's breath skips, and Flora's attention returns to the puffy lips and soft cheeks. Flora has the acute sensation that she did not exist until this very moment.

"We'd love to plan another trip," her dad says on the phone. "Maybe once Connor is back. How long is that now?"

"A little over two weeks," Flora replies casually, as if she isn't keeping track down to the hour.

"That's soon!" he says, and Flora verbally agrees but inwardly deflates. Two weeks might as well be two decades.

She stands at the kitchen counter just beside the refrigerator, picking at a large brick of white cheddar cheese. When she couldn't find any crackers, she opted instead for some pretzels from the back of the pantry that she now realizes are very stale. But she eats them anyway.

"How's it all going?" her dad asks. "Are you 'sleeping when the baby sleeps' and all that?"

The question fires her up with rage, but the logical part of her knows it shouldn't. A wall of misunderstanding stands between them; her father is a product of his generation. He probably didn't change a single diaper when Flora was a baby and, thus, has no frame of reference for her current situation.

So, instead, she just says: "Yeah. *And all that.*"

Flora realizes that her mom's experience as a new mother might not have been so different from her own. Her husband wasn't deployed, sure, but he also wasn't hands-on. Having a partner who is there but not really *there* must breed its own kind of loneliness.

Her dad changes the subject to an article he read recently in a psychology journal about growth mindset versus fixed mindset. She finds herself mesmerized by his voice, the cadence a lullaby. Hearing adult words out loud has a soothing effect on her mind, though she isn't actually comprehending anything he says. Normally, conversations with her father are filled with lively debate and scientific back-and-forth, but her brain at this moment is sticky. Slow.

She takes another bite of stale pretzel,

where are those rice crackers Esther bought

and follows it up with a too-large chunk of cheddar. Her mouth chews with great effort, mimicking the gunk in the gears of her brain.

Her dad hasn't noticed her silence. Or maybe he has and doesn't know what to do with it. He says, "I'll send you the article. You can let me know what you think."

"Cool, yeah, that'd be great, Dad. Thanks."

She stands by the fridge for a long time after they hang up. Or maybe not such a long time; she's not really sure. Outside the window above the sink, she can see the backyard, where the tree line at the edge of their property glows. Every night, as the sun approaches a particular angle, the trees shine gold for a few magic moments.

Maybe she'll have a glass of wine on the porch. She could bring a blanket in case of an autumn chill and watch as the stars appear one by one. Before Iris, she loved spending time out there. The house is in a heavily wooded area of Vermont, and the world within the trees sings its own tune at night after the sun goes to bed. She used to love this time of day.

Now, though, it fills her with dread.

It's right around this time each evening that she hits her lowest point. Maybe it's a hormone dip. Maybe it's the notion of staring into the abyss of the never-ending night, when she will get very little sleep and will have to pry herself from her warm duvet to feed Iris. Each successive feed/pump session gets harder, the four-o'clock one being the most difficult. By then, she is so exhausted that she has to pinch her thighs to keep herself awake as the machine, immune to the time of day, plugs away as normal.

She won't go outside to have a glass of wine. If she actually gets a spare moment, she'll fold the laundry. Or empty the dishwasher. Or wash the pump parts. Or open the new pack of bibs. Or fix that clicking noise in the swing. Or

these pretzels are disgusting

Flora throws them in the trash. She then washes her hands, careful around the dry patch on her knuckles that has now expanded into a scaly lesion, and opens the fridge to replace the cheese back in its drawer.

There, neatly stowed beside the milk on the top shelf, is the box of crackers.

7

Flora has just fallen asleep when a crushing, deafening noise fills her ears. Like metal gears screeching and clashing. She tries to stand and investigate, but she cannot move.

And then it hits her.

it's happening again

Her body is deadweight. Her legs, arms, torso, head—all of them frozen in place, stiff like rigor mortis. Only her eyeballs can dart around in their sockets.

Sleep paralysis.

She hasn't experienced this since she was a child. She figured she had outgrown it long ago. But as the familiar feeling sinks in, fear snakes itself around her limbs like living ropes. Flora tries to use her rational, adult brain to will away the terror.

this is just a nightmare just your brain playing tricks

But the fear lives in her body, which is now rigid with memory as the paralysis attack follows the same pattern it always did when she was little. Her arms are tight against her sides, as if she is wrapped in a cocoon, her chest tightening. She feels the warm trickle of a tear down her cheek.

And then comes the peak: a heavy weight she has long thought of as the Night Hag, who sits on her chest and stomach, crushing her organs until she knows the insides of her body will soon be on the outside.

Flora can't help but picture the scene: her flesh and guts and torn skin exploded all over the room, like an overfilled balloon that finally burst. Even the smaller parts of her, the fingers and teeth and eyeballs, strewn about like forgotten candy from a broken piñata. And her baby, helpless and alone, crying, smelling the coppery fresh blood of her mother mixed with splashes of breast milk that erupted from Flora's exploding ducts.

WHOOSH! Now, just like when she was little, the sound of running water deafens the world around her—louder and louder—as if the sound itself could fill and sabotage her lungs—until finally: the release.

As quickly as the paralysis came on, it recedes.

Breath escapes Flora's lips, and her entire body buzzes as blood returns to circulation, the weight lifting, the chest un-squeezing. Her head is light with the dizzying speed at which all of this just happened.

She brings her fingertips to her face, touching her warm skin and wiping away the sweat that has accumulated on her hairline. Her fingers trace the shapes of her profile, confirming that her body is still whole, half expecting to feel slimy muscles and tendons there, as if she has been turned inside out.

Now wide awake, Flora feels suddenly persuaded toward productivity. Plus, she needs to get out of that bed, out of that room.

She slinks quietly through the hallway and down the stairs, like an intruder in her own home. The house is so quiet, it seems that even the furniture itself is sleeping. The floor complains with every step, and Flora feels strangely unwelcome down here.

She decides to organize the pile of toys on the armchair. As she begins, she considers what just happened. Why, after all these years, has her sleep paralysis returned? Why is the Night Hag back? It's like she spent a lifetime believing in the boogeyman, only to finally outgrow that belief and now be told as an adult that she had been right all along. And what's more—that boogeyman is back. *Here.* In her *house.*

Flora shivers.

She focuses on the toys, packaged in fortresses of plastic and cardboard and zip ties. The waste of it all is depressing, but Flora must admit that gathering the refuse and collecting it in a trash bag is oddly satisfying. She feels quite accomplished.

She arranges the toys into piles: things Iris might use soon, things worth sticking in a closet until she's a few months older. Suddenly, her bubble of awareness expands as the dark around her is lit up like a rave, flashes of colored lights assaulting her unadjusted eyes.

"IT'S A BARNYARD SINGALONG!"

Flora's heart rips through her chest. She must have bumped one of the large buttons on the activity cube. She didn't realize it even had batteries; Esther must have put them in while she was here.

shut up shut up shut up

Though she knows Iris is far enough away and buffered by the blasting sound machine, Flora's brain is still wired to maintain quiet in the house. She scrambles for the off button but can't find it. Instead, she plunges toward the nearby coat closet under the stairs and tosses the singing cube into its dark depths. The lights and music continue, unfazed, but their effects are muted by the thick puffer jackets around them. She closes the door and abandons the toy.

Any hopes she might have had of returning to sleep are now dashed. Her heart is racing like she's had three cups of coffee. She returns to the toys—the mercifully silent ones—and finishes her organizing.

Flora holds a wooden abacus, feeling its edges and weight, which are surprisingly familiar. Then she realizes: they had this same abacus in the lobby at the office. A tug of nostalgia takes hold. She doesn't miss that job, but part of her does miss the kids.

After getting her master's in genetic counseling, Flora decided to work in pediatrics, consulting with parents of sick infants and children to recommend genetic tests and interpret the results for the families. But Flora grew to dread the job as her main role quickly became Deliverer of Bad News. She spent hours on the phone with grieving parents, often acting as their therapist. Telling a parent that his child has a lethal diagnosis and probably won't live beyond the age of seventeen—well, does that ever get any easier?

It was Connor who was the first to point out how unhappy it made her. "It's wearing on you," he said.

"Okay, sure, but how must those families feel? Their children are *dying*. Me being uncomfortable seems irrelevant in comparison."

"Does it?" he asked. "Why?"

Flora didn't have an answer. As was his point, she realized that her suffering didn't lessen the families' suffering. And by convincing herself that it did, that it somehow paid some moral price, she was putting herself on a pedestal that she hadn't earned. And it was coming at a cost—one that seemed to be unique to Flora. Her coworkers could perform the job without holding their hands below the table to hide their shaking. They did not run to the bathroom post-meeting to vomit into the toilet. And they did not lie awake at night envisioning with imaginative detail their patients' next few years of grief.

She called her mom soon after putting in her notice.

"I'm just disappointed," her mother said. "For *you*," she added as an afterthought. "Since, you know, you spent so much money and so much time."

"I know, but I'm not happy," Flora said.

"Okay, Flora," Jodi replied tiredly. And somehow, hearing those two words, Flora felt as though she had broken her mother.

Flora's father had always been the translator between the two key women in his life, softening Jodi's words in midair as they made their way to Flora. He was the joint that connected two immovable bones. But when her parents divorced just after Flora's high school graduation, her relationship with her mom became even more fraught. Suddenly, they had no referee, and no holds were barred.

"Was this Connor's idea? Leaving the job?" Jodi asked.

Flora felt a screw loosen within her. Her mother saw her as weak. She believed Flora needed someone else—a man, no less—to tell her how she felt. "Mom, *what*?"

"It's just not like you. You're usually so indecisive."

Flora snorted. "Okay, and for once I'm putting my foot down. Maybe we could see that as progress." But as soon as the words were out, Flora knew they were all wrong. She was suddenly a child again, so small. "I mean, not *putting my foot down* per se, just…looking out for myself. You know?"

"It's so uncharacteristic of you to give up; that's all I'm saying."

Flora lay awake that night scrambling her mother's words on the ceiling. Was her mom right? Was Flora giving up?

When she asked Connor the next morning, he took a bite of his everything bagel with a thick layer of cream cheese and chewed slowly. So slowly, in fact, that it became obvious he was holding something back.

"What is it?" Flora asked.

He held up his hands in surrender. "I'm not saying anything."

Flora's relationship with her mother was a typical point of contention between them. Even though she usually agreed with Connor, she often felt that primal need to defend her mom and make excuses for her. Even at Flora's own expense.

"Tell me," Flora said. When he again shook his head, she added, "You're not saying anything, but you obviously have something to say."

"Sometimes," he started, "I worry she doesn't..." He paused, choosing his words deliberately. "You're such a bright light, Flora. And when she's around, or whenever you talk to her, that bright light dims."

This time, she didn't argue with him. She chewed on his words, tasting them for days. It wasn't just that she knew he was right. It was that his sentiment birthed a new worry within her. If she continued to enable this dynamic with her mother, at some point her light wouldn't just be dimmed; it would be altogether extinguished.

8

"I 've been thinking about my mom a lot lately," Flora tells Connor during their video chat the next day. Iris lies awake in the lounger beside her on the couch while she pumps. Her laptop is perched on the coffee table, angled in such a way that the bottles and flanges are out of view. She doesn't need Connor's military mates watching her nipples get sucked to death by a wheezing machine.

"You have?" he asks. Then, raising an eyebrow, he adds, "I mean, I guess that makes sense."

"It does?"

"Sure. You just had a baby. You're a mom now. It's gotta be natural to think about your own parents."

Flora reaches over to Iris and rubs her belly. Connor's assessment is logical but oversimplified. Flora's sudden dwelling on memories of her mom feels more complicated. Loaded, somehow. But she can't say this to Connor. He's not a man of nuance; he struggles to see the grays in his world of black and white.

"I guess I've been wishing she was here," Flora says.

"Really?" he asks, surprised. Then he catches himself. "I mean, I don't mean to—it's just—you guys never really got along. I wouldn't have thought..."

"I know," Flora says, "me either, honestly. But it's my *mom,* you know?"

"Yeah, I do know," Connor says. "Sorry, Flo. I wish things were different."

Flora fills her chest with air. "Me, too."

Connor tells her as much as he can about his own life these days: the wind that whistles and howls all night long, the bunkmate who cries in his sleep, the water that tastes like sulfur. Every detail widens her awareness and reminds her that the world is still turning beyond the confines of her endlessly repetitive routine. It's so easy to forget that anything else exists.

When they hang up, Flora unhooks herself from the machine and pauses. She flutters her fingers in front of Iris's face and strokes her head. Like Connor, Flora is surprised that she wants to connect with her mom after all this time. It's probably some deeply ingrained evolutionary desire. After all, society seems to promise this maternal connection will finally bond her with Jodi. Or maybe it's just the chemicals in her brain or her hormones or some psychologically embedded drive or—whatever the reason, Flora hates herself for wanting that connection with Jodi, but she does. She does want it.

She reaches for her phone and navigates to the settings, where she finds the long list of blocked contacts. Most of them are random robocall numbers, but she scrolls to the bottom and sees "MOM." When she blocked the number four years ago, she told herself she was setting the boundary she needed in their toxic relationship. But maybe she had been protecting herself in a different way; maybe she knew, after her wedding, that her mother would never reach out again. If the number was blocked, Flora would never know whether or not her mom had tried calling. This way, she could assume the narrative that *she* was the one in control. That this was *her* choice.

Her thumb hovers over "MOM" and then delicately swipes until a bright red button appears that reads "unblock." She hesitates but presses it. Her mother disappears from the list of blocked callers.

She has no intention of calling Jodi. No way. Maybe a text? But what would she say? Her thumbs bring up a new, blank text chat. The cursor blinks in the top bar, willing her to type the recipient's name. She types "M-O" before abandoning the task and pressing "cancel."

Flora shakes her head and replaces the phone on the coffee table. She grabs Iris and the freshly pumped bottles, heads to the kitchen, and sets the milk in the fridge. As she walks back toward the stairs—

"IT'S A BARNYARD SINGALONG!"

ouch shit shit shit

Her toe throbs where she rammed it into the brightly colored activity cube.

Her breath catches. Didn't she put that in the closet? She must have unknowingly knocked it out when retrieving her coat earlier today.

Flora squats at the knees, careful to keep Iris level in her football hold, and fumbles around for the off switch with her fingers. This time, she finds it on the underside of the cube and slides it to the left. The music abruptly stops, returning the house to its typical quiet, which feels even more silent in the absence of the singing cube.

Once upstairs, Flora places a swaddled Iris in the crib. The late afternoon light slants in and illuminates the floral art prints she ordered for the nursery. The room is admittedly large; one of the corners is essentially bare. But she has done her best to make it feel as cozy as possible with artwork, an elephant-shaped hamper, and hand-painted drawer pulls. She takes one more look at Iris, who has turned her head so she's sleeping on her left ear. A favorite position, apparently. Then Flora closes the curtains and walks out, leaving the door open just a crack.

Downstairs, the singing activity cube turns on.

9

IT'S A BARNYARD SINGALONG!"
   Flora goes rigid.

I turned it off I know I turned it off

She stomps back down the hall and stairs, carrying herself with an air of authority that encourages her annoyance to trump her fear.

From the staircase, she can see the purple and green lights flashing alternately. She takes the final step and swings herself around the banister for momentum. The cube's bright voice squeals—"THE COW GOES MOOO!"—just before Flora kicks it.

The plastic skids across the hardwood floor and slams into the base of the couch. She immediately regrets kicking it as the music distorts. Something has dislodged in the inner workings of the toy so that now the tune is slowed down and off-key, like the soundtrack of a spooky fun house.

She lunges toward the couch and, in one swift motion, grabs the cube and falls onto the cushion. That's when she sees the power button is in the on position again. But who could have turned it on?

this is ridiculous no one could have turned it on I must have thought I turned it off and didn't

She flicks the switch with her nail, deliberately moving it to the off position. But the twisted clown music doesn't stop. The once high-pitched voice is now crackly and low as it proclaims: "THE SHEEP GOES BAAAA!"

Flora pads into the kitchen, cube in hand, and heads for the catchall drawer beneath the microwave. She's pretty sure there's a small screwdriver in there somewhere. Her hands push aside a tape measure, loose change, some paper clips, old instruction manuals, an Allen wrench...

"WELCOME TO OUR LEARNING FARM!"

...permanent markers, a small pad of paper, pencils, an X-Acto knife...

the toolbox in the garage

Flora carries the activity cube with her through the living room to the opposite side of the house. She passes the walk-in pantry, where she remembers she's running out of trail mix, and opens the door to the garage. The cement floor is cool beneath her bare feet, and the faint smell of gasoline makes her nostrils twitch. She makes her way to the steel shelving on the back wall, where nondescript boxes and sports gear live. On the second shelf from the top is a red toolbox, given to her by her father.

She finds a screwdriver and finagles the small door off the bottom of the cube. When she finally pulls out the batteries— "IT'S A BARNYARD SINGA"—the music abruptly stops.

Her chest loosens. She didn't realize she had been holding her breath.

On her way back into the house, she flicks off the light before pausing and considering the now-defunct activity cube in her right hand. She turns the light back on, walks again toward the wall shelving, and places the toy beside a container full of stationery. The cube's big orange button with the face of a pig smiles at her. She slides the stationery box in front of the wide grin and leaves before she can give it another thought.

10

I t's almost midnight, and small grains of sand scratch Flora's eyes beneath her lids. She is atop her pumping perch, the only light in the room emanating from the timer on the sucking machine. Her head snaps back when she almost nods off, but then

what's that noise

Adrenaline pops her eyes open and sharpens her senses. She hears the soft pitter-patter of a whisper. Like someone speaking just under his breath so that Flora can make out the percussive consonants and nothing else.

Maybe it's something in the pump. As much as she is using the machine, she expects it to have some technical glitches. She will call the support line tomorrow and see if they can help her troubleshoot over the phone.

Her pulse is just starting to slow when the noise is back—the *puh* of explosive *p*'s and the *tah* of syncopated *t*'s—like a fly buzzing beside her ear.

Flora leans back slightly to get the momentum needed to hunch forward and switch off the pump. But leaning back allows streaks of milk to escape her flanges, down the sides of her torso. "Shit!"

she cries out, lurching herself forward quickly to avoid any more spillage. She then carefully unscrews the right bottle from the connector and places it on the coffee table. As she reaches for the lid, her forearm grazes the bottle and sends it crashing to the floor.

All she can see is the huge puddle of milk on the hardwood below, the slightly translucent white fanning out quickly against the dark boards. She wants to scream. And so she does. She grabs the nearest pillow and screams into it—really fucking screams—as loudly as she can.

There's no other way to put it: this is so unfair. It's unfair that nursing was hell and that her husband works across the world and that she's all alone in this and that she has naturally higher sleep needs than the average person and that she smells like dog shit all the time. Her milk on the floor is the highest form of cruelty the world can deal right now, since the

there it is again the whispering

The pump is off. So it must be a voice she's hearing. She throws on a loose sweater that, given the scratching against her throat, is on backward. But that doesn't matter right now. Because right now she hears a man's voice speaking softly and slowly and there's not a man in this house; there *shouldn't be* a man in this house.

She holds herself as still as she possibly can, but it's useless, because she can't hear anything through the deafening hum in her ears. Is that the blood rushing in her veins? She shakes her head to stop it, but that doesn't help.

Flora's mind is on hyperdrive. Someone is in her home. She is paralyzed with indecision and fear. What should she do first? Retrieve Iris? Call the police? Search downstairs? Flora closes her eyes tightly as a reset. And when she does, she feels a familiar hand slip into her own. Just like it did all those years ago whenever the loneliness was all-consuming. Whenever the world roared.

Zephie.

Her imaginary friend has returned to her.

Flora gives Zephie's hand a squeeze of thanks as she looks at her. The girl is half Flora's height, with eyes trained on the living room and her hair pulled back tight in a French braid.

A newfound confidence lifts Flora's foot for one step and then another, back toward the mysterious male voice. She assesses the darkness, Zephie with her inch by inch. Her eyes rove over the low coffee table with pump parts scattered across its surface, the fat beige couch sinking in the corner where she always sits, the matching lamps she found at a discount store.

She feels a deep squeeze of her hand just as her eyes land on the baby monitor, perched atop the end table she pulled from the garage for her pump gear. Zephie is telling her something. That squeeze says more than any words can.

That squeeze says: the voice is coming from the baby monitor.

someone is in Iris's room

She flies up the stairs faster than she even would have guessed possible. Her feet barely touch the ground. Until, that is, her left toes get caught on a leg of her mother's curio cabinet in the hallway and send her entire body careening forward.

Flora lands hard on her hands, her wrists taking the brunt of the impact. A sharp jolt travels from the center of her right palm to her elbow. She instinctively cradles it with her left hand and crawls on her knees the last few steps to her daughter's room.

The door is slightly ajar, just as she left it. At least, how she thinks she left it. When she pushes it with her left hand, it creaks and opens to reveal a bright room. For a moment, she thinks the lights are on, that the intruder has had the audacity to flick the switch. But no, that's just the moonlight coming through Iris's windows, painting the crib and rocking chair in a sinister hue.

Her eyes furiously scan the room for a human figure, but they find no one. As she stares, her wrist throbs with a steady pulse of pain.

A flicker of movement from the window catches her eye, but she can't make sense of it. She pushes herself to standing, which takes more effort than it should. Her body is stiff and tight and aching.

As she puts weight on her feet and straightens her legs, the world goes black momentarily. She should eat. Or drink.

Slow, deliberate steps bring her to the window, where her eyes adjust and send a delayed message to her brain about what she sees there.

Bugs. Lots and lots of bugs.

A line of beetles marches up the outside wall of the house and into Iris's window.

who opened this window

The beetles move in a single-file line across the windowsill, down the eggshell wall, over the beveled hump of the baseboard, across the wood floor, over the folds of a forgotten pair of dirty pajamas, up the sturdy leg of the crib, over the rounded front edge of the

it was me I opened the window because Iris's diaper pail had stunk up the place

The beetles' legs—so many legs—move in tandem. This must be what she was hearing. Her body is frozen, her feet hardened in cement. Flora's eyes follow the line of beetles where it leads to the crib.

Zephie stiffens beside her. "Where are they going?" the girl asks.

And even as she is asking, they both know the answer. They both know and neither wants to see, neither wants to confirm. Regardless, Flora propels herself forward, a motherly instinct that cannot be stopped, and places both hands on the edge of the crib.

She looks over the side and sees Iris's mouth wide open, her wails snuffed out by the endless line of insects crawling into her mouth, down her throat, through her small esophagus into her intestines, where Flora is certain they will gnaw at her baby from the inside.

Flora reaches desperately for her daughter, the jarring motion tweaking her sore back, and uses her fingers to stretch open Iris's mouth. She feels around inside for the beetles, scooping them out with fervor, throwing them in all directions. As they land on the surrounding surface of the mattress, they struggle to flip off their backs, then return quickly toward the baby, drawn like magnets. But Flora manages to finally wipe Iris's mouth clean, allowing her unmuffled voice to scream with a pulsing wail that only a newborn can emit. Still, Flora knows there must be more bugs in there. Deep in there. She again thrusts her fingers into her daughter's tiny mouth, and this time they reemerge covered in white spit-up.

That's when Flora feels Zephie's arms around her waist, guiding her to pick up the baby, to press her to her chest, to sway her back and forth in a comforting motion. The three of them stand together, rocking in tandem, until Iris eventually calms, her desperate cries downgrading to pathetic sniffles.

When things are finally quiet, Zephie says, "I think maybe we were wrong."

For a moment, Flora doesn't understand. But then she looks back at the window and sees—there are no beetles. The crib is empty, the mattress clean, save for the wet spot of Iris's puke.

There were never any bugs, only Flora's sleep-deprived mind manipulating her.

She holds Iris tightly. As she does, Flora stares at her own fingers, messy with spit-up and vomit, evidence of the violation. She thinks about how these tainted hands have only one job—to protect Iris from the world.

11

It's not until after Iris has finally fallen back asleep that Flora realizes she should have relocated the baby to the bassinet in the master bedroom. She doesn't want to be more than an arm's length away—she *can't* be, not tonight, not after all that. But she also doesn't have the heart to move Iris again after the first unnecessary disruption. So instead, Flora pulls a yoga mat, blanket, and pillow into the nursery and settles herself on the hard floor beside the crib.

Zephie lies with her, sharing the limited space under the warm blanket. She wears Flora's favorite childhood pajamas, a soft pink set peppered with mermaids and shells. Her fine brown hair is still pulled into a French braid, but it has loosened so that wisps of hair now delicately frame her face.

Even though Flora knows the girl isn't real, it is comforting to feel Zephie's body press against her own. Flora is afraid to close her eyes. If she sees beetles crawling down her daughter's throat when she's awake, what will she see when she sleeps? The thought pricks the hairs on her arms to attention.

"You're not going to leave, are you?" she asks Zephie.

The girl shakes her head and smiles. "Not a chance." Her

fingers wrap around Flora's in a familiar hold, even though Flora's hands have grown since they last saw one another. Still, they *fit*.

"I'm afraid to be alone," Flora admits.

Zephie doesn't say anything; she just snuggles in closer.

Flora breathes in the scent of her friend: grapefruit and coconut. The smell brings her right back to childhood, which is not a comforting place but is at least a familiar one.

And there it is again: Flora's childhood. First, the Night Hag. Now, Zephie. Is her acute loneliness summoning these visitors from her past?

She lies snuggled with Zephie for a long time. So long, in fact, that Flora loses sensation in her right arm. Her head has been resting on it, cutting off the circulation. She tries to roll onto her side, but she can't move the right arm at all. Flora uses her left hand to reach across her body and retrieve the deadened limb.

It is an odd task: searching for a part of her own body that she cannot feel. When her left fingertips finally graze the gummy flesh of her right arm, she picks it up and moves it like she would a prosthetic.

She feels nothing. It's such a strange sensation that she can't help but giggle, which makes Zephie giggle in response. Then the girl reaches for the hand of Flora's dead arm, and this time, the touch registers in Flora's brain. She can feel Zephie's fingers interlaced with her own.

The irony of this is not lost on Flora: that she cannot feel what is there but she can feel what is not.

Flora feeds Iris in front of the big patio windows that look over the backyard. Her eyes burn with exhaustion, and she rubs them harshly in response. The bright sunlight irritates her.

Flora can't shake the image of the beetles. She hasn't seen any more in the kitchen since last night, but she did look for some Raid in the garage this morning. No luck, though she found a spray bottle of some other toxic-looking substance and figured that would do the job. It's perched on the kitchen counter, ready for attack.

A part of her wonders, though…if she imagined the beetles in Iris's room, did she imagine those in the kitchen, too?

Maybe she should have taken Connor up on his offer to hire help.

But no, they can't afford it.

"And what—you just let a stranger take care of your baby?" Zephie asks.

Flora nods. Zephie is right. That's preposterous.

Flora grabs her phone. Twice this morning, she called her mother's number but immediately hung up before ever hearing a ring. She angles the phone's screen away from Zephie, though she should know this is pointless.

"It's a bad idea," Zephie says, reading Flora's mind.

But Flora stares at her mother's contact information. She looks at it so long that the phone eventually blacks out with inactivity.

She could write her mother an email. A call would be aggressive and a text too casual. But an email strikes the right balance. Yes, she can do that.

"Bad idea," Zephie repeats, this time in a singsong voice. But when she sees that Flora is unfazed, she tries another approach, pouting her lips and whining. "*I'm* here. Isn't that enough for you? Why do you have to have her, too?"

"Look," Flora replies, "I love having you here. But you can't change diapers or organize bottles or wash bedding."

Zephie lowers her eyes and gives Flora a *come on* look. "Like *that's* why you want her to come."

Flora ignores this quip and opens her email app. She sets down Iris's bottle, props the baby against her chest for a burp break, and clicks "compose" on the screen. Her thumbs start in on a new draft. Quickly, so that she doesn't have time to change her mind.

From: **Flora Hill** <florahill@we.mail.com>
To: **Jodi Martin** <jojo943@we.mail.com>
Date: September 29, 2024, 10:41 AM
Subject: Iris

Hi Mom…
I miss you.

I can't believe the last time I saw you was at my wedding. That feels like ages ago. I wish I had handled things differently. I should have reached out sooner, I know, but I was angry and confused and hurt. And maybe even embarrassed.

I've probably been thinking about this so intensely because I am a mother myself now. I had a little girl, Iris, on September 2nd. She's beautiful and perfect and amazing. But also…wow. This is HARD. Connor is deployed right now, and Dad was here with Esther for a bit, but they had to go back to their lives. I'm doing it all alone. And I'm drowning.

I think my brain is broken. Does the organ change in childbirth? I can't remember anything. I keep brewing coffee pods without a cup under the spout. I heard a man's voice in the baby monitor. And honestly, I don't think Iris likes me.

I mean, I know she *loves* me, since I'm the human keeping her alive. But I really think if she had her choice, she'd prefer someone who isn't constantly failing the test, someone who doesn't find this all so impossible. And I don't blame her for wanting a mom who "gets it," you know?

I love her so much. I would do anything for her—which feels like an insane thing to say and really mean. But I do mean it. *Anything.* I just also sense this constant background hum, this persistent fear that her stroller will be siderailed by a truck while we're on a walk, or that I'll drop scalding soup on her head while eating with her in the carrier, or that she'll suddenly, without any reason whatsoever, stop breathing and cease to exist.

Are these feelings normal? Is it just because the love is so intense?

If motherhood comes with an automatic update to our human hardware, then mine is corrupted, I swear. I could really use your help. I wish you were here.

I'm sorry for disappearing.

I miss you, Mom.

Flora

12

Flora pushes the stroller through the streets of her neighborhood. Iris lies flat in the bassinet, bundled in a cozy onesie and warm sleep sack. The air is sharp and stings when Flora takes a deep breath. But something about the action is relieving, as if the cold could bring her back to herself.

The neighborhood is sprawling, homes speckled around dense woods. The trees are a mixture of beech, birch, and maple, and around the time she gave birth to Iris, they painted the sky in vibrant oranges, reds, and yellows. Now, though, most of the leaves have fallen. The branches are half-bare, and the ground is littered with rotting maroons and dirty golds. Still, Flora finds it beautiful, this untouched piece of earth.

The roads are wide and mostly empty; the only people driving through are those who live nearby. As the stroller bobbles on the gravel below, it produces a white noise similar to Iris's sound machine. Flora lifts the shade and peeks at her daughter, whose sleeping eyes move gently beneath their lids. Her cheeks are pink, her blood working to keep her face warm in the cool weather.

Flora returns the bassinet shade to its position and looks

ahead. Out here, away from the claustrophobia of the house, she can pretend things are normal. She can pretend her wrist isn't aching from yesterday's fall. She can pretend she didn't hallucinate a string of flesh-eating beetles. She can pretend she hasn't been counting and recounting her daughter's toes, convinced she saw six on the left foot when she pulled her from the crib this morning.

Out here, she's just a regular mom walking her regular baby through her regular suburban neighborhood.

with my regular invisible friend following close behind

Zephie giggles.

Flora's leg muscles engage as the road slopes upward, and her injured wrist throbs as the stroller requires more effort to push. She's wearing an old pair of thick black sweatpants that balloon where she has tucked them into the upper flaps of her fuzzy boots. Her winter coat is snug around the waist, where she still has about twenty-five pounds to lose before she's back to her prepregnancy weight.

if that's even possible

Her wavy hair is clipped at the base of her neck with a tortoiseshell claw. She has chewed off all her nails, and when the ground levels out again, she continues to rip at the cuticle of her right middle finger with her teeth.

"Oh my goshhhhhhh!" An eager, high-pitched voice squeals from behind her. "Is that the *baby*?!"

Flora knows before turning that this is Wanda, her extremely fit neighbor who is perpetually single and perpetually in want of a child.

"It is," Flora says, plastering on a smile, which feels so odd that she's quite sure it must look more like a grimace.

oh my God I've forgotten how to smile

"How old now?" Wanda asks, approaching the stroller and trying to get a glimpse inside.

Flora answers a slew of questions about life as a new mom,

all the while staring at Wanda's flawless skin and silky, conditioned hair. It's not that she is particularly beautiful, or even that Flora envies her appearance, it's simply that the glowing skin and bright eyes indicate that Wanda is a creature who sleeps. Flora finds herself in awe of this anomaly.

"You're not still *working*, are you?" Wanda asks, as if this would be some kind of heinous act worth reporting to child services.

"No, I'm on maternity leave," Flora says.

"Oh, that's *wonderful*."

"Yeah, well, it's unpaid."

"You're kidding!" Wanda's jaw drops at the travesty of it, and, while Flora absolutely agrees with her, something in her resists giving Wanda that satisfaction.

"Oh, I'm just a contractor, so, you know..."

When Flora left genetic counseling, she took on a remote research job. It was always meant to be the in-between gig, but Flora still hasn't figured out what the next venture will be. The work is fairly mindless and, thankfully, requires none of the taxing patient interface. But that's also what makes it mind-numbingly boring.

Wanda cocks her head to one side. "Can I—do you need some help?"

She points to Flora's chest, where Flora has absentmindedly reached her left hand under her coat to massage a burgeoning clog in her right breast.

"Oh, Jesus," Flora says, pulling her arm out and replacing her hand on the stroller. "That's embarrassing. Sorry. I just—my boobs. They're like rocks. I should get home. This one is burning up with a clog."

Wanda half nods, probably counting in her head the number of conversations she's ever had with Flora, wondering what has qualified her to hear such information. "All right, well, have a good one!" she says. Then, leaning toward the bassinet: "You take care of your mommy, little Iris!"

Zephie pipes up from behind Flora, snickering in her ear, "Isn't that a fucking joke! No one takes care of Mommy."

Flora balks in surprise. She doesn't remember Zephie ever cursing before.

But then Flora spots her neighbor's horrified expression. Was it actually Flora who said those words out loud? Flustered, she wraps her hands around the stroller bar and pushes back toward home.

"Nice to see you!" she sings over her shoulder as she hurries away before she can say anything else and before her swollen breast detonates like a grenade all over Wanda's moisture-wicking athleisure.

engorgement
noun [s]
1. when the breast tissue overfills with milk, blood, and other fluids, leading to swelling and tightness
2. when life is too much and you're moments from bursting but there's no relief because a helpless human depends on you for literal survival

Iris is still sleeping when Flora wheels the stroller through the front door, so she parks it in the living room away from the window and turns on the portable sound machine. She frees herself from her layers of warm clothing, under which she is sweating. Pit stains mark large half-moons beneath her arms, and the back of her neck at her hairline is wet.

She drops the coat on the floor and piles her sweater and shirt on top. Flora leans against the doorway between the foyer and living room to take off her shoes, again wincing at the dull ache in her wrist.

"That lady has weird teeth," Zephie says.

"I think they're veneers," Flora replies.

Earlier today, Flora asked Zephie why she is still a child. They had always been the same age when Flora was growing up.

"I'm stuck at the age you abandoned me," Zephie told her.

The realization slapped Flora with a pang of guilt. Around the age of ten, she had considered herself too mature for an imaginary friend, so she had ignored Zephie until the girl gradually disappeared, like a pencil sketch that fades over time until eventually it is gone entirely.

In the wake of this news, Flora now feels especially grateful that Zephie has seemingly forgiven her and returned.

"What are veneers?" Zephie asks about Wanda's perfect Chiclet-gum teeth.

But before Flora can answer, her eyes land on the living room coffee table. Square in the middle is a tiny, squishy, bright orange pig. Flora has never seen this toy. It wasn't in the pile from Esther. So how did it get into her living room?

someone was in the house

She looks around the space warily, but nothing else is out of place. The idea of an intruder sneaking in to simply set a small plastic pig on a piece of furniture is ludicrous, she knows. But what other explanation is there?

"Did you do this?" she asks Zephie, even though she knows Zephie cannot manipulate objects. Zephie is not *real*.

Flora steps toward the pig slowly, as if a sudden movement might inspire it to attack. She keeps her gaze on its triangle ears and broad smile and large white eyes with tiny black dots at the bottom. Something about all of this feels familiar. Like she has seen this face before. And then she remembers. She *has* seen this pig's face before. It's the same as the one on that activity cube she hid away in the—

"IT'S A BARNYARD SINGALONG!"

13

Flora snatches the pig and stomps toward the garage. This is ridiculous. It's all ridiculous. There was no one in the house. The activity cube has not miraculously turned itself on without batteries. Everything is in her head.

"Except you are holding that pig," Zephie says, right on Flora's heels. "That's real, at least."

"I know, but—" And then Flora stops herself, because she's about to argue with an imaginary person.

Zephie does have a point, though. The pig in Flora's hand is indeed real, a shape of plastic she can feel and hold and squeeze. And she has never seen it before in her life, of that she's sure... Isn't she?

Flora flicks the lock of the garage and opens the heavy door, stepping out onto the wooden steps and marching down three short flights to the cement floor below. It's cold in here, and she's reminded that she's not wearing any clothes from the waist up, besides her thin nursing bra, which has expanded under the pressure of her huge, full breasts. The right one is throbbing, the clog solidifying, and a bright red streak has appeared on top.

Her sweatpants drag on the floor and get caught underfoot as she makes a beeline for the metal shelves. Of course the activity cube is now silent, but the box she had placed in front of it has been moved so that she can clearly see the big orange face of a pig.

She was right: the squeaky pig from the living room looks just like it. She bends at the waist and holds the two pigs side by side. Their smiles are wide and deep and slightly maniacal. Flora leans in close to inspect them, but she is instantly startled and flinches away.

did this pig just fucking wink at me

She stares, daring the pig's snout to wiggle, challenging her own brain and the eyes that she no longer trusts. Plastic pigs don't breathe, they aren't alive, they don't wink, they don't even have expressions—

"THE PIG GOES—"

Flora shrieks and instinctively smacks the cube off the shelf, simultaneously jettisoning the small pig in her hand across the garage.

"Did you hear that?" she asks Zephie, because it makes perfect sense that she would ask an entity that doesn't exist if she, too, heard a potentially imaginary noise.

"Yes," Zephie says, and it's the only confirmation Flora needs. That means someone replaced the batteries, moved the stationery box, positioned the plastic pig on her coffee table, and God fucking knows maybe even put the crackers in the refrigerator.

Flora runs back into the house, locking the heavy door of the garage and sliding a nearby bench in front of it. But as soon as she does, before she can even catch her breath, she is doubting herself.

locking the garage won't be enough

She needs to destroy the cube. And so she pushes the bench

aside again and reopens the door. Flora is sweating as she gallops toward the shelves and wrangles the hammer from her red toolbox. Her sweatpants again trip her up, so she pulls them off with concerted effort in great frustration. Stripped down to her bra and adult diaper, she stalks the activity cube across the garage. It's silent, but the bright lights blink and illuminate the smiling pig in alternating half-light, half-shadow.

She lifts the hammer high above her head, squats, and swings. The hammer barely makes a dent in the hard plastic, so she brings it up again and swings harder. This time, a small piece of the corner flies off. For leverage, she places one foot on a nearby utility bucket weighed down by fertilizer, and then swings and swings and swings. It's cathartic, the whacking, even as the lights continue to blink their bright colors. Flora's eyes go wide in wonder and disbelief; how does this thing still have a heartbeat?

Another piece flies off, this time coming at Flora and sticking—*thwack!*—right into her arm. It's about an inch long, with jagged, sharp edges that lodge in her skin like a dart in a dartboard. Blood immediately beads to the surface and drips down her arm in a single dark streak. Flora barely notices as she continues to smash the cube.

When it finally breaks in half, she uses her left hand to hold the bigger piece in place as she brings the hammer down. But the tool hits her thumb,

motherfucker

and the pain throbs loudly. She pauses, bringing her thumb to her lips, sucking on it like she did as a child, trying desperately to minimize the pulsing hurt. She will definitely lose this nail. Might she lose the whole thumb? That's hilarious. She laughs, loud and shrill, as she imagines losing a thumb because she wanted to dispel some evil spirit from a child's activity cube.

In her moment of pause, she hears the doorbell from the main house. And something about this feels perfectly natural. Why, of course she has a visitor. Why wouldn't she?

She tosses the hammer aside, unceremoniously rips the sharp plastic from her forearm, and wipes at her brow like she has just finished a long day of manual labor. She glides through the living room and foyer feeling lighter somehow, and even Zephie has a glow about her.

Flora smiles to herself as she approaches the front door. She reaches for the knob, her euphoria outweighing the throbbing of her thumb and the calcifying of her milk ducts and the steady bleeding of her forearm.

She opens the door, the outside chill prickling her naked bare skin, and there, standing before her, is her mother.

Flora's lips part and her eyes go wide. She can barely croak out a word.

"Mom?" she manages, and then Zephie is there, very much there, fiercely protective, her energy buzzing like an electric fence between Flora and the world.

Jodi stands beside an efficient gray suitcase. Her white hair is in a bun, and she wears a black wool jumpsuit over a simple cream-colored top.

Her right eye twitches twice. A tic.

She looks at Flora with mild disgust. "You might want to put on some clothes."

PART
2

14

F lora regains her voice. "You...you came."

"You wrote to me," Jodi says, one hand on the suitcase. "You don't remember?"

"No, I do remember, of course—"

"You said you wished I was here."

Flora's mouth opens, then closes, then opens again. "I did, yes. I *do*."

"You said you needed me. And so here I am."

Zephie snorts. She mutters under her breath, "First time for everything."

But Flora ignores the girl's remark. Instead, she stares at her mother. Her mother, *here,* on her doorstep. Her mother, *here,* after four years of no contact. Her mother, *here,* responding to Flora's desperate plea without hesitation. Flora doesn't know if her body can contain the feelings beginning to bubble and spring within her.

"Can I come in?" Jodi asks. "It's cold."

Flora shows Jodi to the kitchen and is suddenly hyperaware of the surrounding mess. The table and countertops are littered with dishes, half-eaten snacks, and spare pump parts. A giant bag of clean laundry sits atop a chair waiting to be folded. Flora steps on something sticky near the refrigerator.

"Do you want some coffee?" she asks her mother.

Jodi casually takes in the space and instead points out, "You're leaving a trail. Should we be concerned that your arm is leaking?"

what a funny way to think about bleeding

"Oh," Flora says, looking at the gash in her forearm, open and exposed. She has indeed left a line of blood droplets in her wake.

"Where's Iris?" Jodi asks, and just hearing her daughter's name on her mother's lips activates an electric jolt in Flora's bones.

Zephie, too, perks up at the question.

"She's sleeping," Flora says.

Jodi nods. "Sit down," she instructs, and Flora doesn't hesitate. When she takes the weight off her feet and settles into the hardback chair, every part of her body aches. "You should put Iris on that breast," Jodi says, pointing to Flora's inflamed cantaloupe chest. "Or you could get mastitis."

"She's not—we're not..." Flora's cheeks flush first with shame and then with frustration at that shame. "I'm pumping."

"You're not breastfeeding?" Jodi asks, dubious.

"Well, I pump milk from my breasts and feed it to my baby, so, *yes,* I am breastfeeding."

Jodi frowns. Flora's breath gets shallow as she falls into this familiar dynamic with her mother. Maybe Zephie was right. Maybe this reunion is doomed to fail.

But Flora steps out of her body to assess herself: no shirt, no pants, bleeding arm, purple thumb, greasy hair, red eyes. Perhaps Jodi *should* be doubting Flora's capabilities as a mother.

Jodi searches the kitchen, opening cabinets and gathering

first aid tools. She sits beside Flora and cleans her arm wound, which is deep but narrow. Flora watches her mother work, mesmerized by the new wrinkles around her nose and the additional age spots that have sprouted on her forehead near the hairline. Her cheeks are redder and more raw. Her eyebrows are thinner and lighter, disappearing halfway unless looked at from just the right angle. Her right eye twitches again and unsettles Flora.

As if reading her mind, Jodi points to it and says, "I don't know what that's about. Started a couple years ago. Just another old-age thing, I guess."

Flora has many questions, but she is too spellbound by her mother's touch to disturb the moment. Her mom is taking care of her. Even Zephie doesn't have a quippy retort. Flora closes her eyes so that she doesn't cry.

When her arm is bandaged and a clean set of clothes has been retrieved from the laundry bag, Flora leads Jodi to the bassinet in the living room. Iris is awake now, and one of her arms has broken free of the swaddle. Flora gently unwraps her and ceremoniously hands her to Jodi.

As she does, Flora's breath catches in her chest, so that she has to take short, quick inhales. She thought she'd never see this. And now that she is, a peach pit forms in her throat. She stares at her mother and Iris, both of whom, she is realizing now, share many traits: the round eyes, the large forehead, the small folds at the tops of the ears. Jodi smiles at the baby and then at Flora. For this moment, none of the baggage between them exists. The only thing that's real is this miracle Jodi is holding, this tiny human who is all that matters in life.

And this time, Flora lets herself cry.

Sometime later, after putting Iris to bed, Flora stands at the sink of the bathroom with her hand pump. The electric pump doesn't have suction strong enough to budge a clog this stubborn, and this way she can pop in the hot shower if she needs the heat for reinforcement. She works the clog with the fingers of her left hand, minus the thumb, which turns a darker purple with every passing hour. Her right hand cramps with each aggressive squeeze of the device. Every so often she pauses to shake out her sore wrist.

Her breast is bright red and hard. The pain is unreal as she pushes directly into the pressure point, but it also feels satisfying to strongly knead it with her knuckles. She even uses the butt end of her electric toothbrush to apply vibration and agitate the mass. At least forty-five minutes pass before she finally feels something start to loosen. And after many more squeezes, her nipple stretching unforgivingly far into the flange, the clog bursts open.

Relief crashes over her as the dam breaks. A stream of milk shoots like a hose, and when she has pumped nearly double what she normally does, she sees the bloody clog floating in the bottle of pink liquid.

strawberry milk

15

Downstairs, Flora finds Jodi on the couch, feet tucked under the thick crocheted throw blanket. Zephie isn't here. Flora wonders if she's keeping her distance now that Jodi has arrived.

"I've become somewhat of a night owl," Jodi says. "I guess that happens when you get old."

Flora sits beside her and spots a mug on the table. "Or maybe it's because you're drinking coffee."

Her mother shrugs. "Caffeine does nothing for me anymore."

Jodi then returns to her task: trimming around her nails with cuticle nippers. As she pulls off the dead skin, she flicks it onto the floor below.

"So you're staying?" Flora asks.

Jodi looks up briefly. "Shouldn't I?"

It's an unanswerable question with a multitude of variables, and something deep within Flora resents that Jodi is putting the onus to answer it on her.

"Connor will be home in six days," Flora says instead.

"Okay, then I'll leave in five," Jodi replies.

"That's not what I meant..." But maybe it is what she meant. She knows Connor would not approve of her mother being here. Still, Flora brought this on herself. This is what she wanted— isn't it?

Jodi blows a small piece of dead skin off the clippers and looks at her daughter. "I'm here to help. But I can leave if that's what you want."

"It's not," Flora says quickly. Then, softly, "It's not what I want."

Jodi nods. She drinks her coffee and offers Flora some, who surprises herself by taking a sip. It's so sweet it makes her teeth tickle.

"Oh my God, that's disgusting," Flora says, laughing. "How much sugar is in that?"

"Four packs," Jodi says, then nods to her small zipper pouch full of artificial sweetener packets. "I never leave the house without them."

"*Blech*," Flora says dramatically. "Your sweet tooth has gotten even worse."

"Or even...better?" Jodi smiles.

Flora notices how yellow Jodi's teeth have gotten. Her mother's health has clearly declined in the last few years. Jodi's head bobbles ever so slightly on her neck, like one of those dashboard toys. Her fingernails are brittle and stained. And then, of course, there's the eye twitch. Flora tries to ignore the incessant blinking, but it sometimes produces an involuntary tear that streaks down Jodi's face and leaves a trail in the makeup on her cheek.

"Are you okay? Health-wise, I mean?" Flora asks, but Jodi waves her hand dismissively.

"Oh, let's not talk about all that. We're here for you. Tell me about the labor."

And so, Flora does. She tells her mom the truth about the birth, nothing like what she told Wanda; this conversation is raw and honest. She laments the fact that she's still wearing diapers. She talks about waking in a sweat thinking she has suffocated the baby. She recounts hearing Iris's cries from across the house when the baby is actually fast asleep.

Still, though, she does not tell her mother about the activity cube, the return of her invisible friend, the trail of beetles.

She does not tell her she is afraid she's losing her mind.

That night, Flora dreams she is on a cobblestone street in Italy. The stones are large and smooth with fat spaces between them. The ground is a rainbow of grays. The alley is narrow, and the buildings are squished together like a charming accordion.

Her hands rest on her large belly. She is still pregnant. Connor walks with her. They are on vacation, filled with ease and hope and admiration for the unfamiliar world around them.

To their left, Flora spots a small shop with its door open.

"Should we go in?" she asks Connor, and he nods.

The shop is small, the walls lined with shelves of unique trinkets. Many are made from colorful glass, while others are miniature stone and wood carvings. As Flora and Connor look around, the owners of the shop appear. A husband and wife. They are short and squat, two-dimensional cartoon figures with eyes more like slits because their squishy faces are in perpetual smiles. Some level of Flora's consciousness realizes that the female owner of the shop resembles her own mother, Jodi.

The cartoon people seem surprised and satisfied that anyone has wandered into their shop. A young boy, their son, also a cartoon person, appears from the back room. At around the same time, Flora notices a baby rattle on the floor. It's a worn soft blue. Just a couple of feet from the rattle is a bunny-rabbit lovey, gray and sweet.

Something isn't right. A memory tugs at the back of Flora's mind. A fragment of information that feels vital but she can't quite place. Everything within her says to leave.

She gestures toward Connor, indicating that she's walking out and he should follow. He nods and starts after her. When she steps back onto the cobblestone street, Flora realizes what had been bothering her. Just that morning, she heard a news story. Babies around the neighborhood were going missing. She knows instantly that the toys she saw on the floor belonged to those missing babies.

Flora turns toward Connor to tell him about her revelation, but he's not there. Panicked, she steps back inside the shop to find that the cartoon people have magically turned her husband into a baby. He lies, swaddled, atop the large butcher block table in the center of the room, wailing. Flora tries to speak but has no voice. What have they done to her husband?!

They toss aside his little baby hat, adding it to the pile of paraphernalia on the floor, and the Jodi look-alike lifts baby Connor into the air. She summons her son, and then she proceeds to feed baby Connor to him like a thick sub sandwich. When the boy protests, she force-feeds him until baby Connor is completely gone, swallowed whole.

The boy licks his fingers. The Jodi look-alike smiles. Flora screams.

16

The next morning, Jodi somehow wrangles enough ingredients from the cupboards to make a batch of pancakes. Flora sits at the kitchen table, Iris wrapped up tightly against her chest, and watches as her mother whisks cream-colored slop in a bowl. Jodi never enjoyed cooking when Flora was growing up (*You'll see—once hobbies become chores, they're ruined forever*), but she was always a natural. Now she pulls three different spices from the cabinet and folds them into the mixture with a spatula.

"We should get groceries," Jodi says. "I started a list." She nods toward the countertop, where a small notepad rests.

"We can have them delivered," Flora replies.

"What about produce? You really trust those people to pick out the freshest berries? They'd just pick whatever's on top, even if it's all mushed and moldy."

Flora shrugs. "It's for the convenience, Mom. And I really don't think they'd deliver moldy berries."

Jodi raises her eyebrows and shakes her head. "Whatever you want." She scoops some batter into a measuring cup and pours it onto the hot pan.

Flora remembers a time when she was very little—perhaps one of her earliest memories—when her mom was making home-made barbecue sauce. A curious toddler, Flora had pushed one of the dining chairs over to the stove and climbed on top to see what her mother was doing. Jodi showed her each step of the process and even let her stir. Flora was enamored with her mother's swift and confident movements. As the liquid bubbled in the pot, Flora giggled, entranced by the bright red circles of the stove's burners. Then, curious, she touched one with her right hand.

Over the next few days, the burn blistered and peeled away, and it was her father who tended to it, dressed it, applied the necessary creams. He'd shouted at Jodi when he'd learned what had happened.

"She's two years old, Jodi! *Of course* she was enticed by shiny, bright circles on the stove—"

"I only stepped away for a second to grab the brown sugar—"

"—she cannot be trusted near a boiling pot, especially not *by herself*! You have to watch her!"

Jodi shook her head and touched Michael's facial hair with her fingers.

"I know, I know. You're right," she cooed.

Flora had tried for days to reconcile her mother's version of events with what had really happened. Because as far as she remembered, her mother never stepped away. She didn't take her eyes off of Flora. So why was she apologizing? She didn't do the bad thing her father thought she did. She'd never left Flora's side.

It was only when Flora was older that she realized the truth was far worse than Jodi's account. Her mother had actually seen everything: she'd watched as Flora had gotten the idea and reached her hand toward the burner. It wasn't that she didn't see it happen; it was that she *did* and simply didn't stop it.

"Syrup?" Jodi asks as she carries a plate of pancakes to the table.

"Mmm…not sure we have any…"

"Honey works, too," Jodi says, already searching the higher cabinets for a jar.

The pancakes are, of course, delicious. They have a hint of nutmeg and taste like fluffy pumpkin pie. Flora easily eats three before her mother has even touched one.

"Oh," Jodi says, as if she has just gotten an idea, but Flora knows that whatever is coming is something Jodi has been thinking about for a while. "Do me a favor and don't tell your father I'm here, okay?"

Flora's mouth flattens and her eyebrows scrunch together. "Huh? Why?"

"It's just none of his business," Jodi says casually.

"Mom, that's so weird."

Jodi slowly chews. "Is it?"

Flora licks honey from her fork. "What if he calls? I'm supposed to pretend like you're not here?"

"I just don't see why you need to tell him," she says calmly, rising to refill her coffee cup. Flora knows there's no sense in pushing; this is not destined to turn into a productive conversation. And while she doesn't understand her mother's request, she doesn't have the energy to fight it.

she'll only be here a few days anyway

"I hope so," Zephie whispers. Flora almost jumps at the girl's sudden appearance. "We hate her."

no "we" don't it's more complicated than that

Zephie huffs in defiance and slinks into a kitchen chair, dejected.

Jodi asks, "How is your father? Is he happy?"

This is a land mine of a question, so Flora takes a giant bite of her remaining pancake to buy time.

"Uh, yeah," she says after finally swallowing. "Yeah, I really think he is."

Jodi nods with an imperceptible expression.

Iris continues to sleep against Flora's chest in the wrap as Flora clears the table and Jodi washes dishes. They work silently in tandem, assuming a familiar rhythm, even though her mother has never been in this house. There's something about their dynamic that feels like muscle memory. Flora and Jodi have slipped into a well-choreographed dance.

Flora is drying the skillet when the monitor crackles from the living room.

didn't I turn that off

Her hearing sharpens. Iris is safe against her chest, breathing in and out steadily and cozily in the warmth of Flora's body. But still, an unease creeps in as she again hears the whispering voice of a man. She closes her eyes and tries to calm herself.

those were bugs last time there's no man

From the table, Zephie clicks her tongue in disagreement. "There weren't actually any bugs, remember?"

Flora freezes, skillet in midair.

Jodi looks at her sideways. "What is it?"

Flora comes to and shakes her head. "Huh? Oh, no, nothing. Just got distracted."

They return to their work in silence until the kitchen is cleaner than it has been in weeks. Maybe even months. And all the while, Flora tries desperately to ignore the man's whisper coming from the monitor that she is confident she turned off. The whisper that has become clearer the longer she ignores it. The whisper that has been asking, in an increasingly irritated voice, "Where's my good girl?"

17

Dead leaves crunch beneath their feet as they walk through the woods behind the house. Jodi tried to convince Flora to nap while she got Iris some fresh air, but the idea of being alone in the house gave Flora shivers. Jodi did insist on carrying Iris, wrapped against her chest, to at least give Flora's back a break, and Flora is, admittedly, grateful for the respite. She pauses on the walk, closes her eyes, lifts her head toward the sunshine peeking through the bare tree branches, and takes a deep breath of cold air. Being out here rejuvenates her and sharpens her mind.

"They didn't have these things when you were a baby," Jodi says, referring to the carrier.

"I'm pretty sure women in other cultures have been carrying their babies like that for centuries," Flora replies.

"I'm here to help, you know," Jodi says, pausing to inspect a patch of moss on a fallen log. "You don't have to fight me on every little thing."

"It's not a fight; it's a fact." Even as Flora says it, guilt tugs at her chest. She knew perfectly well how that response would come across. Try as she might, she cannot silence her inner angsty teen while in her mother's presence. "But okay, you're right, sorry."

Zephie follows Flora right on her heels, and Flora is a bit annoyed that out here, with all this space, Zephie insists on remaining this close. So much for keeping her distance.

As Jodi pulls out ahead and leads the way, an image pops into Flora's mind. She imagines Jodi tripping on a hidden rock and falling forward, all her weight landing on Iris, crushing her baby's head—*splat*—like a runny egg.

"Mom," she says, "are you sure you don't want me to carry her?"

"No, we're fine, why?"

"Just making sure."

Jodi stops, turns, and stares at Flora with her mouth in an open, sly smile. "Is that why you came with us? To babysit me?"

"What?" Flora's cheeks flush. "No. That's not—really, that's not it."

"You don't trust me to be alone with her?"

Flora feels ridiculous, though she shouldn't, since this is not the reason she came with her mother, but something about Jodi's tone of voice and raised eyebrow feeds her insecurity. She is exposed, mocked, as if her mother is assuring the world that it need not take Flora seriously.

"It's not that I don't trust you," Flora says, her voice thin. "It's that I don't trust myself...to be alone in that house."

Jodi's demeanor changes. Her chest puffs out and her eyes narrow. "What do you mean?"

no walking this back now you gotta tell her

"Things have been...misplaced. And moved around. And... I've been hearing noises. Well, really—a voice. From the monitor. I thought it had stopped, and then this morning—"

77

"Flora!" Jodi throws her hands in the air, which invites an unhappy grunt from the baby. "Oh my God! Do you think— I heard a story on the news a few years ago about a man who was squatting in someone's house. They didn't even know he was there for months!"

Flora had forgotten about her mother's flair for the dramatic. No one was more prepared for a juicy story than Jodi. She was the kind to thrive on conspiracy theories and couldn't resist a creative spin on neighborhood gossip.

"No, Mom, I don't think someone is secretly living in my home."

Although, now that the words were out there, she found herself doubting them. Was there a chance someone had set up shop in the garage or spare room? Flora had been so preoccupied with Iris. But no, those clickbait stories might dominate the news, but their likelihood in her small, boring life is closer to nil and none. Flora needs to get a grip and bring her mother back to reality.

"Well, what does it say?" Jodi asks.

"Huh?"

"The voice. In the monitor. The man's voice. What does he *say?*"

Jodi sits on a nearby stump and waves Flora closer. Jodi's eyes are wide and engaged, her body leaning instinctively forward in interest and fear.

"It wasn't really words," Flora says. "At least, not until today. But then earlier...while we were doing dishes, I thought— I thought I heard him say something like 'Where's my good girl?'"

There is a long silence as Jodi takes this in. The sun disappears behind a cloud, and the world turns gray. Flora hugs her arms together and blows into her hands for warmth. Finally, she can't take the quiet any longer.

"Mom?" she asks. "Am I going crazy?"

"Well, I'm probably not the person to ask." Jodi laughs. "But listen, this could be serious. Does your monitor use Wi-Fi?"

"Yeah." Flora nods, impressed that her mother would know there is a distinction between monitors with and without internet connection.

"A friend of mine, her daughter went through something exactly like this. She heard a guy's voice from the monitor and realized that it had been *hacked*! He was *watching* the baby whenever he goddamned pleased! Some old-man pervert."

Flora wants to write this off, wants to believe that this is another of her mom's strange conspiracy theories, but she suddenly realizes it might not be that far-fetched. And she also suddenly wants to throw up.

"Oh my God," she says. "Do you really think...?"

"You need a new monitor. One that doesn't use internet." Jodi stands from the stump, on a mission.

"This is surreal," Flora says. "My mother giving me technology advice."

"Ha ha," Jodi says, already walking back toward the house. "We need to disconnect that monitor right away."

"But what will I use instead?" Flora walks side by side with her mother, more quickly now, Zephie on their heels.

"Flora," Jodi says, "I never used a monitor when you were a baby. You don't need a monitor."

Flora wants to argue but decides against it. Her mother has taken the reins, and something about that is comforting. Flora doesn't have to make all the decisions alone. She has a partner in this impossible task of raising a life. A partner who has done this before.

Zephie's voice hisses in her ear. "Yeah, but do you really wanna do it the way she did?"

Flora continues walking in step with Jodi and pretends she hasn't heard.

baby monitor

noun [s]

1. an electronic device that enables a person to see or hear a child who is in another room

2. one of many products you cannot live without because you as a parent are not enough, will never be enough, to keep your baby safe

18

As Flora reaches awkwardly behind the crib to unplug the monitor from its outlet, she has a sudden pang of doubt.

"What if I'm wrong?" she asks Jodi, who still holds a squirmy Iris in the carrier nearby. "Should we wait? See if you can hear the voice, too?"

"I don't see a downside to unplugging the thing either way," Jodi says. Iris is complaining full on now, clearly getting hungry, so Jodi bounces and dances to distract her.

Flora pauses with her hand on the plug. Her body is squeezed between the crib and the wall, torqued so she can reach the outlet. And then, as if answering her very question, the man's voice crackles from the camera.

"...Iris, my girl...night-night..." The smooth, quiet voice emerging from the whispers would almost be comforting if it wasn't so horrifying.

Flora's eyes flash toward the camera. It's pointed toward the empty crib, so the man has no idea she is standing mere inches from the lens.

"Unplug the damn thing!" Jodi shouts.

81

"So you can hear—?" Flora asks as she simultaneously loosens the plug from the outlet with a hurried back-and-forth motion.

"Yes, of course I can hear that! He knows her *name*! How long has this been going on? I can't believe you let him watch her for as long as you did."

Mission accomplished, Flora stands and frees herself from the confines of the space behind the crib.

"I didn't *let* him do anything. I didn't...I wasn't sure if it was real. The first time, I came up here and there were all these bugs..." Her voice trails off. She's barely making sense to herself. Maybe this *is* her fault. She's the one who picked the monitor. She should have known this could happen—she should have at least guessed. She didn't read enough reviews. She didn't do enough research.

Jodi pulls a now-screaming Iris from the carrier and says to Flora sternly, "She needs to eat."

"I know, yes, okay. Let me warm up a bottle." Flora makes her way out of the nursery. Iris's cries pulse in a steady rhythm of complaint behind her.

"Can't you just put her on your breast?" Jodi asks as she follows Flora down the stairs.

In the kitchen, Flora grabs the pitcher of pumped milk from the fridge and assembles a bottle. As she sticks it into the warmer, she takes a deep breath to keep herself from unraveling.

"Mom. I told you. Nursing didn't work for me."

"I just don't understand that," Jodi says, wrestling Iris into the nearby baby swing. "How does it not *work*? Breastfeeding was the most natural thing in the world for me."

"Well, gold star for you, then." Flora stares hard at the warmer's timer as it clicks down. The hot water swirls around the bottle.

"It just seems cruel to make her wait," Jodi says. "And isn't the bond with nursing important? I felt so *connected* to you when I breastfed."

Jesus Mom I fucking get it I feel shitty enough about this as it is

"Yeah, I don't know. I worried about that, too. But. You know. My nipples were infected. Literally infected, so."

The timer still has two minutes left on it, but Flora pulls the bottle out to feel the sides. Warm enough. She's more in a rush to shut up Jodi than the screaming baby.

She leads Jodi to the living room, drops a burp cloth on her lap, and turns quickly back toward the swing. Iris is now red in the face. Flora grips her strongly, then lifts and places the baby into her mother's lap. Iris immediately takes the bottle, her face pruning into a tight contraction as she sucks with so much force that she has to pull off and cough within only a few seconds.

Jodi coos, "I know, sweetie, you were so *hungry,* weren't you? You shouldn't have to wait, I agree." The words are obviously directed at Flora.

Flora collapses into the neighboring love seat and takes out her phone, where she's immediately pulled into a deep rabbit hole of cybersecurity and hacking horror stories. Her stomach twists with repulsion and fury. Some man somewhere in the world has been watching her baby daughter sleep, has been whispering things to her. Has Iris already internalized his words on some deep subconscious level? Is she already traumatized? This perfect, untouched creature already wounded by the world—and all while her mother was under the same roof, tricked into believing she had been keeping her daughter safe.

"I wonder if we need to disconnect the Wi-Fi," Flora says, and Jodi looks up as if she had forgotten Flora was in the room. "It looks like since that guy was able to hack into the system, other people could, too, so we need to reset things—passwords, something about IP addresses. I don't really know."

"Whatever you think," Jodi says, her attention back on Iris.

"I'm asking what *you* think," Flora says, annoyed. "Connor usually deals with this stuff."

"So just turn it off until he gets home. We can go without internet for a few days."

Flora's gut flutters. "Can we, though?"

She thinks of all the times she has asked Mother Google for advice. The 5G signal is weak here at the house; she won't be able to browse the internet without Wi-Fi. What if Iris spikes a fever? What if her poop suddenly changes color? Flora hastily takes screenshots of various feeding charts and sleep cycle diagrams as insurance.

"Yes, Flora, we'll be fine. Although"—Jodi looks up and smiles—"we might have to buy our own groceries."

"Mom, this isn't funny. I'm kinda freaking out," Flora says.

"Okay, then, don't turn off the internet. I thought you wanted to. I don't know what I'm supposed to say here, Flora." Then, quieter and more playfully to Iris, "I never know what I'm supposed to say, do I?"

Flora sighs audibly. "Never mind, I'll figure it out, it'll be fine."

She heads for the cabinet that houses the router when another thought emerges: she should try to call Connor one more time. Once the Wi-Fi is off, he won't be able to reach her.

"I'm just gonna call Connor and let him know. So he doesn't worry," she says to Jodi, who continues to stare at Iris. Flora doubts her mother has heard her.

In fact, it is becoming increasingly apparent that Jodi would be content if Flora wasn't here at all.

19

As Flora boots up the video-calling app, she notes the time. It's not even noon. How is that possible? The days get longer and longer.

She used to wish for more hours. Back when she was working at the hospital, she used to curse the clock for moving so quickly. How would she ever get caught up with all the test results and patient calls and internal emails? Even her remote research job quickly ate up the hours of the day, despite its tendency toward the mundane. But now the days drag imperceptibly slowly, and although she has a mountain of housework to get done, she is usually chained to a small human who renders her immobile. So the days are not only long but also unproductive. It's a deadly combination.

The video turns on and Flora's face pops on to the screen. It's a shocking sight. Her hair is thinning around her face, and the spaces beneath her eyes sink farther inward every day. Even her lips, which are cracked in two places, have lost their color.

She makes a feeble attempt to improve her appearance: pinching her cheeks, licking her lips, fastening her baby hairs down

behind her ears. But it's useless. She decides, instead, to apply a
filter through the app and play it off as a joke with her husband if
he notices.

The ringing tone goes on for almost a minute without an
answer. Flora immediately tries again, but she knows the chances
are slim that Connor is available to talk. Usually, he's the one to
initiate the calls. She doesn't even know what time zone he's in.

Flora opts to leave him a video message that he can view next
time he's at the computer. She tells him about the monitor being
hacked and having to switch off the Wi-Fi. She also tells him
about the falling leaves on her walk, the bloody clog she pumped
out, and Wanda's hard-to-digest enthusiasm and newly trimmed
(unflattering) bangs.

She does not mention her mother.

She almost does; she considers it, almost allows it to slip out
while recounting the walk in the woods, but she stops herself.
Connor would be upset—frantic, even—if he knew Jodi was
here. He never trusted Jodi, but the wedding was the final straw.

They were married at a farm in central Virginia, not far from
where Connor spent his childhood. The wedding itself felt like
a huge family affair, since many of the vendors were Connor's
friends. Flora loved it. She had always dreamed of having a big
family. Both she and Connor were only children, but Connor
grew up in a small town with tons of neighbors. It was like having a dozen cousins just down the street. Flora's family never
extended beyond their tiny threesome.

Flora knew her mother probably thought the whole
home-grown-wedding vibe was tacky. And Jodi said nothing to
correct that assumption. In fact, she spent most of the day sulking. At one point just before the ceremony, Flora spotted her
mom at the edge of the property looking out at the approaching

storm clouds. Her shawl blew behind her in the warm summer breeze, and she held her arms close to her chest. There was a heavy sadness about her, and Flora was drawn to her by an invisible string. She joined her mom by the rotting yet charming log fence and placed her hand gently on Jodi's lower back. Jodi turned and smiled the saddest smile Flora had ever seen. There was no joy in her eyes.

Flora was then whisked away for the ceremony. Just after she and Connor exchanged vows, the rain started. The wedding party grabbed umbrellas and held them over the bride's and groom's heads as everyone dispersed and ran into the barn, laughing and skipping through the torrential downpour.

It was perfect.

Throughout the reception, whenever Flora caught her mother's gaze across the room, it was full of grief and sadness. A small smile would spread across Jodi's lips, as if she were saying *I'm so sorry.* Finally, when a bus arrived to take the first wave of guests home, Flora couldn't take it anymore. Her mom shouldn't get to ruin this day. She shouldn't get to be all mysterious and sad and lurk in the shadows as a punishing reminder that Flora would always be part of a small, fucked-up family and would never *really* fit in with this boisterous, huge, loving family of friends to which Connor belonged.

Flora found her mom outside. The rain had stopped during the reception, and Jodi was standing near a puddle attempting to wipe mud from the bottom of her shoe.

"What's going on?" Flora asked, suddenly catapulted by vigorous energy. "What has been so horrible about this day that you haven't been able to smile once?"

"What are you talking about?" Jodi said, looking around to see if anyone could hear them. "I haven't said a word."

"You don't *have* to," Flora said. "That's the point. It's in your face. You're clearly upset about something, and you obviously want me to ask. Because, of course, you just can't stand that this day is about me so you've got to make it about *you*—"

"I'm tired, Flora. I'm getting on the bus."

Flora could have left it at that, could have shrugged and walked away, but something about her beautiful white dress and the sparkly lights and the champagne bubbles in her head gave her the confidence she needed to let it all out.

"You spent this entire day wanting to leave! Counting down the minutes until you're free."

"I did not—"

"And I guess I shouldn't be surprised, since that's how you've been my whole life. Always *waiting*. Waiting to be *done* with the pesky task of mothering."

"I don't know where this is coming from," Jodi said, looking down to fiddle with her shawl.

"Oh, Mom," Flora retorted with a bite in her tone, "you clearly never wanted to be a mother. It's so *obvious*. You always acted like you had to give something up to be my mom, some grand life." Flora gestured wildly with her arms, as if finally breaking free from the ropes of her mother. "I don't know what I did to make you so miserable, but you know what? *Go*. Do what you've always wanted to do: *leave*. I don't care anymore. I *can't*. I don't have the energy it takes to be enough for you or to prove to you that I'm worth it. So just *go!*"

Jodi stared at her daughter. She reached out and took Flora's hand, the first time that entire day she showed any sign of compassion. Her eyes softened, and the moment was intimate. It was what Flora had craved since that morning, since putting on her wedding dress and walking down the aisle and becoming a wife.

"Okay, Flora," her mother said. She reached up and lovingly wiped a stray hair from Flora's face. "If that's what you want."

And then she left.

Flora doesn't blame Connor for being protective. And normally, she appreciates his efforts to act as a buffer between her and Jodi.

But telling him that her mother is here would only worry him. And, perhaps even more importantly, she doesn't want him to tarnish whatever connection she and her mother are miraculously managing to salvage.

Flora can feel it: this time is special. She asked for help, and her mom delivered. She showed up.

This time is different.

20

After Flora finishes her video message to Connor and triple-checks that the Wi-Fi is disconnected, she makes her way downstairs. She has a sudden craving for a crisp BLT on toasted sourdough, but she knows none of those ingredients are in the house.

Her mother is no longer in the living room when Flora returns, and Iris's bassinet is empty. Flora's body jumps to high alert. Where could they have gone? She writes an epic narrative within the span of a few seconds that involves her mother kidnapping her baby, Flora hiring a private investigator, and Iris being found years later living under another name in a different country.

Then she hears a clattering noise from the garage.

Flora finds Jodi rifling through a couple of boxes in the far corner. Iris lounges content in a bouncer nearby.

"What happened here?" Jodi asks as Flora enters. She's pointing to the destroyed activity cube.

"Oh, uh—" Flora is supremely self-conscious. Her fingers automatically find the wound on her forearm and graze the fresh bandage she switched out this morning.

But Jodi has already moved on. "I was thinking there were

some old baby toys in one of these boxes I sent you when I moved." She returns to the task, bent over a large cardboard box, her arms disappearing deep within its contents.

"I honestly haven't looked through those in ages," Flora says.

"Well, that much is obvious," Jodi retorts.

Guilt pangs at Flora; her mother carefully packed those boxes years ago, assuming Flora would get use out of her old things. But Flora barely took inventory of them before placing them in storage. That guilt, though, is quickly followed by annoyance; her mother knows Flora doesn't like to collect stuff, and yet she shipped it on over when it was no longer convenient for Jodi to keep around.

Flora sits on the cold concrete floor by the bouncer and lightly taps it with her fingers. Iris bobs up and down as Flora watches her mother.

"Do you remember these?" Jodi asks, holding up a large pink and purple toy cupcake. She sticks her fingers through the top and flips the edges out and over, and the whole thing turns into a girl wearing a dress. Like a reversible jacket.

Zephie squeals with excitement and squats down next to Flora. They used to love these and called them their hidden fairies.

"Oh my God, I wonder if they still make these things," Flora says, reaching for the doll. She instinctively sniffs it, remembering how it used to magically smell like cake batter. Surprisingly, it still does. She holds the doll up for Iris to see, showing her the mechanics of the toy's transformation.

Jodi joins Flora on the floor, moving slowly onto one knee and then the other. Her hair is pulled again into a taut bun today, a stark contrast to how she always wore her hair when Flora was growing up: loose and billowy. As Flora watches Jodi settle onto the concrete, her attention wanders to the twitching eye. The involuntary spasming irks Flora even though she knows it shouldn't. Perhaps it's because it is yet another reminder of her mother's age; that eventually, these frailties will grow and unravel her seventy-year-old body, probably long before the two of them are able to find some kind of equilibrium.

Flora is suddenly profoundly grateful they have this time together.

"What is that?" Flora asks, distracted by a small object under a stuffed alligator in the box.

A flicker of recognition crosses Jodi's eyes before she stifles it, shrugging. "Oh, huh, that shouldn't be in here," she says, reaching for the strange object. She sets it on the ground behind her, like she'll find a place for it later.

"What is it?" Flora asks again. "Can I see?"

Jodi holds it up. "It's just a hippo's tooth."

Flora reaches for the six-inch arched piece of ivory and pries it from her mother's grasp. "*Just* a hippo's tooth?" She inspects the artifact. The back of the tooth is silky smooth, whereas the front is adorned with inscriptions. Lions and human figures with lion heads that wield knives. One depiction is simply a pair of long legs attached to a circle at the top. In another, a large bird carries a knife on its back. Flora rubs her thumb over a series of hieroglyphic characters.

"Why do we have this?" she asks. "Where did it come from?"

"It's called a 'birth tusk,'" Jodi says. "Meant to ward off evil forces or something. I don't know, your father got it for you when you were little. I think he found it on a work trip."

"This does not seem like something Dad would buy," Flora says skeptically.

"In Pennsylvania, maybe? Probably at the Egypt museum there."

Flora nods. "Oh, okay, that makes more sense. Like a gift-shop trinket."

"No," Jodi says, shaking her finger. "It was more than that. He put that thing under your crib. Like it would actually work."

Flora laughs. Nothing about this story seems credible. "Dad?! *Science is the only reliable road to truth* Dad?"

Jodi shrugs. "I wanted to get rid of it. I didn't even *want* to know what the hell kinda voodoo he was pulling."

Flora exhales in disbelief. "I don't get it. Why would Dad want something like this?"

Jodi raises a shoulder before returning to the box of toys. Flora can tell her mother is done with the topic, but Flora continues to stare at the tooth in her hand, flipping it over. The tip is worn and used, and she wonders what history it bears.

Why would her father buy this? And why would he place it under Flora's crib? These actions are completely incongruous with the Michael that Flora knows. But then, why would Jodi lie about the tooth's origins?

When her mother is distracted, Flora slides the birth tusk into her own pocket and makes a mental note to ask her father about it.

From the bouncer, Iris wails, announcing her hunger, and that's when Flora remembers her own grumbling stomach. Flora pries the baby from her seat and makes her way back into the house. It's only then that she realizes Iris's bare arms are ice-cold—how could she have been so stupid? It's freezing out here in the garage. Iris should have had a jacket.

She tells Jodi as much, and her mother replies, "I said that. When you first got out here. Remember? I said she needed a sweater. I didn't know where they were."

"You did?" Flora asks, her voice trailing.

Jodi nods.

Behind her, Zephie scoffs and sings under her breath. "Liar, liar pants on fire."

21

The rest of the afternoon passes in a blur of laundry, pumping, feeding, and vacuuming. Shortly before dinnertime, Jodi retreats to the guest room for a nap, and Flora has to use every bit of restraint not to flip the coffee table in rage. Why does her mother get to nap? She resents that Jodi's actions even suggest she is more tired than Flora.

"No one on the planet is as tired as we are," Zephie says, and Flora can't help but chuckle that even her imaginary friend is exhausted.

"Stop calling me that," Zephie whines. She is perched atop the dryer, her short legs swinging off the edge.

"Calling you what?" Flora stands in front of the washing machine waiting for the load to finish.

"'Imaginary.' I hate that word."

Flora doesn't know how to respond. Was Zephie always so self-aware?

She turns her attention to the next batch of laundry, spraying the items with stain remover. Iris had a blowout yesterday, and the onesie has been soaking in water that is now yellow with floating chunks of poop that resemble cottage cheese. She pours the water in the nearby utility sink and wrings out the stained outfit. Then she sprays it liberally.

"It stinks in here," Zephie says.

"Why do you think Mom came?" Flora asks, surprising herself with the question. She didn't realize it was on her mind. "Like, why she *really* came."

"Well, you sent her an email telling her you were going nutso," says Zephie. "Maybe she wanted to make sure you were okay. Or maybe she wanted a front-row ticket."

"Or maybe she doesn't trust me to be a good mom," Flora says.

"Oh, she for sure doesn't," Zephie agrees.

The washing machine clicks off, and Flora bats Zephie off the dryer so she can load it. She takes a quick pause to step into the hallway and listen for Iris's cries. Down here in the utility room, which is nestled in the back of the home by the garage, Flora can't hear what's happening in the rest of the house. She wishes she still had a working monitor. But only silence emanates from upstairs, where both her mother and her daughter are clearly sleeping.

When she has finished transferring the load, she places the next batch of clothes and sheets into the washer before heading to the living room. Her right hand subconsciously finds the birth tusk in her pocket and rubs its indentations.

Flora pulls out her phone to research the tooth but then remembers she doesn't have internet. Frustrated, she snaps a picture of it with her phone and texts it to her dad. *Found this in the garage. Do you remember getting it?* She watches the send bar load painfully slowly.

Flora enters the kitchen in search of something sweet. She

finds a box of expired granola bars in the cabinet above the coffee maker and just about cracks her incisor trying to bite into one. She tosses the box into the trash with a satisfying thud and then finds the Nutella, spooning it directly from the jar into her mouth. She is, once again, wearing only a nursing bra on top. She looks down at the flabby, loose skin on her belly. It's nearly impossible to believe that her stomach was stretched out three times this size a month ago.

Her phone buzzes with a call.

"Hey, Dad," she answers, licking the spoon clean.

"You said you found that in the garage?" he asks. There is tension in his voice. Or maybe he's out of breath.

"In a box of stuff from the old house," she replies. "What is it?"

"Not sure," he says quickly.

"Mom said you got it when I was little. Said she found it under my crib."

The moment the words are out, she knows her mistake. She's not supposed to tell Dad that her mother is here.

"Your mom told you—?"

"A while ago, I mean. When she sent the boxes," she says. "She mentioned maybe you got it in Pennsylvania. At a museum?" There's a long pause. "Dad?"

"Yeah, I remember," he admits.

"Well, what is it? I tried to look it up online, but without internet—"

"What happened to your internet?"

"It's out. I dunno," she lies. She doesn't feel like admitting to her father that a stranger has been stalking her baby. "Can you tell me anything about the tooth?"

"I didn't get it at the museum," he says. "I was leaving the museum when I saw a woman on the street selling them. She was…well, she looked like some kind of witch, honestly. Like you'd see in the movies. I'm sure it was all part of the marketing ploy. The *costume,* if you will. She talked about the teeth and how they used them in the Middle Kingdom to protect children." He clears his throat. "I didn't believe any of it, obviously. I just thought you might like it. So I threw her a few bucks for the souvenir."

He's lying about that last part. Flora can tell.

"If you didn't believe her, why did you put it under my crib?"

"Why are you so curious about this thing all of a sudden?" He's agitated, flustered even.

"I don't know why you're getting upset," she replies. She tightens the top of the jar back onto the Nutella. "I just found it and was curious…"

He changes the subject. "You doing all right? Since you don't have internet, you need me to send you some food?"

"That would be great, actually," Flora says.

"I'll do that," he says.

There is a long silence then. But Flora does not fill it. She wants the silence to be productive. She walks to the table and sits, resting her elbows on the tabletop. Her fingers tug and twirl a front section of her hair.

Finally, after a long while, her dad says, "She had a tough time when you were little. Your mom."

"What do you mean?" Flora presses the phone to her ear, as if the closer it is to her skin, the more likely she is to hear the truth. "How did she have a tough time?"

"She was hospitalized, you know that."

Flora scrunches her eyebrows together. "Yeah, I know. For dehydration, right? She spent the night to get an IV and some rest."

"It wasn't for dehydration," he says heavily. "And it wasn't just overnight. She was there for ten days. In the psych ward."

Flora is grateful she is sitting, because suddenly the world spins. It's like her universe is a speck of dust floating in the atmosphere and someone flicked it casually, sending it spiraling in the opposite direction.

"The psych ward? How did—why didn't I know this? This seems like something I should have known."

"I always thought your mother should be the one to tell you."

"Well, she and I don't really talk, so—"

"I know, no, of course, I know."

A tightness blooms in Flora's ribs just below her left breast. She takes short, successive inhales to try to dispel the ache.

Her dad continues. "She hadn't slept in days, and she was acting strangely. I took her to the ER. They did checks and everything seemed fine, so they told us to go to the psych institute instead. They put your mom on antipsychotics and within a week she was back to normal."

Flora opens her mouth, but no sound comes out.

After another minute, her dad finally asks, "You still there?"

"Yeah," she croaks. "Uh, sorry, Dad, Iris needs me. I'll call you later."

She hangs up. The cell phone is warm in her hand. She presses it against her nose and bites the corner of her silicone case as she stares. When she finally blinks, her eyes are dry.

"I guess we know why she's really here, then," Zephie says. She leans against the wall that separates the living room from the kitchen. "To make sure you don't end up in the psych ward like her."

Flora nods slowly. "Yeah," she says. "Or to make sure I do."

22

Bags of bagels, pints of deli sides, and a tray of meats, cheeses, and cookies cover the kitchen counters. All delivered first thing this morning. Clearly, Flora's dad felt guilty about dropping that emotional bomb on the phone last night.

"This is all from your father?" Jodi asks when she arrives downstairs and sees the spread. Then she purses her lips. "You told him I'm here, didn't you?"

"No, Mom, I didn't. I just said I could use some food."

Jodi snorts. "Some?" She eyes the breads and meats. "Always going above and beyond, isn't he?" Catching herself, she adds under her breath, "Well, for you, anyway."

Flora does not take this bait. She finishes her breakfast at the table while Jodi prepares a cup of coffee, once again adding four packets of fake sugar to the cup. Flora winces.

She slept even less than usual last night, her mind replaying the conversation with her father on a loop, trying to make sense of the truth that her mother was institutionalized. She wishes she had the kind of relationship where she could ask Jodi about that time, but that's a surefire way to kill the conversation before it even starts. Her mother shares on her own terms, and if Flora seems too interested, Jodi will sniff it out and clam up.

"Do you want a cup to go?" Jodi asks.

"To go?" Flora repeats. Then she remembers they discussed taking a walk through the neighborhood. "Oh, sure, good idea."

Iris's eyes are wide open as they bundle her up; she has become more alert to the world around her in the last few days. When they've settled her into the stroller's bassinet, Flora packs a bottle of milk and throws some extra diapers in the storage basket. As she slips on her fuzzy boots and long winter coat, she glances toward the living room. There, atop the coffee table, in the exact spot where it was before, is the tiny plastic pig.

"How did that get there?" she asks, pointing to it.

"What?" Jodi follows Flora's gaze. "That pig thing?"

"Yes, the pig thing," she says frantically.

Jodi buttons her coat slowly and stares at Flora. It's this stare that confirms that Jodi is testing her, *watching* her for signs of instability. It's all making sense now. Jodi doesn't have the backbone to tell the truth about her time in the psych ward, but she also doesn't trust her daughter to handle motherhood and all its tribulations.

"I don't know, Flora," Jodi says carefully. "I guess I put it there?"

"You guess?"

Jodi raises an eyebrow, and Flora hates this, hates everything about this. She doesn't want to be analyzed and watched in her own home. She hates knowing that she's always one step away from—what? Would Jodi put Flora away? Would she take Iris?

"I think I found it in the garage," Jodi says. "Yesterday, when I was going through the boxes. I thought it was cute and brought it inside for Iris."

"And you put it in that *exact spot?*" Flora asks, sounding increasingly anxious but unable to stop herself. What are the chances her mother would place the pig in the exact same spot it was in before?

"Let's get outside," Jodi says, directing the stroller toward the front door. "I think some fresh air would do you good."

As they walk along the edge of the road, Flora pushes the stroller with her forearms so she can wring her fingers and crack her knuckles. She rubs her fingertips together nervously.

"Cold?" Jodi asks, and Flora nods absentmindedly, going with the narrative her mother has suggested.

Flora has questions,

so many questions

and she doesn't know where to start.

The sky is gray, and the cold carries with it a weighted silence, like the world is wearing earmuffs. Flora focuses on the steady crunching of her boots on the gravel and tightens her grip on the stroller's push bar. She's craving normalcy.

"How's the condo?" she asks her mother.

During the divorce, Jodi bought a condo in a small complex, and Flora had liked the idea that her mom wouldn't be alone. It was steps from the beach in the Outer Banks, somewhere Jodi had always wanted to live. The family went every summer while Flora was growing up. Her mother came alive at the beach. Flora always felt a bit like the ocean was the only thing her mother truly loved.

"The condo is the same." Jodi shrugs but then remembers something. "Oh, someone died in the building!" she says excitedly.

Flora gasps. "Not Belinda?"

That's the only person Flora knows her mother to be friendly with in the complex. A similar-aged woman who was recently widowed when Jodi moved in.

"No, not Belinda," Jodi confirms. "Another woman. I don't think you ever met her." Jodi lowers her voice slightly, as if letting Flora in on a secret. "She shot herself."

"Jesus," Flora says. "That's horrible."

Jodi nods solemnly but clearly enjoys laying down the gossip. "They didn't find her for days."

"Days?" Flora pushes the stroller a little too hard in her shock, and her wrist flares up in pain.

"Isn't that tragic?" Her mother shakes her head. "No one checking on her. The only reason they even found her was because the person below started to complain of a smell in the vents."

Flora cringes. "Well…if she was that lonely, that might have been part of why she did it."

"Maybe," Jodi agrees.

They continue to walk for a moment in silence before Jodi remembers another tidbit. "You know, when they finally went into the apartment, they found beetles eating her dead body."

Flora stops in her tracks. "Beetles?"

Jodi continues, unfazed. "A whole trail of them. They came in through the window. 'Flesh-eating beetles' they're called. Who knew? Some of them were even crawling into her mouth, eating her from the inside."

I'm going to throw up I'm going to throw up

"Flora?" her mother asks. Jodi gestures ahead, suggesting they continue their walk. After a moment, Flora complies, lifting her leaden feet to carry her forward, her eyes trained on the road but seeing nothing of her surroundings. She can only see the beetles in Iris's room.

"Anyway," Jodi continues, "it all got me thinking—would anyone even know if I died in my condo?"

Flora rolls her eyes. Her mother has, of course, found a way to make this about her.

"Oh, Mom, we would *know,*" Flora says.

But as the words escape her mouth, she realizes that her mother may have a point. Until now, Flora and Jodi hadn't spoken in years, and her dad doesn't make a habit of keeping in touch. Unless her mother has friends Flora doesn't know about, maybe it really would be days before anyone noticed. The thought is impossibly heavy to Flora, murky with guilt and sadness. But she won't admit this to her mom.

"Belinda still lives there, right?" she points out. "She would check in on you."

Jodi raises an eyebrow in half agreement. "I suppose you're right."

She avoids eye contact, which is her way of brushing off the topic. And that's when Flora realizes this is something her mother actually worries about—dying alone.

In the bassinet, Iris's eyelids become heavy. Flora should get her home for a proper crib nap, but she wants to capitalize on this moment. She doesn't want to risk shutting her mother down the one time she is sharing about her life.

"Belinda's gone a lot, though," Jodi tells her. "She goes on retreats. Travels for tantra workshops and—"

Flora barks a laugh. "Isn't she, like, seventy?"

"What does that have to do with anything?" Jodi retorts.

"Okay, fair, fair," Flora admits. "I didn't know she was into that kind of stuff."

"Oh yeah, Belinda is very woo-woo. Spiritual. We've been to a few psychic fairs together."

Flora raises her eyebrows. "Together? So you believe in that stuff now?"

"Oh, Flora," Jodi says, "you're still young. You're still under the illusion that the world is not mysterious."

Flora has no idea what that's supposed to mean, but before she can respond, the sky breaks open, and a violent deluge of water falls from above. Jodi yelps, and Flora instinctively leans over the bassinet to protect Iris from the cold, pelting rain. Together, Flora and Jodi turn the stroller and run back toward the house, their bodies bent against the storm.

23

By the time they get back home, the rain has soaked Flora's clothes all the way through, and she can't stop shivering. She and her mother give Iris a bath in the kitchen sink before Jodi sends Flora upstairs to reset her internal thermometer with a warm shower.

Flora lathers a giant blob of shampoo between her palms and, using her nails, massages her scalp with the foam. She doesn't remember the last time she luxuriated under the water like this. Knowing that Iris is taken care of, she is able to fully relax, to feel the warmth as it runs down her body. It massages her muscles, which are sore from carrying Iris as well as sitting uncomfortably to pump.

Her mind returns to her mother's story about the lady who killed herself in the building. Flora is filled with sadness at her mom's fear of dying alone. But that sadness is also distracted by her own curiosity. Since when is her mother interested in the "woo-woo," as she called it? Has her mom changed that much since they last spoke, or has she always had this hidden side to her?

The rain beats down on the roof, and Flora can hear it even

over the rush of the shower water. She had no idea such an intense storm was coming. But then, how would she? She doesn't have internet. And even if she did, she'd have little interest in the weather report. Her entire life takes place within a small blueprint of earth. The daily precipitation rate is irrelevant.

Flora rinses her hair and, because she can, reopens the shampoo bottle for a second application. As she again massages her scalp, she fantasizes about a past life. She imagines prepping for a dinner out with Connor. They'll go to a small local spot with charming fairy lights on the patio and split a bottle of Malbec. On the drive home, she'll reflect on her empty schedule for the weekend ahead. Absolutely nothing she *has* to do, no one depending on her. The thought is intoxicating.

How long will it be before she has that feeling again? Maybe never. She is absolutely tethered to another human being. And she has no one to blame but herself.

She feels like a shit mom when she has these thoughts. The truth is, she has never loved another living thing the way she loves Iris. So how can such competing feelings coexist within her simultaneously?

When Flora finally gets out of the shower, the mirror is covered in steam. She wipes away the residue to reveal her blurry face. She takes her time swabbing her ears, plucking her overgrown eyebrows, applying lotion to every last square inch of her skin. She combs the knots from her hair and sprays on leave-in conditioner that smells like coconut.

Flora slips into a soft pajama set that kisses her skin when she walks. She wraps her hair in the towel and considers walking downstairs to relieve her mother before pausing in the hallway. Her mom has things covered. Flora doesn't need to rush. Instead, she walks to the guest bedroom, where Jodi has been staying.

She listens one more time for footsteps on the stairs and, hearing none, slips inside the room.

It's largely untouched, but there are still obvious signs of a visitor: the unmade bed, the open suitcase on the floor, the unique items on the nightstand. Flora doesn't know what she's looking for or even why she's here, but she feels called to explore and touch the items that belong to her mother. As if she could grow the intimacy between them by holding her mother's things in her hands, by understanding their shapes and edges.

She runs her fingers over the cover of a slim, worn book titled *The Yellow Wallpaper*. The picture on the front is a beautiful textured floral pattern in yellow with a woman standing in a dress of the same material. Beside the book is a thin pair of black reading glasses. Flora picks them up and rubs the lenses with her soft pajamas, disappearing a few smudges before replacing them on the table.

The suitcase is sparsely packed. A couple of cozy jumpers, a few sweaters, socks and underwear. No makeup, no accessories. Her mother's style has clearly been pared down. Even the color palette of her items is muted: grays, blacks, creams. As if she wants nothing more than to blend in.

Flora wishes she had a sibling she could text. *Mom goes to psychic fairs!* It's the kind of thing she needs to gossip about.

She remembers a time when she was six or seven. Her father was driving the family Volvo with her mother in the passenger seat and Flora in the back. She was wearing headphones plugged into her Discman, but she pressed pause on the music when she noticed her father's knuckles turn white on the wheel.

"Jesus, we're having this conversation again?" she heard her mother ask.

Flora pretended to listen to music as her father replied, "Think about Flora."

"I do think about Flora. That's exactly why I don't want to have another one."

"Jodi—"

"She's got headphones," her mother said defensively. "She can't hear me."

They rode in silence for a moment. Flora tried to make sense of what they were saying. Her mother busied her hands by adjusting the bright blue scarf around her neck.

Finally, her father said, "She asks you for a sibling all the time."

"That doesn't mean anything," her mom said. "She doesn't know what she's asking."

"Of course she does." Her father paused, then added, "We could get help this time. It wouldn't be like it was with Flora."

"Michael. I'm not having another child. And frankly, after all that happened, I can't believe you're still asking. It's not *safe* for me, for us—you have to stop. You just have to."

Her father was silent the rest of the drive. Flora found the conversation curious; she'd always assumed it was her dad who didn't want another kid. That's what her mom had insinuated. But this made it seem like the opposite. And it also seemed like it was Flora's own fault she didn't have a sibling. *I do think about Flora. That's exactly why I don't want to have another one.* Flora was drenched in guilt. She never heard her parents discuss the topic again, and that was the night she officially gave up on any fantasy of having a brother or sister.

But today, the conversation comes to her in a new light. Was her mother referring to her stay in the mental hospital when she said it wasn't safe for her to have another? For the first time, Flora empathizes with Jodi.

"Don't feel bad for her," Zephie says, startling Flora back

to the guest room where she's digging around in her mother's things. "She's not a nice person."

Flora frowns. "It's not that simple."

The more days that pass, the more real Zephie feels. Flora no longer has to summon her the way she did when she was little. Lately, Zephie appears of her own accord, and her opinions are not always in line with Flora's.

maybe we're just out of sync like any old friendship that is revived

Flora is about to stand and return downstairs when something in the suitcase catches her eye. She reaches for it and finds a tiny baby hat made of soft pink yarn. It reminds Flora of the hats they give out at the hospital. Was it hers when she was a baby? Did Jodi bring it as a gift for Iris? Flora returns it to its spot. Asking her mom about it would mean having to admit she snooped around in her stuff.

"Kinda like how she was snooping in your boxes in the garage?" Zephie asks.

"That's different. Those were boxes she sent me years ago. She already knew what was in them," Flora says.

Zephie rolls her eyes.

Flora ignores her, though internally she can't help but recognize how she is falling back into that old pattern of defending her mother without pause.

24

I t's nearing Iris's bedtime, and she has been crying for twenty minutes. Flora's best guess is that the baby is overtired. There is a cruel irony to this, in that if she misses the ideal window, Iris will be *so tired* that she screams her lungs ragged rather than fall asleep.

Flora stands with the baby near her crib as Jodi watches the storm outside. Here in the nursery, the rain echoes ominously, falling crooked from the sky so that it beats directly against the window. A nearby tree's branches tap on the glass, as if waiting patiently to be let inside.

"You know, just once, when you were little, I put some whiskey on your pacifier," Jodi says.

"Just once?" Flora asks dubiously. Jodi shrugs.

Flora rocks Iris back and forth until she finally has to admit defeat.

"Think we have to leave her in here to figure this out herself," Flora says.

Jodi continues to stare out the window and doesn't reply. A flash of lightning briefly illuminates the room before it plunges back into darkness.

Flora lays Iris on her back. Her face is bright red and wet with tears. Flora hates to leave her daughter like this, but there's nothing to be done. Holding her isn't helping and, in fact, may be making things worse. Plus, Flora's back and legs are killing her from standing and rocking for so long.

As Flora and her mother exit the room, another flash of lightning is followed by a loud crack of thunder. Iris wails harder, despite the sound machine blasting white noise beside the crib. Flora takes the stairs slowly, as if they, too, might be wet with rain, and fiddles with the birth tusk, which she slipped into her pocket earlier today.

"Are you hungry?" Jodi asks.

"Always," Flora replies. "I think it's all the pumping. I'm perpetually starved."

In the kitchen, Jodi assesses ingredients in the fridge while Flora cleans pump parts.

"I don't know how you have the patience to do that," Jodi says, nodding toward the growing pile of washed connectors and valves and bottles.

"I wouldn't call it patience. More like I don't have a choice." She pours more vinegar into the large bowl and swirls it with hot water. "It sucks, to be honest. And look. My hands are all dry and cracked."

"A real labor of love," Jodi says.

labor of love

phrase

1. a task undertaken or performed voluntarily without consideration of any reward

2. a guilt-fueled endeavor that not only feels mandatory but is also a ginormous pain in the ass

A bit later, Jodi holds a lemon in one hand and rifles through the silverware drawer with the other. "Where are the knives?" she asks.

"Where they always are," Flora says.

Jodi shakes her head. "Nope. Not here. Actually, most of the silverware is gone."

"What do you mean it's gone?"

Flora joins her mother at the drawer, which she now sees is sparsely filled: only a few forks and spoons rest where there would normally be piles of each.

"That's weird," Flora says.

"You emptied the dishwasher this morning," Jodi reminds her.

"I did?" Flora asks. "Oh, yeah, I did…"

"Do you know where you put them?"

"I definitely put the silverware back here."

Jodi raises an eyebrow. Flora is at a loss for words. Confused, she begins walking the length of the countertop and opening each drawer. It isn't until she reaches the far end of the counter that she finds the utensils. They're in a drawer typically reserved for food storage items like chip clips, rubber bands, and silicone bags. Jodi approaches and looks down where Flora is staring.

"Huh," she says, "why do you suppose you put them there?"

"I absolutely did *not* put them there," Flora says, then turns to her mother. "Are you messing with me?"

Jodi snorts. Her bad eye twitches. When Flora doesn't laugh, Jodi raises her eyebrows and parts her lips in disbelief. "Wow. Just. Wow."

"Well, it wasn't me!"

"And so the next logical explanation is that I'm deliberately toying with you? Yeah, you caught me, Flora. You don't talk to me for years, then I take the high road and show up here to help you but—surprise! I'm really here to *rearrange your silverware!*" Jodi shakes her head and walks away.

Flora thinks fast, trying to replay the morning's events in her mind but coming up blank. "I mean, Mom, I didn't..." But what can she say? The truth is, she barely remembers emptying the dishwasher at all. So much of how she operates these days relies on autopilot. "Sorry, I know you're not—I don't even know what I'm saying. I must have had a massive brain fart."

"Those seem to be happening a lot lately," Jodi retorts.

Flora sits at the kitchen table as her mother returns the silverware to its proper drawer. It clatters loudly in Flora's brain, hitting the sensitive spot in her left temple where migraines occasionally sprout. She rubs it with her fingers and takes a deep breath.

She doesn't hear Iris wailing upstairs anymore, which could mean the baby finally fell asleep or—more likely—the freight-train-loud rain is muffling her cries. The water pelting the house also pelts her skull and fans the flames of a headache. It's not so much the sound of the rain but what it means: she needs to place towels under the lip of the back door, set up a bucket in the garage where the ceiling leaks, and set the faucets to dripping so the pipes don't freeze overnight. But she doesn't even have the energy to get up from the kitchen table and pee, let alone prep the house for a massive storm—something she has never done on her own. Google would be a helpful tool in this moment. Fuck that stalker guy haunting her baby monitor. She briefly imagines jamming a fork in his eye, the utensil meeting no resistance as it slides through the center of his white jelly ball.

"With all these 'brain farts,' as you call them, should I be worried?" Jodi asks.

Flora snorts.

Her mother turns to her. "Is something funny?"

"I didn't know thunderstorms could happen in the cold," Flora says.

Jodi scrunches her eyebrows. "What?"

"Thunderstorms. I thought they were a warm-weather thing."

"Flora," Jodi says, joining her daughter at the table. "Did you hear me? Do I—do *we* need to be worried? You seem off."

"Maybe I'm just *dehydrated,*" Flora says, then starts laughing. Her own laugh makes her left temple throb, but it really was a clever retort.

"I'll get you some water," Jodi says, standing again.

Flora sighs loudly. "No, don't you get it? Remember when you went to the hospital because you were"—here she makes large, exaggerated air quotes with her fingers—"*dehydrated??*"

Jodi freezes in place.

"Secret's out! I know you were in the psych ward," Flora says.

Jodi shakes her head disapprovingly. "I knew you told your father I'm here."

"I did not! I did *not* tell Dad you're here! And who cares if I did? That's not the point. The *point* is that you were in a mental institution and you never told me!"

"Why should I tell you?" Jodi asks.

"Because it's a huge deal! And it's relevant to *my* medical history."

Flora winces. She shouldn't have made this about her.

But Jodi doesn't react. She grabs a glass from the cabinet and fills it with water before carrying it back to Flora and placing it in front of her. "That was not a happy time in my life. I was very alone. Your father—I know he's this perfect man in your eyes, but he wasn't there for me the way he has been there for you. He was never..." Jodi swallows. "Anyway, why should I sit around and think about the unhappy times? Why should I dwell on them?"

Flora's anger is trumped by the emptiness in Jodi's eyes, which fills Flora with regret that she ever felt entitled to her mother's story. Perhaps it really never was Flora's for the taking. Perhaps it would have simply been a privilege for her mother to share. Instead, she has stolen it from Jodi without permission and wielded it as a weapon against her.

"I'm sorry," Flora says. "I'm so sorry."

Jodi's eyes fill with tears—or, at least, the good one does. The twitching eye remains dry. "Is your arm bleeding again?" she asks, pointing to the spot that was impaled by the activity cube.

The bandage is soaked from underneath. Flora peels it off slowly to reveal that the deep cut is infected. Thick yellow pus pools at the surface of her skin and pulls off in long, sticky strings as she removes the bandage.

"Something's gotta give," Jodi says as she cleans Flora's wound.

"What do you mean?" Flora could fall asleep right here, mid-conversation.

"You're not taking care of yourself. Who knows how long this has been infected. You barely leave the house. You were hysterical over a small plastic pig—"

"You don't get it, that was *weird,* it was—"

"—and now with the silverware. You don't even remember emptying the dishwasher. It's concerning, Flora. What if something happens to you? What if this forgetfulness affects the baby?"

Her mother's words hurt far worse than the inflamed divot in her arm. Especially because she knows Jodi is right. Her mother is seeing all the things Flora wants to ignore.

"And I still don't even know how you got this injury," Jodi says, wiping the cut with a cotton swab.

"It was…" Flora starts.

Her mother looks up at her with the same expression she has had since Flora was a child. An expression of expectation and subtle disappointment. And suddenly, Flora is seven years old again, caught sneaking Halloween candy from the stash a few days before the holiday.

"One of Iris's toys wouldn't turn off," she says. "Even after I took out the battery. So I smashed it with a hammer."

Jodi doesn't say anything. She doesn't have to. Flora can feel the shame emanating from her mother's core, traveling like radio waves toward her, seeping into and poisoning her body.

25

F lora opens her eyes to find herself lying on the couch. Her back is stiff, and her lids are half-glued shut with sleepy gunk. The house is still, but the storm continues to rage outside. She opens and closes her palms, then rubs her fingertips together and cracks her knuckles. Where is her mother? How long has she been on the couch? The last thing she remembers is being in the kitchen with Jodi.

Flora shifts her weight and brings her feet to the floor. The rain pierces with a sharp, tinny tone. It must be getting colder out there; this sounds more like hail.

The room around her is vacant, and she realizes the entire house is dark. It must be the middle of the night. Or maybe it's seven p.m. She really has no clue, and the storm outside seems to have plunged the world into eternal darkness.

"You fainted." Jodi enters from the garage. "So there might have been something to that notion of dehydration, after all."

"I *fainted?*" Flora can't believe it. "How long have I been on the couch?"

"Not long," Jodi says, wiping her hands on her pants. "Maybe an hour? I'm not sure. And I don't know what time it is because the power went out."

Flora realizes this must be why the house is so dark. Then a worse realization hits. "Oh no," she says. "No, no, no. How will I pump?"

"Do you need the electric pump?" Jodi asks.

"I mean, I can technically do it by hand but, God, that'll take hours. I can't do that. I can't..." Flora starts to cry. "There has to be a way...we don't have a generator, but have you checked the circuit breaker? It's in—"

"—the garage. That's what I was doing. No luck. But you're welcome to try it yourself."

Flora deflates. Her breasts are already feeling full. She nudges them with her fingers, feeling their soft bounce, checking for sore spots. None yet.

And what will happen to the milk in the fridge? She can't afford for it to go bad.

"I'll help you," Jodi says. "Hopefully the power will be back on soon."

But as the hail pelts harder outside, they both know this is wishful thinking. Flora reaches for her phone and sees she has missed a call from her dad. Noticing the battery is in the red, she instinctively reaches for the charger on the end table before remembering the electricity is out.

"We have to leave," Flora says. "Go to a hotel or something."

"There's no way we're driving in this weather," Jodi says. "Especially not with a baby in the car. You're too tired. You just fainted, for God's sake. And my eyesight is already terrible, especially since this twitch started. Paired with the blinding rain, it's just not possible. We have to stay here."

Flora whimpers like a kicked dog. She curses the storm. Why

couldn't it have held off for just two more days? Connor will be home then, and he would know what to do in this situation. These things don't stress him out the way they do her.

Zephie what do I do this is so unfair

But Zephie doesn't show up. In fact, Flora hasn't seen or heard from her since their little tiff earlier in Jodi's room.

Although her mother is only a few feet away, Flora feels very alone. She knows this is unfair; Jodi is here for the sole purpose of helping. But still, Flora feels helpless, completely at the mercy of the world around her, a plastic bag in the wind.

Flora sits on the edge of the bathtub, the cool porcelain hard against the bones of her butt. She is naked from the waist up, cranking a hand pump on her right breast. Her hand cramps. The stream of milk is still going strong after forty minutes of continuous squeezing. And she hasn't even started on the left breast. This is in no way sustainable. She's desperate for electricity.

Flora cries. Her shoulders heave forward, and she abandons the pump in order to hold her head in her hands. Her thighs turn red from the pressure of her elbows as she watches the tears fall to the floor below.

I am failing in every way in every way I am failing

This has become her mantra.

She stares at the marble floor. Its design paints unintended pictures on its surface. Like finding shapes in clouds. She spots a resting camel with a large hump, a rabbit ready to pounce, an elegant Venetian mask.

"That's a candle with a flickering flame, do you see it?"

When she hears Zephie's voice, Flora's whole body exhales. She lifts her head and sees herself at ten years old. Hazel eyes, dry skin on the forehead, baby hairs that curl around her ears. It's like stepping through a time machine. Zephie smiles, and Flora sees the space between her upper teeth that braces will later fix.

this makes sense Zephie is me I am Zephie

Flora smiles and lifts her arms to hug the child version of herself, but suddenly something is very wrong. Her body feels heavy, weighed down.

wet I'm soaking wet

The bathtub is overflowing. Her pants are sopping wet, cling-ing to her body. The water falls over the edge of the tub with fervor, quickly accumulating on the floor. Zephie looks suddenly scared. She is wet now, too, and her hair sticks to her face and neck. The lightweight dress she's wearing was only moments ago a soft baby blue and has now been darkened by the water.

"Flora?" she asks, but her voice sounds like she's underwater.

Flora reaches out for Zephie, but her muscles are rubber. She is forced to watch as the water level in the bathroom increases and the *whoosh* of the overflow gets louder. Zephie starts to cry, and then she opens her mouth to scream, but no sound comes out, only a huge gush of water like the end of a firehose has been opened—

"What is it?" Jodi snaps her fingers in front of Flora's face. "Flora? Hello?"

Flora blinks, and the bathroom is back to normal. The tub is not overflowing, because it was never on. The floor is dry. She has regained mobility in her body. Zephie no longer sits on the floor in front of her.

"Did you see that?" she asks Jodi, even though she already knows the answer.

Jodi looks around the room. "See what?" Then, after a moment of silence, Jodi frowns. She clearly has much to say but steels herself. "Iris is crying. I think she's hungry."

Flora takes in a slow breath. "Can you do it? Feed her? There's milk in the fridge. We should use it...before...before it goes bad."

Jodi nods, then looks around the room one more time, as if someone might pop out from under the sink and explain everything. Finally, she exhales. "Sure. I'll feed her."

And she leaves.

Flora inspects her hands and clothes. She feels under her butt for water. She even places her hands on the floor, rubs her fingers over the image of the flickering candle that Zephie found, but there is not even one drop of water.

"What was that?" she asks out loud, praying that Zephie will answer. "Am I hallucinating?"

"No," Zephie says from behind her.

Flora whips around and sees Zephie sitting in the tub, her knees pulled tight to her chest.

"You're not crazy," the girl says.

"But I have to be. This is...none of this is real. *You're* not real."

"Stop saying that!" Zephie shouts, and her voice reverberates so strongly around the room that the mirror on the wall vibrates.

Flora stands, trembling. "You're scaring me," she says in a tiny voice.

Zephie mimics her, like that childhood game of copying whatever the other person says. "You're scaring meeeee," Zephie sings. "You're scaring me! You're scaring me!"

"Stop," Flora begs. "Stop it, Zephie. Why are you doing this?"

"*I'm* not doing *anything!*" Zephie retorts. She buries her face in her knees, balling her body until it is impossibly compact, and cries. Her shoulders move up and down with her short, heaving breaths.

Flora's fear dissipates and is replaced by guilt. Zephie is just a child. If anyone is scared, it's probably her.

"I'm sorry," Flora says. She places her hands on the edge of the tub and kneels down beside it. "Zephie?" Flora gently touches Zephie's arm, a desperate plea for connection. "Can you look at me?"

But when Zephie complies and lifts her head, it's not tears that Flora sees coming from Zephie's eyes. Instead, with each great heave, a line of beetles emerges from her black sockets.

Flora jumps up and back, bruising her spine against the countertop and sink. Zephie screams again and reaches her tiny hands up to her face, digging her nails into her cheeks to scrape up the bugs. Blood drips down to her chin, but the beetles keep coming. Flora watches as Zephie's body decomposes in fast motion. The beetles are feeding.

"What's happening to me?" Zephie shouts as her body deteriorates. "What's happening?"

But Flora doesn't answer. Instead, she flies out of the room, slamming the door shut behind her and racing down the hallway toward the stairs. She skips every other step and nearly slips toward the middle, but she finally reaches the bottom and finds her mother with Iris in the living room. Flora doesn't say a word, just runs to her mother and falls at her feet, grabbing her legs and pressing her face into Jodi's body. Her breath is shallow and hoarse.

Jodi runs her long, brittle fingernails through Flora's hair, massaging her scalp. After a moment, she coos, "Let me help you."

Flora doesn't pull her head away from her mother's touch; she just nods agreement with her whole body.

"Yes," she replies. "Yes."

26

Flora has completely lost track of time. She doesn't know how long the power has been out; she only knows that it has not yet returned. The storm outside continues to rage, condemning the world to darkness.

She has not moved from the couch since the incident in the bathroom. Jodi has fully taken the reins, feeding Iris every few hours. Flora hand expresses for comfort when her breasts are unbearably full, but she doesn't have the energy to manually pump. She knows this will kill her supply, but nothing can motivate her muscles to move. Her body has melted into the cushions.

She smells rancid. A blended brew of spit-up, body odor, dried milk, sweat. Even the wound on her arm stinks, which must mean the infection is getting worse. But again, Flora doesn't care. She has reached the ultimate lethargy, and it is surprisingly freeing. Her anxiety has kept her in fight-or-flight mode for so long that now the pendulum has fully swung the other way—absolutely nothing matters, everything is pointless, effort in any regard is a total waste. And it's lovely. It's weightless.

Zephie has been tugging at the hem of Flora's subconscious.

Flora can feel her, waiting at the edge of awareness, desperate for attention. There's an urgency to her presence, but Flora is content to ignore her. She makes a concerted effort to banish the images of Zephie in the bathroom: empty sockets for eyes, tears made of beetles, water shooting from her mouth. She can't begin to imagine why Zephie would punish her like that.

Flora lies belly-up, feet planted on the soft cushion so that relief blossoms in her lower back as she presses through her heels. If she turns one degree to the right or left, her breasts throb in pain. She can't help but wonder what Connor would think if he were to walk in right now. He would see his wife, half-dressed and incapacitated on the couch, with rock-hard red boobs spilling out of her nursing bra and an arm bruised from its oozing laceration. He'd see sporadic piles of dirty laundry (burp cloths, onesies, socks, sweats), scattered kitchen bowls crusted with remnants of days-old snacks, diapers and wipes and changing pads and the snot sucker and the baby nail file and blankets and clean towels and

I'm so thirsty

Flora's mouth is dry, like she has been chewing on cotton balls. The sensation shivers her spine. She closes her eyes, and when she opens them, Jodi is standing above her. The rain must have muted her footsteps. Flora blinks hello, and Jodi crawls onto the couch, placing Flora's head in her lap. Using the lightest touch, she drags her fingertips back and forth across Flora's face.

The gesture transports Flora to childhood. She remembers the first night she tried to sleep without her baby doll, uniquely named "Baby." She marched into her parents' room shortly after bedtime and handed over her lifetime lovey. She had thought hard about it and decided she was too old to sleep with dolls. When she placed Baby on the large armchair in the corner of her parents' room, she announced, "I need independence."

In school, they were learning about *being independent,* and the notion felt novel and grand. She couldn't wait to prove to herself how independent she could be.

Her dad smiled a somewhat sad smile and said, "All right, bunny."

Her mother said nothing.

An hour later, Flora still couldn't fall asleep without her comfort item. She padded silently out of bed and down the hallway to her parents' room. Baby was exactly where she had left her, so she gently pulled her from the chair and hugged her close. Before Flora turned to leave, she heard her mother crying. Soft, barely perceptible whimpers. When her mother realized that Flora was in the room, she brought her finger to her lips, *shhh,* and pointed toward the hallway.

Flora's mother followed her back to her room and climbed into bed beside her daughter.

"What's wrong, Mommy?" Flora asked.

"I'm feeling sad," her mother said. "And since you came to get Baby, I wonder if you were feeling sad, too."

Flora nodded and cuddled in closer to her mother, who began to lightly stroke her face. Flora didn't want the moment to end. In that snapshot of time, she had the rare sensation that she was a part of her mother's world. She was on the *inside.*

Now, Flora has that same feeling, her face once again in her mother's hands.

"Thank you for coming," Flora says, the words half-strangled in her dry mouth.

"I'm happy to be with my babies," Jodi says, and Flora doesn't cringe at her mother referring to Iris as hers. Instead, it feels like they are part of something together. Like Flora matters.

"Why didn't you have another one?" Flora asks.

Her mother's fingers stop.

"I just mean," Flora continues, "didn't Dad want another kid?"

"He did," Jodi admits. Her fingers restart as her gaze moves to the nearby window. "Well, he said he did."

"But?"

"But..." Jodi flinches slightly at a crash of thunder. "He knew it wasn't a good idea."

"Because of your time in the hospital?" Flora asks.

"That's right," Jodi says, adjusting her legs beneath Flora's head.

They sit in silence, and a lull in the rain echoes their own quiet.

Finally, Flora asks in a tiny voice, "Was it scary? The hospital?"

Jodi thinks. "At first," she admits, "but then..." Her demeanor changes. She gets serious, moving her gaze back to Flora, her bad eye twitching constantly. "I didn't lose my mind, Flora. But they want to take your baby away. You hear me? That's what they want to do. And so you have to play their game. You have to say you were the crazy one. That you've changed."

"But you didn't? Change, I mean?"

Jodi ignores this question. Or maybe she's inwardly puzzling out the answer. Finally, she says, "You stopped talking to me after your wedding."

"Mom..." Flora says like a teenager whining *come on*. When Jodi doesn't respond, though, Flora asks more gently, "Did you even care?"

Jodi's expression is blank. "How can you ask me that?"

"You had a miserable time at my wedding. You didn't want to be there."

"That's ridiculous."

"And when I told you it was obvious you hated being a mother,

you didn't argue with me. You didn't"—Flora's voice cracks—
"you didn't tell me I was wrong."

Jodi shakes her head. But when she opens her mouth, it's not
to give an apology.

"And yet, you became a mother yourself." Jodi's good eye
begins to tear. Her voice is strained. "Why couldn't you understand? Why couldn't you see?" When Flora doesn't answer, Jodi
repeats herself. "Why couldn't you see?" She asks it again and
again, more hysterical each time.

Overcome with disbelief, or maybe shock, Flora leaves her
body, watching the tableau of her and her desperate mother from
the outside. She has the sensation she is falling, as if someone has
knifed the strings of her parachute.

She wonders if she is dreaming.

27

Flora wakes in bed with no memory of having walked upstairs. Her shirt is soaked with milk, her breasts so over-full that they have leaked drop by drop to form a massive puddle on the sheets. This tragedy would normally get a reaction from her, but right now she is numb.

The room is awfully quiet. No pelting rain, no crashing booms of thunder. She props herself up on her elbow and looks toward the window, but the curtains obscure her view. Her mother must have pulled them closed. Flora has been wanting to replace them. They were inherited with the house, and they are not at all her style: a dark gray with an ugly orange quatrefoil pattern.

She lifts herself with great effort, swinging her legs over the edge of the bed. She pauses here in the hopes of stilling the spinning room. Her muscles are stiff.

Her feet carry her to the window, where she slides the curtains to the far edge of the rod. She scrunches her eyes in immediate discomfort. The whole world is white. There must be two feet of snow on every surface. And it's still coming down, a wall

of white dumping from the sky. Like a static screen on a mal-
functioning television.

"You're awake," Jodi says from the doorway.

"Iris?" Flora asks.

"She's downstairs in the swing. I just left her for a second
when I heard you walking around. It's adorable; she discovered
the mirror on the mobile above her head. And the spinning animals. She follows them with her eyes." Jodi smiles.

Flora shivers, still wearing the milk-soaked shirt. "We must
be low on milk in the fridge," she realizes.

"We're doing all right," Jodi assures her. "You don't need to
worry."

"What day is it?" Flora asks. Her phone died ages ago.

"Connor gets back day after tomorrow," Jodi says.

Flora remembers her mother had said she would leave before
Connor returned. But how can she in this weather? Jodi doesn't
have her own car, and Flora assumes taxi services aren't running
in the storm. They wouldn't have a way of calling one even if they
were. Which means Jodi will be here when Connor returns. The
thought punches Flora in the gut.

well she has been helping so he should be grateful

"Why don't you shower and come downstairs?" Jodi asks. "I
can make you something to eat, and you can play with Iris while
she's awake."

Flora nods in agreement and watches her mother leave. When
Flora looks down at her hands, they strangely do not feel like her
own. She doesn't recognize the lines on her palms or the curves
of her fingers.

After she has showered, she ventures downstairs to find Iris
content in the swing. Her small eyes dart back and forth as she
follows the spinning mobile with her gaze. She looks healthy,

her cheeks a rosy pink, her fingers gripping the strap across her chest. Her lips pucker around a blue pacifier with a hippo on it, and she sports an adorable bear beanie. That's when Flora realizes that the house is freezing. Of course, because the heat isn't working without power.

"How hungry are you?" Jodi calls out from the kitchen.

"Starved," Flora replies. Then she lowers her voice and whispers to the baby, "I'll be back, my love."

In the kitchen, Jodi assembles a sandwich with food left over from the delivery. She stacks it high with lettuce, bacon, and tomato.

The moment Flora sees it, her mouth waters. "Oh my God, I was *just* thinking the other day how much I wanted a BLT." Had she told her mother? She doesn't remember.

Jodi smiles in response and brings the sky-high sandwich to the table. When Flora takes a bite, mayonnaise squeezes out the sides, and she uses her right index finger to swipe it up. She licks the mayo with a satisfying smack and goes in for another bite. It's the best sandwich she's ever had.

Iris starts to cry. Flora thinks about getting up, but Jodi stands first. "Finish your food. I'll take her upstairs and feed her before her nap."

Flora swallows a half-chewed bite. "Thank you," she says.

Alone in the kitchen, she takes her time eating, tasting every ingredient smashed between the toasted bagel halves. The flavors are so strong, her taste buds so alive. It's like a sudden superpower.

three cracks of pepper two rotations of salt four thin slices of watery tomato

When she has finished, she wants another. She opens the fridge and grabs the bag of bagels, the remaining half of a tomato in a baggie, the mayonnaise. Just as she's about to close the door, she spots the pumped milk on the top shelf. Her eyes narrow in confusion. The pitcher is almost full. How is that possible? She hasn't pumped to empty in…a long time. She was planning to hand express after eating to make sure Iris had enough for the next couple of hours.

what has Mom been feeding the baby

Panic sets in. "Mom?" she calls out.

But no answer. And then another thought hits her: Jodi didn't prepare a bottle before leaving the kitchen.

she is starving her

Flora abandons the food on the counter and flies upstairs.

she wants to kill my baby

But when she reaches Iris's room, things are quiet. Calm. Flora enters slowly, not wanting to startle her mother. She just needs her daughter safe in her arms.

"Mom?" she says again.

Jodi has positioned the rocking chair closer to the window for a view. She sits with her back to Flora. "Shh," Jodi whispers, not bothering to turn. "She's getting sleepy."

Flora takes a step into the room. Then another.

"Did she eat?" She tries to keep her voice even and casual.

"I'm feeding her right now," Jodi says.

Flora seethes at the lie. A floorboard creaks under her foot as she gets closer to the window. But when she reaches the rocking chair, the air around her thins. She struggles to breathe as she stares at her mother in horror.

Jodi is naked from the waist up. Her skin is papery and flecked with age spots. Dry patches adorn her upper chest, and crusty scabs—warts?—dot her neckline like a chunky piece of jewelry. Her sagging, deflated breasts hang down to her belly button. And attached to her left nipple is Iris, who sucks and sucks, her eyes closing, her arms hanging by her sides.

"What are you doing?" Flora finally manages to scream.

"Don't shout like that!" Jodi whisper-screams back.

"Stop! Stop it!"

Flora lunges forward to grab Iris, but Jodi turns her body and uses her free arm as a defense. "She's not done feeding!"

"What are you *talking* about?" Flora is hysterical. "You don't have any *milk,* Mom! You're starving her!"

"Flora, you need to calm down." Jodi tries to shelter Iris, but the baby still pulls away from the nipple and cries. And, to Flora's horror, there on Jodi's huge, scaly areola is a bead of milk.

"It's called relactation," Jodi says. "It's perfectly natural."

"It's disgusting!" Flora retorts.

And suddenly, every bite of that delicious sandwich is rocketing up her esophagus. She brings her hands to her stomach, bends over, and vomits at her mother's feet. Pieces of bacon sprinkle the chunky pile.

"You're not well, Flora," Jodi says. "Iris needs to be taken care of."

"Yeah, by her *mother,*" Flora spits. She drops to her knees and dry heaves, her throat burning.

"You can't breastfeed," Jodi says. "Iris needs that *bond.* You're depriving her—"

"Get out!" Flora shouts. "Get the fuck out!!"

She tries to stand but slips in her own cold-cut upchuck. Her forehead smacks the armrest of the wooden rocking chair on the way down.

"Flora!" Jodi shouts, concerned. She jumps up and places a crying Iris in her crib before returning to Flora. She crouches down beside her, pushing Flora's hair out of the way so she can see the point of impact. "You're bleeding," Jodi says. A drop of blood lands in Flora's eye. She blinks, and the gesture is imitated by Jodi's bad eye twitching in response. "We have to check that you don't get—"

"You need to *leave*," Flora spits through clenched teeth. "I'm serious! Get out!"

Jodi recoils and stands. She sighs dramatically before reaching toward Iris's crib.

"Don't touch her!" Flora shouts.

"I'm taking her with me," Jodi says.

Flora forces herself to all fours, pausing in a tabletop position. She burps and swallows back the nausea. When she stands, the world goes briefly black.

"Taking her where?" she asks, adjusting herself so that she's blocking the room's exit.

"Downstairs," Jodi says. "Where else?"

"You're trying to take my baby away from me," Flora says. Another drop of blood drips down through her eyebrow.

"If I don't," Jodi says, "*they* will."

"They who?"

"You're not well," Jodi says.

"Stop saying that!"

Iris cries in her crib. Jodi takes a step toward the baby, and Flora screams. It's bloodcurdling and makes Iris cry even louder. Jodi can't help but turn back toward her own daughter. She extends her arms in front of her in a stance of caution.

"I can take care of her while you get better," Jodi says. "No one else has to be involved."

"How convenient for you," Flora spits.

Her mother takes a step toward her, and Flora looks around for something with which to protect herself. But she's an island in the middle of the room.

what do I do Zephie where are you what do I do

And then she's reaching into her pocket for the birth tusk. She hadn't realized it was there. When did she put it in her pocket?

But she doesn't let the question slow her down. She holds up the tusk, wielding it like a weapon. The pointy end of the hippo's tooth could do some real damage.

thank you Zephie thank you

"I've been looking for that—what are you doing with it?" Jodi asks. Her eyes bulge and her feet immediately plant in place. "That thing is cursed."

Flora laughs a high-pitched, cackly laugh that even she doesn't recognize. "Cursed?"

"Flora, you don't understand. Listen to me."

Jodi takes three more steps toward her, and, as she does, Flora swears the birth tusk warms in her hand. Like an over-worked cell phone, it has become hot to the touch. She tightens her grip anyway and extends her arm once again toward her mother, who looks scared.

"Okay, Flora," Jodi says, recoiling. "Okay. I'll leave, but only if you give me that tusk."

"Why?" Flora holds it in front of her for protection as she sidesteps away from the door. The two women circle each other like lions in the wild, each waiting for the other to make a move.

"Because it's dangerous. Just give it to me, and I will leave."

"Fine, take the fucking thing! I don't care! Just get out!"

Flora throws the tusk beyond her mother, out the door and into the hallway. Jodi turns and runs for it, fetching it like a dog, and Flora rushes to slam and lock the door behind her.

Finally safe, she returns to the crib and holds her daughter.

They both cry.

28

I ris sleeps in the crib, where Flora has climbed in beside her. The light in the room has shifted, from either the passage of time or a change in the weather. From Flora's cramped fetal position on the mattress, she twists to look out the window but can only see the sky and treetops. It appears the snowfall has stopped.

Flora watches Iris's chest rise and fall, her tiny lips forming a yummy pout. The baby's breath skips, and Flora instinctively holds her own breath, listening for Iris's exhale. When she finally hears it, she, too, can breathe again. Moving slowly and carefully so as to not rock the mattress, Flora works her way to a seated position. She leans her back against the slats of the crib and stretches her neck.

Jodi is probably somewhere downstairs, moving freely about the house while Flora is holed up in the nursery like a prisoner. She wants to force her mother out. If the roads were drivable, if her mom had a car, if Flora could charge her phone...but Flora will just have to stay here with Iris, in this crib, until Connor gets home. One eye always watching to ensure the door stays locked. She read once that ducks sleep in groups, taking turns so that at any given time, at least one duck has an eye open to look out for predators. She's not sure if it's true, but she likes the idea.

And anyway, she's gone this long without sleep, what's another day or two or three?

"I'm scared," Zephie says, huddled in the opposite corner of the crib. She pulls her knees close to her chest. "Is she going to take Iris?"

"Connor will fix everything," Flora says. "He'll be home soon. We just have to wait here."

Zephie bites her lip and pulls self-consciously at her delicate yellow dress. She shakes her head and asserts, "I told you inviting her was a bad idea."

"Okay, you were right. Is that what you want to hear?"

"We need to do something," Zephie says.

Flora takes a deep breath. Her bones are tired. "There's nothing to do, Zephie."

"You have to listen to me this time! We can't just sit here!"

This moment tugs at Flora's memory. Zephie's insistence, her fingers fiddling with the hem of the yellow dress. Flora tries to place it, this feeling of déjà vu, and then it slams into her with an unforgiving force.

Moose. This is exactly what happened with Moose.

When Flora was six, she went to a classmate's birthday party where the coveted last gift was a brand-new puppy. The dad brought out the small brown dog with a large blue bow around its neck. His tail wagged incessantly as he traveled from kid to kid, licking their faces and making them squeal in delight. After that, Flora begged her parents for a dog.

She'd find ways of sneaking it into conversation. She'd draw dogs and stick them on the fridge with dog-shaped magnets. She even pretended to be a dog when her mom came to get her out of bed one morning.

"Wake-up time, Flora," her mother said as she parted the curtains.

"I'm not Flora," she panted, "I'm a chocolate Lab!" Flora sat up on her hind legs and held her arms out like limp paws. "Woof! Woof!"

"Okay, well, that makes breakfast easy, then," her mother said. "You can pick scraps from the trash can."

Flora frowned. The game was suddenly a lot less fun.

As human Flora shoveled blueberry waffles into her mouth, her dad explained how much work it was to have a dog. Her parents loved to run through all the reasons they couldn't grant her one-and-only wish in life.

But then, shockingly, her mother arrived at school early one day to pick her up. She drove Flora to the nearby animal shelter and introduced her to their new dog, Moose. Flora didn't know what inspired this change of heart in her parents, but she didn't dare question it.

Moose was a one-year-old shepherd mix who had been surrendered to the shelter a few weeks before. His mouth was perpetually covered in slobber, and he leaned his whole body weight against anyone who pet him. Flora was in love.

She spent every spare minute with him. Cuddling with him on the floor, rubbing his belly, preparing his food with care. She even built forts in the living room that were big enough for the two of them.

But soon, Zephie started to complain. She pointed out that Jodi, too, was in love with Moose—so much so that Flora had to compete for her mother's attention. Flora hadn't particularly noticed this, but the more Zephie talked about it, the more Flora saw it for herself.

"It's like we're invisible when Moose is around," Zephie said.

And it was true. The dog had instantly bonded with Jodi, who didn't even care about dogs before Moose came along. He would follow Jodi everywhere, even to the bathroom, and he wiggled his way into her bed every night. He cried when Jodi left the house, whimpering and lying by the front door until she returned. And he even had a secret stash of her dirty socks hidden beneath his bed so that her smell lingered there at all times.

The obsession grew to be reciprocal. One night, they were running late getting home, so Jodi told Flora she was going to feed Moose as soon as they walked in the door.

"But I'm *starving*," Flora said at Zephie's suggestion.

Truth was, Flora had eaten a late snack that day and wasn't hungry at all. But this was a test. And Jodi failed it. She made a beeline for the dog the second they got home and delayed Flora's dinner until he was fed and satisfied.

"See?" Zephie whispered. "She loves him more."

Her mother brushed Moose every night before bed, at the same time she used to brush Flora's hair. When Flora pouted, Jodi scoffed. "You hate it when I brush your hair!"

Flora couldn't argue with that, since she did often complain when Jodi ran the bristles through her knots. But this was different.

Her mother added, "You're old enough to do it yourself now, anyway."

Zephie shot Flora a look like *told you so.*

Jodi had a particularly busy time at work about eight months after getting Moose. She was helping part-time at a nearby university with fundraising, and it was their big event of the year. This meant she was away from the house most nights for a few weeks. And Moose was not happy.

He started taking his frustration out on Jodi's items:

pantyhose, underwear, silk pajama pants. One night, when Jodi arrived home late from work, she turned on the light to reveal a living room full of Moose's damage. He had completely destroyed two television remotes; pieces of plastic were sprinkled all over the floor and couch. Jodi frowned.

"Moosie boy, what have you done?"

Flora was hiding nearby, watching the interaction from around the corner when she should have been in bed. She swallowed a giggle when she heard her mother curse under her breath as she collected pieces of the destroyed gadgets.

"You gotta stop this, little man," Jodi continued cooing to the dog. "Please tell me you didn't eat any of this. That would cost a fortune in stomach surgery." She looked down at Moose, who wagged his tail in happy oblivion. "If you keep this up, you won't be able to live here anymore. You gotta learn to be a good boy." Her words were harsh but her voice was light and soft.

Jodi abandoned her cleaning task and crawled onto the floor with Moose. She lay down and let him lick her face, laughing like a child. From their hiding spot, Flora and Zephie frowned. Flora wondered when, if ever, her mother had shown her that much affection.

From that moment forward, she hated Moose.

"We never should have gotten a dog," she told Zephie that night in bed.

"We need to do something," Zephie agreed.

"Like what?" Flora asked, defeated. "We can't do anything."

"Why not? This is our chance," Zephie said. When Flora bit her lip and scrunched her eyebrows together, Zephie added, "You said yourself you hate him!"

Zephie had a myriad of plans: letting him escape out of the open gate, blending a bunch of grapes into his food (her mother told her grapes are poisonous to dogs), throwing his ball into the street as soon as a car whipped around the corner onto their cul-de-sac. But none of these ideas sat well with Flora. The truth was, she didn't want to hurt Moose. She wanted to hurt her mother.

"That's brilliant," Zephie said in response. "We need *her* to get rid of him herself. She even *told* Moose that he needs to stop destroying things…"

Together, they hatched a plan.

A few days later, Flora snuck into her mom's closet and ran her fingers over the clothing collection. Vibrant colors, soft fabrics. She landed on a long duster her mother had purchased in Rio. The pattern was mesmerizing, the fabric delicate. It had some sentimental value, though Flora didn't know why.

"This is perfect," Zephie said.

When Jodi found the shredded sweater, she cried. Moose tried to comfort her, but Jodi closed herself in her room. The dog turned to Flora and stared at her with his giant dark eyes. He knew. He knew exactly what she had done.

Flora felt icky. Maybe her plan hadn't been so brilliant after all. Ashamed, she bowed her head and fiddled the hem of her yellow dress between her fingertips. She would never wear that dress again.

Within a week, Moose was gone. Jodi said he had separation anxiety, so she found an old man two towns over who never left his house. The man continued to send her photos of Moose until the dog died a decade later. Moose lived a great life.

For Flora, though, nothing changed. Her mother never returned to brushing her hair at night, and she never wrestled on the ground with Flora like she had with the dog. She was just a sadder version of Jodi, no more interested in her daughter than she had ever been.

Moose, Flora realized, was never the problem.

29

I hate that dress," Flora tells Zephie, who fiddles the same yellow hem in her fingertips now.

"It used to be your favorite," Zephie says.

Flora reflects on her time with Moose and wonders if maybe it had never been about Jodi. Maybe Zephie didn't like the fact that *Flora* had a new friend. And so she manipulated her into getting rid of him.

The thought is frightening—what it means for the past but also what it means for today. What are Zephie's intentions? Why did she really show up after all these years? Flora shakes her head, dispensing with the notion that anything sinister is afoot. Next to her in the crib, Iris stirs. She's going to be hungry soon.

"We have to go downstairs," Zephie says. "To get her milk from the fridge."

"I'm not going down there," Flora replies.

She tries to straighten her legs in the crib, leaning back on her tailbone and extending her bare feet toward the sky. Her toes are tinged blue from the cold, and she wishes she had a pair of socks in here.

"Then what will Iris eat?" Zephie retorts.

As if on cue, Iris opens her mouth and wails. Flora bites her lip. She doesn't have a choice: she has to nurse. She pries off her bra, and her heavy breasts, now riddled with clogs, ache without the support.

Flora tries to convince herself that she can do this. But as she brings a crying Iris close to her chest, her mother's saggy breasts flash in her mind. She blinks hard, trying to disappear the image, and adjusts Iris crossways in a cradle hold. Then she cups her left breast in her hand and brings it to Iris's wide-open mouth.

The latch is shallow and immediately pinches Flora. She winces and pulls the baby off.

"Downstairs," Zephie chants. "Downstairs. There's milk downstairs!"

Flora ignores her and tries a second time to latch the baby. Once again, Iris's lips clamp down on the nipple, but Flora curls her toes and breathes through the pain. The sucking motion is unbearable against the rock-hard clogs. Flora uses her pinky to break the seal and pull Iris away. She can't take it.

Iris's mouth is red with Flora's blood. Her nipple wounds have reopened.

This won't work. Zephie is right.

"Of course I am!" the girl sings.

Flora climbs out of the crib and rifles through the closet, where she finds a large fabric wrap that one of Connor's friends sent them before Iris was born. Flora most definitely needs a video tutorial explaining how to use this thing, but she'll just have to make do with winging it. She wraps it again and again around her waist, then throws it over her shoulders and back around. Iris continues to cry as Flora finagles the baby into her makeshift carrier. She holds her hands beneath Iris's butt for extra support so there's no chance of her slipping out. Flora then finds a baggy open-front sweater on the floor of the closet and layers that on top.

"What if Mom tries to talk to me?" she asks Zephie, dreading the thought of running into her mother downstairs.

"Stick a fork in her neck," Zephie says.

Flora rolls her eyes. "Thanks for the help."

"I'm not joking."

A chill snakes its way up Flora's spine. She thinks of Moose and the violent ways in which Zephie suggested they *rectify the problem*. Flora then tries to *not* think about stabbing her mother in a major artery.

Downstairs, there's no sign of Jodi in the living room. Flora heads straight for the kitchen and opens the fridge. The pitcher of milk is almost full, and she exhales in relief. The refrigerator is still slightly cool inside, despite the power having been out, but she can see that the produce is starting to turn. She places the milk on the counter and smells it to be sure it's good, then she gathers a couple of bottles and her manual pump. Just before she's about to turn around and leave, she thinks to chug a giant glass of water and grab herself a few snacks.

With a complaining Iris wrapped tightly against her chest, Flora places all the items in a large salad bowl for transport. She's about to head back upstairs when she decides to check the breaker box. She snuggles a hat on top of Iris's tiny head and carries her to the garage, sets her in her bouncer, and heads to the circuit breaker. The cement floor is cold beneath her bare feet.

She examines the board, hopeful that switching the circuits back and forth might produce some kind of miracle. But nothing happens no matter how many times she fiddles with them. Iris cries from her bouncer, and when Flora looks toward her, she notices the shelves on the far wall. They seem different some-how. She narrows her eyes in concentration. An itch sprouts on Flora's brain as she stares.

something is off

She walks toward the shelves slowly, as if approaching a skit-tish animal. The boxes have been rearranged. She's sure of it. Her mother must have been out here again. But what was she looking for this time?

Something *hiss, hiss, hisses* in the wall, and Flora knows it's just the pipes, but the sound still startles her back to the present moment. She needs to feed Iris.

Inside, she situates herself on the armchair and offers Iris milk from the fridge. Flora doesn't do the math of how old the milk must be—a Google chart would surely tell her it has gone bad. But it smells okay, and she doesn't have any other option.

Iris sucks ferociously at the bottle as Flora stares out the back window into the dark void of the night. Her mother must be asleep upstairs. The house is silent save for Iris's *suck suck sucking*.

But then, outside: a break in the clouds. The bright moon illu-minates the backyard briefly. Flora's eyes narrow as she tries to see more clearly. There, in the snow, are footprints. Her breath catches, and a fire ignites in her stomach. The trail of prints goes from the house to the woods, with no sign of returning tracks.

where the hell did you go Mom

Her mother does not have proper footwear. She showed up at Flora's door in simple leather boots that would in no way hold up in deep snow. And did she even have gloves? A hat? She will freeze to death out there.

"So what?" Zephie whispers. "Let her."

Flora briefly considers this before sighing and hurrying Iris through the last ounce of her bottle. Flora burps the baby as she walks to the back door. When she opens it, a gust of freezing air enters the house, and Iris reacts loudly to the sudden temperature plunge.

"Mom?" Flora calls out. "Mom!" She shouts loudly, but her words are immediately swallowed by the snow. There's no way someone in the woods could hear her. What is her mother doing out there? How will she find her way around in the dark?

"This is just like her," Flora says out loud. "The second I'm mad, she finds a way to turn it around and make me worry instead."

Flora stands, knowing what she must do but dreading it, willing her mother's figure to appear suddenly from behind the trees. But as the minutes pass, Flora is increasingly nauseous with guilt. What if something happened out there? What if her mother is hurt—or worse?

She closes the back door to preserve what little warmth they have left in the house. Then she sets about gathering warm clothes for both herself and the baby, bundling Iris tight against her chest. Flora puts on one of Connor's coats that is large enough to zip Iris inside as well. As she shoves her feet into her boots, stamping the heels down to squeeze them in, regret and resentment whirl in her gut.

Her mother better have a good reason for doing whatever she has done.

30

Flora's boots crunch the snow as she walks deeper and deeper into the woods. A theater kid she dated in college taught her that cornstarch packed into a tea towel produces a sound like footsteps in snow.

Memory is a funny thing.

It must be the middle of the night. Or the very earliest hours of the morning. The moon was surprisingly bright in the backyard, but here in the woods it is obscured by branches and what little foliage remains this late in the season.

Iris has fallen asleep, cocooned in the oversized coat. Flora fantasizes about switching places with her baby. What she wouldn't give to be cuddled up warm and safe and lulled into a deep slumber. Instead, her back screams with every step, and her weary legs ache. She curses the snow for making the trek that much harder, but she's also grateful for the road map. Her mother's prints are a clear trail.

Dead branches catch on the fabric of her coat as she walks. Each scratch makes a *zip* sound as she trudges forward. One grazes her cheek, stinging. She wonders if it broke the skin, but her face is too numb to tell. Her nose drips into her mouth, and all she tastes is cold, cold, cold.

Iris stirs slightly in her sleep, turning her head from one side to the other, and, as she does, a warm, wet liquid slides down Flora's chest between her breasts.

you've gotta be fucking kidding me

The spit-up travels quickly down her belly to the waistline of her pants. She's desperate to wipe it off, get herself clean, but it's under layers of clothes and a sleeping baby. There's no way. She takes one exhausted step after another, the spit-up getting tacky and sticky and

I just wanna GET IT OFF

But then the trail of footprints ends. Right in front of her. It's darker here, the woods more dense, and she squints as she wills her eyes to adjust or maybe develop some kind of superpower so she can see through the darkness. And then, to her right: a dull crackling, some lit embers. The afterthoughts of a fire.

She pivots and maneuvers herself over a large log, sitting and swinging her legs around to the other side. And that's when she finds her mother, leaning with her back against the log facing the other direction, eyes closed.

"Mom? Jesus, *Mom*?" Flora jostles her mother's shoulder. Jodi groans just enough of a response for Flora to know she is alive.

Flora surveys the area and finds her mother's boots a few feet away in the snow. Sure enough, when she looks back at Jodi, Flora sees that she is barefoot. Not even any socks.

"Are you insane?" she asks, gingerly crouching down in the snow to inspect her mother's feet.

"Don't...touch..." Jodi murmurs, and Flora can see that her mother's feet are injured, though she can't determine to what degree in the dark.

"What were you doing out here?"

Jodi shakes her head, and Flora again looks around for any clues to her mother's motivations. Something in the ash of the fire catches her eye. She stands, one hand under Iris for extra support, and grabs a large stick, which she uses to dig around in the fire's remnants. The end of the stick hits something hard. She fishes the item out of the embers and pushes it into a pile of snow. Flora touches it quickly with her fingertips to assess the temperature. It's only warm, so she lifts it to her face to see it more clearly.

The birth tusk.

Was her mother trying to burn it? Does she really believe that strongly that it's cursed? The hippo's tooth is made of ivory; of course it didn't burn. And how did her attempt fail so spectacularly that she injured her feet in the process?

Flora stands, her knees popping. She slips the tusk into her pocket. Her mother is not in a state to answer questions right now, but she will. Flora will demand it.

First, though, there is the issue of getting them all home. Through the snow. In the dark. Without the use of Jodi's feet.

She considers walking back to the house, dropping off Iris, and bringing back a sled in order to drag her mother home. But she shouldn't leave Jodi out here for that long, alone and cold and in pain.

"Can you move at all, Mom?" she asks.

Jodi opens her eyes, takes a breath, and nods. She puts weight on her hands and leans forward.

"Great," Flora encourages, "that's great. I'm going to squat down, and I just need you to climb onto my back, okay?"

Her mother nods.

After much awkward finagling and a fussy Iris expressing her annoyance at having been woken up, they are finally back on the trail home, retracing their earlier footprints. Flora leans forward with the weight of Iris on her chest and her mother on her back. Flora's arms hook under her mother's legs, which wrap around Flora's waist and, subsequently, Iris's little body. With her mother's head above her own, and little Iris's below, the three of them are like a generational totem pole.

She thinks of that phrase "it takes a village" and snorts. A village would be nice right now. Real nice.

it takes a village
idiom, proverb
1. the notion that a child's upbringing is a communal effort
2. a phrase people throw around in a way that ultimately belittles how fucking impossible it is to raise a child without support

31

T hings look much worse in the light.

Jodi's feet are gravely misshapen. On the left, her three middle toes are melted together with a large patch of scaly redness on top, the skin peeling back to expose rawness. It's all reds and purples and yellows, the tips of the toes starting to blister and bloat. On the right, her heel is peeling, as though the foot is loosely wrapped in its own skin, like cling wrap on half a sandwich.

"What *happened,* Mom?" Flora asks.

They are at the kitchen table, Jodi's feet propped on a chair nearby. With Iris safe in her crib upstairs, Flora tends to her mother's wounds.

Jodi is more alert now. "It was an accident."

Flora frowns. "I saw the birth tusk. Were you trying to burn it?"

"It's cursed."

"You mentioned that," Flora says.

As they talk, the tusk warms in her pocket, the heat traveling through her thick pants to the top of her thigh.

"You left it there, right? You left it in the fire?" Jodi's eyes are wide and wild.

"Yes," Flora lies. "Mom, you have to tell me what's going on."

Jodi bites her lip and shakes her head. Flora sighs and bends over Jodi's feet again, using tweezers to peel away at the swollen heel. As she sets the remnants on a paper towel, she marvels at the growing pile of human skin on her kitchen table.

"When I threw it into the fire," Jodi starts, eyes trained on her injuries, "it—nothing happened at first. But then…my feet burned."

"Like the flames jumped? You were standing too close?"

"No, no, not like that. My feet just felt really hot and when I looked down there was nothing one minute and then the next— they were covered in flames."

Flora scrunches her eyebrows together. "I don't see how that's possible. Like spontaneous combustion?"

"I don't *know*, Flora," Jodi says tiredly. "I'm just telling you what happened. That *thing*"—she spits the word from her mouth—"is out to get me."

Flora finishes wrapping her mother's feet with gauze. "The tusk? What do you mean 'out to get' you?"

"It's as if we're connected somehow." Jodi takes a deep breath, lifting her chest, and lets the air out slowly. "But it's gone. Out there in the woods. So I'm safe now." She grabs Flora's hands with her own. "*We* are safe now."

Flora's brain is chunky soup. Her mother's story makes no sense. And Flora's thigh is getting hotter with every passing minute. She expects to find a shiny burn mark there. But still, she dares not move the tusk now, dares not tell her mother that it is not actually out there in the woods but, in fact, right here in her pocket.

Upstairs, Iris cries, and, as her voice reaches them at the

151

table, Jodi gasps. Flora looks over to find that her mother's breasts are leaking. A wetness spreads across Jodi's shirt. Flora's own chest, however, is dry. Panic and anger and revulsion steam up in her like a kettle about to sing. This isn't right. It isn't *right.*

"You stole my milk," she says, harsh and accusing.

"What?" Jodi asks.

"You stole it from me!"

Jodi cocks her head to the side. "Now, Flora, that's not how it works, you know that."

"Oh, is it not? Is that 'not how it works'? Kinda like how feet don't just spontaneously combust and people aren't *connected* to inanimate objects?"

Jodi opens her mouth and closes it again. "You don't understand."

"Connor will be home tomorrow," Flora says, and she can taste the relief of her words as she speaks them.

"What do you think women did in ancient times?" her mom asks, ignoring her. "It was *normal,* if a woman couldn't breastfeed—"

"I *was* breastfeeding!"

"—then another nursing mother in the community would help out. It's absolutely natural."

Flora's hands fly into the air. "You are *not* another nursing mother! You are *my* mother!"

She watches as the wet spots on Jodi's shirt expand, and she can't take it anymore. She needs to go upstairs. Needs to be with her daughter. Needs to clean her filthy body and rest her bones, which feel like they are breaking at this very moment, cracking from exhaustion and overexertion.

Silence screams between them, dense and alive like an angry scribble.

Finally, her mother asks in a small voice, "Carry me to bed?"

And, of course, Flora agrees, because for every cell within her that resists, there exists a cell drawn to her mother like a compass to true north.

With her mom in her arms, a role reversal of all the nights her mother carried her to bed as a child, Flora climbs the steps. They do not speak, but their bodies communicate; Jodi's heartbeat thumping against Flora's arm, tears falling down Flora's cheeks. Her mother rests her head on her daughter's shoulder. And as Flora lays her mom in bed, she realizes that the same complex, paradoxical feelings she has for Iris apply to her mother as well. A deep, primal, evolutionarily wired love that coexists with resentment and a desperate need to separate, to individuate.

Perhaps there is no way to break this cycle, after all. Perhaps this is how it was always meant to be.

32

F lora brings Iris into the bathroom and straps her into her bouncer on the floor. With a pacifier in her mouth, she is content to look around the room, wide-eyed.

As Jodi sleeps down the hall, Flora prepares a bath, desperate to wash off the stink and filth and stress of the last few hours. In the mirror, she sees a deranged woman. Her hair is matted, her scalp sore from not brushing her knots for days. Dried blood cakes her forehead where she banged it on the rocking chair. Her cheeks sink in below her eyes, and her arm wound is exposed, now calcified in a yellow crystal scab. Her head pulses; her arms ache. She is moments from total mechanical failure.

Flora tests the water with her fingertips. It's hotter than she can stand, but she wants it that way. She slowly slips over the edge, gently submerging her body. The hot water stings, and she would normally pull away from the sensation, but she is disconnected from it somehow. She feels only an echo of the pain. She wishes she had a fancy bathtub that would pelt her with scalding-hot jets.

Iris complains from her bouncer, and Flora looks over the edge to find the baby staring in her general direction.

"You wanna join Mamma?" she asks.

Iris blinks "yes," and Flora reaches into the cold air for her daughter. She doesn't worry about the water dripping on the floor or getting the bouncer wet. She unzips Iris's onesie and lifts her toward the bath. After opening the diaper and letting it fall to the floor, she rests Iris on her legs, belly-up, with only her lower half in the water. Iris can't smile yet, but Flora knows she wants to.

Flora wonders briefly about the temperature of the bath. But it doesn't feel that hot anymore. She's sure it's fine.

"Doesn't that feel good?" she asks, gently massaging the clean water into Iris's tiny shoulders and cleaning behind her little ears. Her tiny body turns pink in delight.

Suddenly, Flora feels water on her back and a similar massaging sensation, as if she is touching her own body instead of Iris's. But when she looks over her shoulder, she sees her mother on the edge of the tub.

"Mom? How did you—?" She didn't hear her come in, didn't even notice when she propped herself on the nearby porcelain. "Your feet! Did you walk here?!"

"I crawled," Jodi says with a smile.

Goose bumps sprout on Flora's forearms.

"Relax," her mother says, continuing to massage her daughter's shoulders and neck.

Flora leans back, intoxicated by her mother's touch and the weight of her child on her legs. Without warning, Flora begins to cry. The hot water and loosening muscles release something within her that she cannot contain.

"I'm just so tired," she says between sobs.

"I know," Jodi coos. "Shhh, I know."

She dunks Flora's head back just long enough to wet her hair, then lathers a large dollop of shampoo between her palms. Her brittle nails scratch Flora's scalp, and Flora emits a low moan of pleasure.

"I felt the same way," Jodi continues as she washes Flora's hair. "I was so exhausted. At one point, I even convinced myself the baby wasn't real. That she was just a hallucination."

Surprised, Flora tries to turn her head toward her mother, but Jodi dissuades her with her hands, continuing the massage.

"Just listen," she whispers. "Try to relax."

Flora squeezes Iris's hands, twisting her daughter's tiny fingers in between her own.

"My baby wasn't real," Jodi continues. "That's why I would hear cries when they weren't happening. She was a phantom. Trying to trick me."

"That's pretty twisted," Flora says, her voice cracking as she becomes uneasy.

Jodi tends to Flora's hair lovingly. "An evil phantom," she whispers.

"Mom…" Flora's eyes go wide with thought. "Did you try to hurt me?"

This time, Jodi allows Flora to turn her head, and she makes eye contact. "No, Flora. Of course not. I never would have hurt you."

A headache pulses at the base of Flora's skull.

"I was trying to save you," Jodi says, "from that evil. From the *bad* inside."

Flora is lightheaded. "But…"

"And that's what I'm here for now, too," Jodi says. "To save you."

"Save me from what?" Flora asks.

Jodi shifts on the tub's edge, positioning herself in front of

Flora, and suddenly her hands are on Flora's upper chest. She nods as she leans forward and pushes Flora under the water. Flora doesn't resist as her face goes under. She holds her breath as the water sinks into every pore, every crevice. When she tries to resurface, though, she is met with resistance. She holds more tightly to Iris's hands and pushes with her feet to overpower her mother's force.

"What the hell?" she asks when she reemerges. Iris still lies oblivious on her legs.

"I'm trying to save you," Jodi says again. "You and me, Flora, we weren't built for this. We weren't made for motherhood."

And though Flora wants to fight her, wants to disagree, she can't. Because she *is* a failure; that much is clear. And her daughter deserves better. This time, when Jodi pushes her under, she takes her breath a second too late, and the water fills her throat and gurgles and bubbles down to her lungs. She needs to cough but can't, and when she releases air out of her mouth, the water churns and swirls. Her eyes are open this time, and she sees her mother's face, rippling and distorted through the water's surface. Her mother is sad, resigned. She does not look like she enjoys what she is doing.

Flora almost lets her do it, too. She almost closes her eyes and succumbs to the warmth. But then Iris's small head appears under the water beside hers, and she realizes that her mother's plan is not meant only for Flora.

And this—this she cannot allow.

Flora flails her body, knocking her knee against the side of the tub, her leg throbbing up to the hip in response. She tries to lift her hands, but her mother has them blocked with one of her arms, and Flora is weak, so weak. It's as if she has been drugged, but she knows she has not. Her body is just *done*.

She again presses through her feet, and this time her torso shoots up from the water with such force that she headbutts her mother, who falls backward. With her mother on the floor beside the tub, Flora lifts Iris from the water and inspects her. She wails loudly, and the noise is a godsend. She is alive.

But before Flora can do anything else, she feels the pressure of her mother's hands on her torso, and her body falls toward the wall when her feet slip on the slick porcelain of the tub, her shoulder slamming into the tiles and dislocating from the joint.

Her muscles *RIIIIIPPPPPP.*

oh my God I can't move my arm oh my God

She is put together wrong, like a broken puppet.

Iris hangs from Flora's limp grasp, and Jodi lunges forward to retrieve her. Flora takes sharp breaths between her teeth. Jodi lifts the baby from the water and then ceremoniously holds her head in one hand, preparing to dunk her backward like a baptism. Flora leans against the wall with her bad shoulder and screams in pain as she uses the wall to brace herself. She kicks out her right foot and slams it into Jodi's chest, sending her reeling. The baby goes with her, not ideal but the lesser of two evils, at least safe from the water for the moment.

Jodi is disoriented, Iris still in her arms, and Flora uses that very second to reach over the edge of the tub with her good arm and— *SLAM*—whack her hand against Jodi's burned feet. Jodi wails, and Flora whacks them again. Blood sprouts beneath the gauze.

Iris cries, pressed uncomfortably into Jodi's chest, naked and exposed and cold.

Flora's left arm is useless. It hangs limp at her side, and she can't even make a fist with that hand. She needs to pop it back into place. She uses her right hand to lift her left arm, the pain seizing and gripping and threatening to knock her out. But she maneuvers the arm above her head and reaches with her left hand to the opposite shoulder. Then, moving on instinct alone, she swiftly yanks the arm across, relief crashing against her as the joint pops back into place. It's not perfect—a dull ache pulses beneath the surface—but she has regained use of her limb.

The combination of relief and pain makes black spots dance in her vision, and when they dissipate, she sees Zephie. The little girl stands beside the sink, watching Jodi with deep hatred. When she sees Flora exit the daze, she tells her emphatically, "The birth tusk! It's in your pants pocket, remember? *Use it.*"

Flora nods, wishing desperately that Zephie were real, that she could use her own hands to reach for the tusk and pull Iris to safety. But Zephie is here, that is all she can do, and Flora is grateful. She takes a breath and lunges for her pants on the floor. Her wet fingers grapple with the fabric in search of the pocket and finally pull out the birth tusk. She holds it up for her mother to see.

"Look! Look! I didn't leave it in the fire. I have it *right here!*"

Jodi's eyes go wide. She holds on tighter to Iris and scoots her butt toward the wall for support. "Flora. What have you done?"

"What have *I* done? You're trying to kill me! You're trying to kill my baby!"

"I'm not!" Jodi screams, crying now. "I'm trying to *save* you both!"

"No wonder this thing wants to destroy you! It's protecting Iris!"

"You don't understand. You don't understand." Jodi repeats this over and over, rocking herself back and forth, pressing Iris tighter and tighter against her chest.

Zephie is crying now, too, getting more and more hysterical, shouting for Jodi to let go of the baby. Shouting that Iris isn't safe. But, of course, Jodi does not hear her.

"Give her to me," Flora says to her mother, wielding the birth tusk like a weapon.

"I can't do that," Jodi says sadly, climbing onto her knees, with one hand on the floor and the other holding little Iris. She crawls toward the bath.

this is it she is going to drown my baby

Zephie screams, and when she does, Flora feels something unusual. A sense that her body has been here before.

Without hesitation, Flora lurches forward and stabs the sharp end of the birth tusk—*thwunk!*—straight into Jodi's bad eye. The tooth travels through the jelly marble and only meets resistance as it pierces the brain behind it. Jodi falls backward, surprised and uncomprehending.

Flora grabs Iris and holds the wailing baby against her. Skin to skin. Just like she was taught in the hospital.

see I can do this I can do the things they tell me to

She ignores the tears trailing down her own face and ceremoniously towels Iris dry and places her in her bouncer. Flora's movements are stilted, not quite her own, born of repetition and muscle memory rather than any conscious decision.

When she stands, she again feels lightheaded. In the mirror, she sees her wet hair glued to her neck, her left shoulder red and swelling. And then, behind her—movement. Zephie is there, watching, and Flora sees something in her expression. A fear or warning or premonition. And then—her mother appears in the mirror, too. Jodi smiles at Flora through the reflection. The birth tusk is still lodged deep into her bad eye. Flora whips around so that she's face-to-face with her mother and swings her arms up in self-defense when she sees that Jodi is coming for her. Flora's hands claw erratically at her mother's face, the nails scraping her mother's paper skin and drawing blood. But it's not enough to deter Jodi. Flora watches as Jodi's arm rises high into the air, a dense porcelain soap dish in her hand, and arcs downward toward Flora's head.

A loud thunk, a hard smack, and the world goes black.

33

Flora is seven. She walks with her father down an outdoor deck flanked with tiny shops. In the near distance, she can see the water and docks full of waiting boats.

She slips her tiny hand into her father's, feeling his large knuckles and protruding veins. She likes to push on them and move them around under his skin. His large hand is strong, covering hers two times over. And yet, the palm is soft.

Flora watches a seagull arc high in the air and return along a similar path, lazily drawing patterns in the sky. She hears a loud thump as another seagull drops an oyster onto the dock from a great height in an attempt to crack it open.

"Daddy," she says, her eyes still trained on the birds, "why doesn't Mommy like me?"

Her father stops walking. He looks down at her, mouth open slightly. She thinks he looks sad, but she doesn't know why. Maybe she's not understanding.

"Oh, bunny," he says, "Mommy does like you. Of course she does. She *loves* you."

"I know she loves me," Flora says matter-of-factly, "but that's different."

Her father guides her to a nearby bench, where he sits so that they are at eye level. He places his hands on Flora's shoulders and turns her toward him, holding her with a kind firmness.

"Your mom is a person just like anyone else. She's complicated. She has a past. And sometimes that past bubbles up..." He pauses, looks away toward the water again, blinks hard. "Sometimes she feels sad. Really, really sad."

"So does that mean..." Flora scrambles his words in her brain, trying to piece them together in a way that makes sense. "Does that mean—*I* make her sad?"

Her father lets out a long breath. "No, bunny. You don't." Then, looking back toward the water, he says, "Your mother's sadness is all her own. That's the only way she'll let it be."

Flora is twelve. She sits crouched on the floor of her bathroom, crying giant tears into her lap. Her brownish-red-stained underwear and jeans hang over the tub's edge, and the open box of tampons rests at her side.

"You don't have to wear them," her mother's voice says from behind the door. Flora has locked her out. She wants to be alone. "You can wear pads."

"No, I can't!" Flora wails. Joey's birthday party is this weekend, and two very important factors dictate that Flora must learn how to use a tampon. One: it's a pool party. Two: Flora is in love with Joey.

She hears her mother sigh and sit with her back against the door.

Flora bought the tampons on her short walk home from

school. She detoured to the strip mall Rite Aid, hightailed it to the feminine hygiene section, and grabbed the first box she saw. She didn't sigh with relief until the tampons were paid for and safely hidden in her shopping bag.

"Can I come in?" Flora's mother asks after a moment of silence.

"No!" Flora shouts back immediately, horrified at the thought.

"Okay, I'll talk you through it from here, then."

It takes Flora a minute to get herself amped enough to stick a giant cotton wad up some hidden hole between her legs, but she finally does. Her mother talks her through each step, but after three attempts, Flora just can't shove it in there. Is she deformed? Is her vagina unnaturally small? Will she ever be able to enjoy the modern conveniences offered to women, or will she be stuck in ancient times and have to wear rags like diapers and hide in a hut every few weeks while her uterus bleeds?

"Please, Flora, just let me in," her mother begs, and Flora acquiesces. It can't get more embarrassing than this, anyway.

She opens the door and flops onto the closed toilet seat in defeat. "My vagina is broken," she says.

Her mother chuckles—then gasps loudly.

"Flora!" she says, reaching down to the ground. She bends back up, the tampon box in her hand, her mouth open wide. "You bought *ultra* size!"

Flora doesn't know what this means, but her mother breaks out into the heartiest laugh Flora has ever heard. And it's contagious.

The two laugh and laugh, both ending up on the floor, neither able to stop long enough to attempt standing. Whenever a break does come, and they finally catch their breath, one of them snorts and sends the other howling again, starting the whole process over.

Flora is seventeen. She punches the code for the garage door opener and winces as the giant door creaks open. She hopes her parents can't hear it from their bedroom. She is forty-three minutes past curfew, and not even for some scandalous or exciting reason. It's only because her friend Eddie got a flat tire and instead of calling roadside assistance, he felt it absolutely necessary to prove that he could change it on his own. Three hours later, he finally gave up and agreed to ask for help. They didn't even make it to the party.

Still, though, it would be easier to not have to explain any of this, especially because her mother doesn't particularly like Eddie. So Flora pads quietly through the garage and opens the door to the house as slowly as possible. This particular hinge makes a loud squeak when the door is about three-quarters open, so she slips herself through before ever needing to get to that point.

She enters the main house, proud of herself for not disturbing the peace, when she is met with the image of her mother sitting in silence at the kitchen table. Flora braces herself for whatever is coming, ready to prove that this was all because of a flat tire— she forced Eddie to let her keep a page of the receipt in case this very scenario played out—but her mother doesn't say a word. She just takes a sip from a large glass of red wine.

"Mom?" Flora asks, more scared of her mother's calm than she would be of anger.

But her mom looks as if she hadn't even noticed Flora entering. She lifts her gaze and says in a voice barely louder than a whisper, "I don't think your father and I are going to make it."

Flora sits at the table. The room is dark. She imagines her mother sitting here since dinnertime, staring at her wineglass through the sunset, the oncoming dark, the impending blackout. Did she even notice that it was almost midnight?

As shocking as it is for her to hear the words out loud, Flora is not surprised by the news. Probably none of them are, really. Her mother and father had never quite seemed to fit, and Flora felt more and more that they would be happier living separate lives. But she senses a sadness in her mother now. Not knowing what else to do, she tops off her mother's wineglass.

"I'm so sorry, Mom," she says.

Her mother smiles a little, then looks Flora square in the eye. She becomes suddenly serious, her voice firmer now, more emphatic.

"Happiness is a privilege," she says. "And I do not deserve it."

Flora is thirty-two. When she wakes up, her mouth is so dry that the insides of her cheeks are stuck to her teeth. She carefully opens her jaw—*POP!*—and the hinge releases with a jolt of pain to her left ear. Her legs and torso are heavy, weighed down.

blankets

these are blankets

Flora is in bed. Her own bed.

She lies still, eyes darting for answers on the ceiling, and wills her brain to catch up to the present moment. When she tries to sit, her left shoulder screams a pulsing protest. She rolls onto her right side and pushes herself up with her palms. The room twirls, and she closes her eyes to avoid hurling, though it might be inevitable given the hangover-like headache that pounds at her temples and tugs at her raw throat.

How did she get in this bed? She tries to remember. Needs to remember.

water

so much water

She was in the bathroom. She had desperately needed a bath. Desperately needed to get clean. She was so dirty and so, so tired.

Crying. There was crying. She remembers pulling baby Iris into the bath with her.

Iris where is Iris

Flora jerks her head toward the other side of the bed and sees that the bassinet is empty. The house is quiet, the surrounding silence oppressive, shoving the walls and ceiling and floor into one another, trapping Flora like a trash compactor.

oh God what have I done to my baby

And then the door creaks, and Flora's veins whoosh with rage as she expects to see her mother—her mother who she now remembers tried to kill her, tried to kill her baby. Her mother whom she stabbed through the eye and brain and who still stood with enough strength to knock Flora out and do who the hell knows what to Iris.

But it's not her mother.

Flora blinks, the brief confusion rendering her speechless, and then, for the first time in weeks, she feels her muscles relax. Truly relax.

Connor. It's Connor.

"You're awake," he says.

"Connor," she replies, relishing his name on her lips, and then he is with her on the bed, holding her hands and cradling her head. She drinks in his bright eyes. She wants to stuff herself full of him, like a bear preparing for hibernation. But first: "Iris?" she asks. "Where is Iris?" Her eyes ravage his face, searching for clues.

"She's downstairs," he says. "Asleep in the swing."

Flora shakes her head. "No, she's not supposed to sleep there unattended, her airway could get blocked, she—"

"Flo," Connor says, taking her hands strongly in his, "she's fine. She's not alone."

"Who's with her? Oh God, not my mother—" Flora tries to stand from the bed, but she winces in pain at her swollen shoulder, the hurt radiating to her elbow.

His eyes widen and then narrow. "Are you sure you're okay?"

Flora stares at him. Her mother's words itch at the back of her brain. *They want to take your baby away.*

Connor leans in closer. "I found you passed out in the bathtub. You could have..." His eyes glisten with held-back tears momentarily before he catches himself, a small break in his deep voice. "You could have drowned, Flo. Iris could have drowned. She was in your lap, crying, and you were just sleeping through it. Have things been this bad the whole time?"

Her lips open and close a few times like a dying fish.

they want to take your baby away

She chooses her words methodically. "No. I was just so tired."

Thoughts and doubts swim in Flora's head, and she almost thinks she can see them, just in front of her eyes like floaters in the space between what is real and what is seen. She wants to tell him what happened in the bathroom, what her mother tried to do, but

don't tell him

you know what he'll think

And then a deep understanding bubbles underneath her consciousness, like a dead body that works its way up through the dirt and finally surfaces after a long rain.

Her mother wasn't in that bathroom. Her mother was never even here.

Because her mother killed herself two years ago.

PART
3

34

The world does not make sense to Flora. She has many questions about what is real and what is not. But she cannot ask these questions of anyone but herself, for every moment of her life is now a test. Every moment is an opportunity to misstep. She is being watched. Her father and Esther are here to "lend helping hands." Her own husband is examining her for weakness and inconsistencies.

Flora cannot lose Iris. She will not. So she writes herself a new story. And since the best lies revolve around truth, Flora orbits the altered facts around a very real catalyst: sleep deprivation. She tells her family about the benign things like misplacing crackers and forgetting the coffee cup under the spout. Details to illustrate a sympathetic narrative: Flora was just a tired mom doing her best. And when she finally took a moment for herself, the warm bathwater lulled her into such a deep sleep that she didn't hear her baby crying.

But within the private confines of her own mind, Flora tries desperately to puzzle together the blurry facts. Her mother showing up—that was, what? A hallucination? A fever dream?

If so, where did reality end and the dream begin? The singing activity cube and plastic pig—were those real?

And the one thing Flora can't even bring herself to ponder is what actually happened in that bathroom. Was there really a struggle in the tub to save Iris's life? And if there was, whose hands were actually dunking her child's tiny face beneath the water's surface?

There must not have been a struggle. It must have all been in Flora's head. She must be sick. Which is comforting, really, because sick people get better. Sick people can be treated. They can be helped.

Still, doubt creeps and seeps like a steady leak in the drywall.

Flora showers in the guest bathroom because she is afraid of the other. She stands, unmoving, under the water.

Zephie

Zephie would know

It's true. Her childhood friend witnessed everything. But as hard as Flora tries to summon her, Zephie does not come. She hasn't seen her since everything that happened in the bathroom.

Flora brings her hands to the shower wall and leans her weight against them. Her shoulder is less tender now, the swelling subsided, thanks to some pain medication her dad found in the back of a drawer.

As she leans forward, the water hits her back directly, and Flora moans in relief as it trickles down her legs and onto the tile floor beneath. When she again lifts her gaze, her fingers catch her attention. The nails are dirty, grime built up underneath. She squints and brings them closer to her eyes for inspection.

that's not dirt

that's blood

She remembers scratching at her mother's face, the fragile

skin tearing in response. And here it is now: that same blood under her nails. But how is it possible?

She grabs a small nailbrush from the caddy hanging over the showerhead and scrubs. Her left hand works through the dull pain still coursing from that shoulder and moves the hard bristles back and forth with fervor. Back and forth and back and forth until she can no longer feel her fingertips. Until her own blood rises to the surface and breaks through the skin's barrier, mixing with the dried blood already there. Mixing so that Flora can no longer tell the difference between her own blood and that of her mother. It's easier this way, when there is no definition, when there is no barrier between what is real and what might not exist at all.

After her shower, Flora goes downstairs to join the others for dinner. The electricity has returned; Connor worked his magic on the breaker box, and Flora is relieved but simultaneously gutted. If she had just known how to troubleshoot the problem herself, she wouldn't have needed to go all that time without power. She could still be pumping instead of giving Iris formula, which Connor picked up at the store when he realized they had no milk.

Michael and Esther serve up homemade lasagna and arugula salad. Connor spends most of the meal sharing what stories he can from his deployment, and Flora is relieved to have the spotlight on someone else. Especially because, as she sits at the kitchen table, she is plagued by visions of peeling dead skin from her mother's feet.

was that even real

She considers inspecting the trash for remnants of burnt flesh.

"...if you want us to," Esther says.

Everyone is looking at Flora.

"Hmm?" she asks.

Her dad wipes his mouth with a paper napkin. "Esther was just offering our services," he says. "We can stay a couple days."

"I told them how my dad's knee surgery got pushed up," Connor says to Flora. "So since they can't come for a while, your dad offered."

Flora doesn't want the extra pairs of eyes on her. She needs time and space to investigate, to figure out the truth of the last week. But she also can't afford to raise any alarm bells. She knows it will seem suspicious if she denies them. So she plasters on a smile and nods.

"That would be wonderful," she says.

"It must have been so hard for you," Esther says.

Flora realizes this must be the moment they are going to acknowledge and dissect the reason they are here.

"The sleep deprivation," Esther continues. "You know, there's a reason they use it as a torture tactic!" Everyone murmurs agreement in chuckles and *mm-hmms*. "I definitely had the baby blues," she adds.

"That's a thing?" Connor asks. "Like, officially?"

"Oh, yes," Esther says, "many women get them in the early weeks after birth."

They continue to talk, but Flora stares at her fingertips, which are bright red from the scrubbing. She hides them in the folds of her shirt and runs her tongue over her teeth, fuzzy with plaque. She feels like the child at a parent-teacher conference, where the conversation is, in theory, about her but is actually about everyone else's opinions of her.

It strikes her then that this is all that matters now: everyone else's opinions of her. Because if a seed of doubt grows within them that she is not a fit mother, they will intervene. They will take Iris away.

Her mother was right. She was right all along.

baby blues

term

1. feelings of sadness in the few days/weeks after having a baby; symptoms include mood swings, crying spells, anxiety, and difficulty sleeping

2. a cutesy term for yet another way a woman's body will try to rob her of the joy of her child's earliest days

35

F lora sneaks into the guest room before her dad and Esther
come upstairs to unpack their things. Though her logical brain tells her that the room is likely untouched—*must* be
untouched—she has to confirm this for herself.

Sure enough, the room is empty. Or, more accurately: the
room is void of her mother's belongings, like the worn book and
stray reading glasses and softly woven baby hat. Flora sits on the
bed and stares into the empty space, waiting for something to
happen that will answer her questions. But of course, nothing
does.

She crawls toward the pillows of the bed that has been made
for weeks and feels slightly stale as a result. Flora buries her face
in the pillow closest to the nightstand and takes a large inhale.

It's her mother's scent. All of it. Like sunflowers and wet
leaves and fake-fruit candy. The same perfume her mother always
wore.

She brings her hands to the pillow and squeezes, as if she
could wring out the scent and take it with her. But instead, the
fingers of her right hand get entangled in something thin and

wiry and long. When she brings it to her face, she sees that it is a strand of hair. Long white hair. Her mother's hair. It must be.

She fiddles it in her raw, overscrubbed hands and winds it around the tip of her index finger. Around and around and around until the finger's circulation is cut off, until it seems like one more yank would sever the tip with a clean slice.

"Knock, knock!" Her father's voice sends her bolting from the bed. She slips the hair in her pocket for safekeeping and stretches her arms out in a welcoming gesture.

"It's all ready for you," she says as he enters.

"Oh, we're easy, you know that. No need for special treatment." He wheels the suitcases into the room.

"Well, if clean towels is special treatment, your bar is pretty low," Flora quips.

He smiles, and behind it is a knowing, a sadness, that makes Flora want to rip the curtains from the windows in rage. *STOP LOOKING AT ME LIKE THAT!* she wants to shout.

Suddenly, her mother's voice is in her head.

you're not well

Flora has to get out of this room.

She nods at her father and walks out the door into the hall. Over her shoulder, she calls, "Let me know if there's anything else you need."

She takes the stairs down at a quick pace and finds her husband on the couch with Iris. Flora slows when she sees her daughter in his arms. A picture she has longed for, has daydreamed about for weeks. She doesn't want it to be tainted. This is all wrong: her dad shouldn't be here babysitting her; she shouldn't have blood under her nails; she shouldn't smell her mother's scent on the pillows.

"Come sit with us," Connor says, and she does.

The three of them huddle close on the couch, Flora leaning all her weight against Connor as he holds Iris in his arms. He watches his baby's perfect, puffy lips suck the nipple of the bottle, a bead of milk dripping down the side of her mouth and quickly hiding in the folds of her neck. His gaze doesn't flinch; he can't stop staring at his daughter.

And Flora can't stop staring at *him*. Her body warms at the sight of his doe eyes trained on the small creature they created together. She always heard about the magic of motherhood, how out of this world it would be to hold her own baby and know it had grown inside her. But no one had mentioned this: the magic of watching her partner crack and expand to make room for a love his body couldn't formerly contain.

She finally closes her eyes, hearing only the breath of her husband and the sucking sounds of her baby's mouth. She finds comfort in these things, but it's not until her hand slips into her pocket and fingers her mother's stray hair that she feels whole.

36

The next morning, they wake to see that the storm has finally passed, and, though the earth is still blanketed with snow, the clouds have cleared and the bright sun reflects off the ground with fervor.

Flora's dad lies with Iris on the living room floor. He shakes a tambourine and presses giant buttons on a baby-sized keyboard Esther bought.

"Want to join us?" he asks as Flora walks through the room.

Her feet and heart stop. Flora sees her baby's face under the water, fingers holding her little head below the surface.

I might try to kill her

She looks at her father with Iris and longs for the normalcy of it all. But she doesn't trust these hands that sometimes do not feel like her own.

Esther enters from the kitchen, sensing something is up. "I was about to take a walk. Flora, you want to come?"

Flora nods.

They walk through the woods in silence. Flora is exhausted. She should have spent the night sleeping thanks to all the extra help, but instead she scrolled on her phone endlessly, hiding its light beneath the duvet and turning it off whenever Connor stirred. She read mom forums and social media threads and anything she could find about sleep deprivation and its hallucinatory effects. Paired with the imbalance of post-birth hormones, she knows now through her research that it could have all been in her mind.

But...the hair...her mother's smell...the blood under her nails... and then this morning, while emptying the dishwasher, she found a handful of artificial sweetener packets in the silverware drawer.

"Do you or Dad use fake sweetener?" she asks Esther as their boots crunch the snow.

Esther frowns. "No. Or, maybe your dad does sometimes."

If she finds it an odd question, she doesn't say. Flora wracks her brain. Could they have been sent in the food order her father had delivered?

"How are you feeling today?" Esther asks, and Flora wants to push the question right back into Esther's mouth.

"Good, yeah, thanks," she says.

They walk in silence, their feet moving in sync, the crunching a steady rhythm.

"It's probably annoying," Esther says, reading Flora's mind, "hearing that question over and over again."

Flora considers. "A little," she admits.

Esther smiles. "Well, then, let's talk about something else."

"Can you tell me about when my mom died?" Flora asks.

Esther stops in her tracks. But Flora's expression gives nothing away; she acts as though this line of inquiry is as common as wondering what to cook for dinner.

"Uh, well," Esther starts, moving her feet again to catch up with Flora, "what would you want to know?"

And suddenly, they reach the spot that Flora has been walking toward for twenty minutes, whether or not she was conscious of it. The fire her mother built. Or, rather, the remnants of the fire. Two burnt logs. Flora frowns. As she stares at the pile, she realizes maybe it's not the proof she needs. Weren't there more logs here the other night?

"I'm not sure what I want to know," Flora admits. "She and I weren't talking when she died, and I think I just didn't want anything to do with her. Or her death. You know?"

Flora does not dwell on the truth, which is that she was so wracked with guilt over her mother's suicide that she knew she'd never be able to forgive herself. She had told her mother to get out of her life. And so, her mother had complied.

would things be different if

"I kinda checked out," Flora says, cutting off her own thoughts. "I don't even really know what happened except that she shot herself."

Esther nods slowly, turning something over in her mind. "That's pretty much the whole of it."

"Where?" Flora asks. Esther looks at her quizzically, increasingly uncomfortable with the conversation. Flora repeats, "Where did she shoot herself?"

"She was in the living room—"

"No, I mean, where on her body?"

Esther shifts her weight between her feet. "Maybe we should head back. You could ask your dad—"

"I don't want to," she says quickly. Then, covering, she follows up with, "I don't want to stress him out. I just want some of the details, you know?"

Esther bites her lip. Dust dances in the rays of sunlight that shine through the trees around them.

"She shot herself in the head. Or, well, the throat. Like this." She holds the tips of her fingers in a gun shape and presses them under her mouth, pointing upward.

"And the bullet went out the top of her skull?"

Esther's eyes narrow, and she clearly wants to resist, wants to return to the house and wash her hands of Flora's curiosity. But she answers, "Out her eye."

Flora thinks of her mother's tic, her twitching eye. "The right one?" she asks, and Esther nods.

Then, as if hurrying to get this over with, Esther adds, "They didn't find her for a few days. I think..." She makes a sort of *I'm sorry* expression. "I think a downstairs neighbor complained of the smell."

Flora knows this story. Her mother told it to her. The "neighbor" who died. The neighbor whose lonely death had filled her mother with dread. The neighbor whose story Jodi did not want to be her own.

But that *was* her mother's story. She *did* die alone.

Flora is profoundly sad.

The two women have been standing so still that a squirrel meanders by them, smelling the ground in search of food. He is so close that Flora can see the individual hairs on his back, the medley of browns and blacks and whites, his beady eyes that dart around with a singular focus.

And then something else comes to her. An echo of a memory.

"Esther," she says, "I have a weird question."

Esther raises her eyebrows, and Flora knows she must be thinking how *all* of these questions have been weird. Still, Flora doesn't hesitate.

"I need you to be honest with me," she says.

"Okay..." Esther replies, wary.

"When they found my mom...what kind of state was her body in?"

Esther looks confused.

Flora tries to clarify. "I mean—were there any—bugs?"

Esther's expression changes. She looks at Flora with something akin to fear. And then she finally finds her voice.

"Beetles," she croaks. "Flesh-eating beetles."

37

Flora needs to find the birth tusk. If her mother was right, and the tooth is somehow connected to Jodi, then it must hold the key to her questions. And she needs answers *now*. Without them, she doesn't trust herself around her own baby. And that, she is learning, is the cruelest form of torture.

She is searching the garage when Connor finds her surrounded by boxes and tools pulled from the shelves. Her hair is frizzy and half-brushed, her eyes wide with wonder.

"What are you doing?" he asks.

Flora shrugs. "I had the urge to purge!" she says with a laugh that isn't quite her own.

Connor doesn't reply. He just tilts his head to the side, as if he might see things differently that way, as if his wife might suddenly make sense from a slightly altered vantage point.

Flora spent the morning searching, but the birth tusk wasn't in the bathroom or the nursery or her bedroom or—well, anywhere in the house. So she thought it might be here in the garage, where she originally found it.

But no. Flora has gone through the box four times, and four

times all she found were long-forgotten trinkets from her childhood. She chucked the whole thing in the trash.

At lunchtime, her father sits across from her at the kitchen table. Connor and Esther have taken the baby for a walk around the block. Flora eats a turkey sandwich on rye that her father made. It has too much mustard.

"Esther told me about your conversation yesterday," he says, and Flora understands now why Esther and Connor vacated the premises. Her father must have told them he wanted to have a Talk.

"Mm-hmm," she says, wet bread sticking to the roof of her mouth.

"It was probably a lot, learning about your mom's stay in the psychiatric hospital. And, well, it's normal for you to have questions. Is there anything else you want to know?"

Flora stares at a tiny piece of toilet paper that her father has attached to a razor nick on his neck. A drop of blood sticks the paper to his skin.

"Anything else I want to know about what?"

He shrugs. "Any of it. The hospital. Her death."

Flora wants to ask how it's possible she knew about the flesh-eating beetles before Esther told her. How it's possible she knew the bullet went out her mother's right eye. How it's possible she knew the history of the birth tusk before her father ever admitted it.

But, of course, she cannot ask these things. Because this Talk is a test, and those questions would mark an automatic failure.

"No," she says. "Esther pretty much filled me in."

"I don't know if she should have," he says, fiddling with a piece of uneaten crust on his plate. "The bit about the bugs...I hope it didn't upset you."

Flora shakes her head. "I asked."

"I know, but there are some things in life we're better off not knowing." Her father looks at his fingers, pressing his index nail into the pad of his thumb so that it turns white.

"What do you mean?" she asks. "Is there something else I don't know?"

His ears perk like a curious dog's. "Hmm? Oh, no. No, I just meant in general." He presses his hand into the table, a physical reset. "I did want to let you know that I have some things of your mother's at the house. Just a box or two. I saved them after...I thought there might come a day when you would want them."

"Yes," Flora says, her heart pitter-pattering in her chest. "Yes, I would love those."

"I'll bring them next time we come down."

"Can you mail them?" she asks quickly. "As soon as you get home?"

He looks at his daughter for a long moment. "Okay," he says, "I can do that."

Later, Flora tells Connor what her dad said about how she's better off not knowing some things.

"It's just an expression, though, isn't it?" he asks, joining her on the couch. "'Ignorance is bliss' kinda thing."

"But it didn't feel like that. It felt like he was referring to something specific. His mind drifted. He went somewhere else."

Connor shrugs. "Flo, his mind could have gone anywhere. He was probably thinking about something in his own life, from his own childhood."

Connor knows something
they're all hiding something from me

Before bed, Flora pads into Iris's room to watch the baby

sleep. It's the first time she has allowed herself to be alone with the baby since the attempted drowning.

The new monitor is balanced on the nearby dresser. Connor bought one without Wi-Fi but hasn't yet mounted it to the wall. Flora thinks about the man's voice, her daughter's stalker. Connor believed her when she first told him the story, but does he still? Or is he second-guessing that now, too?

She looks at Iris's face, which somehow seems to have changed in just the last couple of days. Every hour she avoids her baby is another hour her baby grows and evolves without her. But she doesn't have a choice. Until she knows the truth about what happened in that bathroom, the only way to keep Iris safe is to stay away.

It's so hard, though. So hard to stay away. She just needs one look, one touch. She is drawn to her daughter like water to a crack. Wherever her tiny baby's body is, Flora's body will find her, will fall into her.

"I'm working my way back to you, little one," she says. "I promise."

And then,

ZAP! Flora's brain conjures an image and projects it behind her eyelids. A tree falls on the roof, wood and shingles and wet caving and collapsing into the crib, the fragmented end of a broken board angling so it slides effortlessly through the soft spot on Iris's head.

get out of here now

Flora backs out of the room and hurries to her own bed, balling her fingers into fists so they cannot act of their own accord.

38

F lora spends the next forty-eight hours cleaning the house.
She vacuums, mops, dusts every book and baseboard,
sanitizes every doorknob, washes every towel and bathmat,
squeegees the windows, triple-wipes the mirrors, takes a micro-
fiber cloth to the television screens. She organizes every drawer,
disposes of old condiments and dried herbs and pantry items,
scrubs the oven and refrigerator shelves.

The cleaning starts as a more thorough search for the birth
tusk, but the effort is not fruitful. There are so many moments
when Flora feels she must surely be on the verge of discovery. But
it is nowhere. Not shoved into the back of any drawer, not hidden
behind the shower curtain, not kicked under the toe space of the
bathroom, not folded in the sheets of her bed, not thrown in the
dirty laundry hamper. Every time she lifts an article of clothing
or opens another door to a hidden nook or cranny, she is convinced the tusk will be there. But every time, her airways deflate
with disappointment.

Nevertheless, Flora is *alive*. She has more energy than she has
had in weeks, maybe even months or years. Her injuries don't

bother her anymore; her achy shoulder has stopped screaming, her once-purple thumb is intact, nail and all, and her forearm is no longer infected. And how electrifying to get her house in order! To scrub away the dirt and grime and sweat and spit and vomit and blood. She doesn't even need breaks! She barely needs to eat or drink!

She leaves the bathroom for last. *That* bathroom. She has been afraid to spend too much time in there. But now that she is here, even this feels good. Her knees are cold against the tile floor. She reaches over the tub's edge and liberally sprays the thick white cleaning agent.

Cartoon bubble figures smile at her from the bottle's label. One of them says in a high-pitched voice, *We've got hydrochloric acid! A leading cause of accidental poisoning in children!* The bubble winks, like *hint hint.* Then a bigger bubble eats that smaller bubble and burps. A moment later, it sticks out its tongue and gets big *X*'s for eyes.

oopsies he's a goner

Esther's voice breaks Flora's trance. "You can probably call it quits." She chuckles and gestures toward the sparkling-clean tub.

But Flora does not. *Cannot.*

Connor finally retrieves her around dinnertime, insisting that she give it up for the day. And it is only then, when she is forced to pause her work, that she sees the others are right. The bathroom is clean. She can move on. Something about the realization flips a switch within her, and her energy is immediately zapped, like cutting the electricity to a lamp. She nods toward Connor, insisting she'll be down for dinner as soon as she changes out of her grubby clothes.

In the bedroom, she stares at an open drawer of shirts, paralyzed by choice. But also paralyzed by the meaninglessness of it all. She feels very, very small. Her effect on this earth is so insignificant that it cannot be measured. She spent two days cleaning a house that will only get dirty again and demand the same of her in a week. Again and again, the dirt will accumulate, and again and again, she will remove it, scrub it, disinfect it. But it's a useless gesture, really. Because it doesn't last. Nothing lasts.

A loud *bbzzzzzzz* pulls her from the undertow of her thoughts. A swarm of bees? She looks to the window and finds nothing. Her head swivels toward the sound—it seems like it's coming from the hallway.

Her feet carry her to the door of the bedroom, where she pauses. The *bbzzzzz* is louder here, and she wonders if Connor is drilling something downstairs. But as she stands there, the noise feels close. And suddenly, she is uneasy. Like a deer in the woods who can sense the shotgun around the next tree.

She takes one step into the hallway. Then another. The house is quiet save for the incessant *bbzzzz,* which reminds her of a dentist's drill approaching her mouth, readying itself to puncture the tooth's enamel and sink in toward her gum.

And then she's there. Back in the bathroom.

Her electric toothbrush is alive, spinning as it stands upright in its charging base.

She has no earthly clue how it would have turned itself on, but she is relieved to find the noise coming from something benign. With an exhale, she presses the black button to silence the tool. She then frowns at the water droplets that have escaped its bristles and sprayed like blood splatter all over the mirror.

When she finishes wiping it down, she turns off the light and leaves. She is only a few steps toward the stairs when—*BLINK!*—the light in the bathroom turns back on. Curious, Flora returns and finds the switch once again in the on position. She places her fingers firmly on the switch and deliberately pulls it down, watching as the light goes dark in response. She stands there a moment, watching the switch, then, satisfied, heads back toward the stairs.

BLINK! The light. Shining again.

The switch has popped back to the on position. That familiar feeling of unease creeps in once more, but Flora does her best to ignore it. Rolling her shoulders back, she stands a little taller and frowns at the light switch as if she could scold it into cooperating. She pulls the switch down, confirms the light has turned off, and quickly heads for the stairs.

BLINK! This time, she runs back, as if she could catch it in the act. But even though the light is on, the switch remains in the off position. Flora's brows come together in confusion, and she flicks the controller up and down, slowly at first and then quickly enough that it should produce a strobe effect—but the light does not change. It remains on, bright.

She stares at the light and the switch and the electric toothbrush. Is there a glitch in the wiring of this room? Maybe something that happened after they lost power?

"Mom?" she whispers. "Is that you?" She stands as still as possible, highly attuned to every hair on her skin. Then another thought comes to her. "Zephie?" she asks, her voice even smaller. "Zephie, are you here? Are you back?"

BLINK! The light goes off, then *BLINK!* comes on. After a few seconds, *BLINK!* it turns off, then *BLINK!* on and *BLINK!* off briefly. Then *BLINK!* on and remains on. Then *BLINK!* off. The pattern feels deliberate.

Morse code

"Flora?" It's Connor's voice from downstairs. And the second he calls, the light goes off. And stays off.

She tests the switch, flipping it up and down, and the light responds per usual.

"No," she says quietly, "no, no, no—what were you trying to tell me?"

"Flora, are you okay?" His voice is closer. He's coming up the stairs.

Flora exhales, angry at the disruption, desperate for everyone to just

leave me the fuck alone

"Hi. I'm okay," she says, stepping into the hallway.

He stands a few feet away from her, his head tilted a couple degrees off-center. A look that Flora is coming to know well. A look that means she is under scrutiny.

"We're outside grilling," he says. "Wanna join?"

She looks back at the bathroom, but nothing happens. Whoever or whatever was here is now gone.

"Yeah," she says, her gut full of snakes. "Let's go down."

Flora joins the others on the back patio and immediately realizes she didn't change her clothes after all. She's still wearing her cleaning garb, which most definitely stinks. But she doesn't have the energy to go back upstairs.

"No big deal," her dad assures her. "No dress code at this bar and grill. I mean, look at this one. She's in her pj's." He nods toward Iris, who is content in his arms.

Out of the corner of her eye, Flora sees Connor's sideways expression. He's probably wondering what she was doing upstairs all this time if she wasn't changing her clothes.

Esther pipes up from beside the grill, where she is buttering buns. "We've got hot dogs and burgers and corn. You want cheese?"

Flora nods. The events of the last few minutes ping-pong in her skull. She reaches into her pocket to finger the piece of her mother's hair. She longs for the comfort of it, the wiry strand that has become a totem to bring her back to herself.

But it's not there.

it has to be here it was here earlier

She tries to hide her panic as her fingers fish around both pockets in search of the hair. And then a horrifying thought occurs to her: What if it fell out while she was cleaning? What if she inadvertently vacuumed it up?

"You wanna hold her?" Flora's dad asks, extending Iris in her direction.

"No, uh," she says, backing away from the baby, "let me—I think I forgot something upstairs. I'll be right back."

She doesn't stick around long enough to see their expressions. She runs upstairs and retrieves the vacuum from the hallway closet. Dropping to her hands and knees, Flora struggles to unhook the compartment that holds the trash bag. When she finally does, it pops with such fervor that dust poofs out around her, covering the nearby area in a thin film of debris. She pours the contents of the bag right onto the carpet. It's a mess.

Flora doesn't think; she runs her hands through the pile of trash, sifting through bits of food and dirt and lint and gunk. She finds plenty of hair and winds each strand around her index finger, pressing each one against her skin, hoping to feel the coarseness of her mother's brittle strand. But none of them are her mother's hair.

"Flora?"

It's a female voice, and for a moment, Flora's heart lifts as she thinks Zephie has returned to her. Zephie, who can explain everything that happened, who knows Flora better than she knows herself. Zephie, who Flora swears was only moments ago trying to send her a message through the lights.

But Flora looks up and sees Esther. Of course it is only Esther.

"What happened?" Esther sees the disassembled vacuum and Flora crawling about in the debris. "What are you doing?"

Flora swallows, then coughs as dust catches in her throat. "I . . ."

Esther watches Flora crumble chunks of dirt between her fingertips. "Do you need some help?"

"My earring," Flora lies. "I lost an earring."

"Oh," Esther replies, relieved by this very normal explanation. A large breath escapes her lips. "Let me help. What does it look like?"

Together, they sift through the vacuum's spilled guts, Esther looking for something that was never there, and Flora realizing now that she may be doing the same.

She does not find the hair. And as these items slip away from her—first the tusk, now the hair—she feels something else slip away with them. Something like a part of her. Something that cannot be replaced.

39

Who's next?" Flora's dad asks the group the next morning. He's making omelets for everyone. Iris is a few feet away in the swing, watching the small animals on her mobile spin around and around.

"You want another one?" Connor asks, pointing toward Flora's empty plate.

She doesn't remember eating it. "Didn't know how hungry I was," she says.

Flora is staring at the floor near her father's feet, where she has just seen three scuttling black figures cross the expanse of the kitchen and disappear through a crack under the cabinets. She didn't see them clearly enough to determine the type of bug, but she has a guess.

Nearby, Esther prepares a bottle of formula. No matter how many studies Flora reads that prove she needn't give it a second thought, she still worries that depriving Iris of breast milk will lower the baby's IQ or permanently weaken her immune system or plant some seed of trauma deep within her that will bloom in late adulthood and point back to Flora as the root of all Iris's problems.

But maybe that would happen anyway. Maybe that is the burden of motherhood: to give all that you can and know that it will never be enough.

She looks at Iris, who continues to watch the dancing animals on the mobile above her, and then,

ZAP! Flora sees Iris fall from the swing, her neck cracking at an impossible angle, and then

ZAP! this time the swing breaks, its heavy metal frame falling on top of Iris's chest and knocking the air from her in an instant, crushing her body like a sandcastle, and then

ZAP! this time Iris's onesie gets caught in the contraption until the spinning mobile lifts her tiny body up, up, up, and she is hanging by her neck with the little animals, spinning around and around, her weight slowing the mechanics and warping the music.

"Ugh, there's another one!" Her dad says from the stove. Flora watches as he retrieves a paper towel and smashes something on the countertop.

"Should I call an exterminator, you think?" Connor asks, joining her father at the sink. Then he turns to Flora. "Have you seen all the bugs? The last few days, they're everywhere, it feels like. I know it's an old house, but..."

"Bugs?" Flora asks.

they see them too

the beetles are back

Flora shrugs in response. "I've seen a few," she says. After all, this could be another test. Safest to stick with a neutral response.

"I'll call someone," Connor says. Then he points to the fresh omelet Flora's dad has just plated. "Flo, sure you don't want another one?"

She shakes her head. "I'll take another coffee, though," she says.

"I'm on it." He smiles.

She thinks of all the days she crossed off before Connor's arrival, desperate for her husband's calming touch and steady demeanor. How often she cursed the calendar that told her she was doomed to another week, another day, another hour tackling parenting alone. And now that he's finally here, it's like she is the one who has left, her mind fighting a battle elsewhere.

Part of her resents that he can't see this. She wants to slap him awake.

Connor brings both Flora and Esther fresh cups of coffee. The second Flora takes a sip of hers, she almost spits it out.

"Oh my God, this is awful. Is yours bad, too?" she asks Esther.

"Mine is okay." Esther shrugs.

"Something is seriously wrong with mine," Flora says. Then she turns to Connor and asks, "Did you put sugar in it?"

Connor gives her a *come on* look. "Like I don't know you?"

"It's gross! Taste it!" She passes it to him.

He reaches dramatically for the cup. "Well, with that ringing endorsement, who could refuse?"

Flora's dad laughs from the stove. They all watch as Connor lifts the mug to his lips carefully. After a second he shakes his head.

"Tastes like regular black coffee to me."

"Let me try yours," Flora says, reaching for his cup. She takes a sip and immediately tastes relief. "Oh yeah, way better. There's something off with mine."

Connor smiles, something like recognition crossing his face. He gives Flora the look he makes when he has won a bet.

"What is it?" Flora asks.

"Mine has sugar in it. That's the only difference."

"Bullshit," she says, calling him out. "You drink yours black, too."

"Not anymore. Base coffee was crap this time. I got used to the sugar. Can't go without it now, it seems."

Flora stares into the cup.

Esther pipes up from nearby, "Maybe your tastes have changed after pregnancy. I think that can happen."

But Flora's limbs go cold and her stomach sinks to her toes. She knows what this means. She takes one more sip of the sugary coffee, hoping to wince in response. Instead, she loves it.

Connor laughs. "I put a lot in, too!" He's enjoying this.

"How many packs?" Flora asks, but she already knows the answer.

no no no no no

"Four," he says.

Four packs of sugar.

just like Mom

Later, Flora is with Iris on the floor of the nursery. Connor has stepped out briefly to find the diaper cream that seems to roam the house of its own accord.

Flora grabs a soft burp cloth from the rocking chair nearby. She gently wipes the cloth over Iris's face—like a curtain from top to bottom—in her own newborn version of peekaboo. Iris lights up every time the cloth uncovers her eyes and Flora reappears.

The last time, Flora pauses just when the cloth is over her daughter's face. She imagines leaving it there, watching as it slowly blocks Iris's airway, her chest moving more and more slowly, Iris still too little to coordinate her limbs to move it off her face. She pictures pulling the cloth so that it is taut, so that she can see the imprint of her baby's face through the fabric.

try it see how it feels

Bile sneaks up her throat, burning.

Flora blinks, and she sees Iris looking up at her, smiling with glee. Flora instinctively tosses the burp cloth across the room. Connor comes back then, and Flora hurries out with some excuse.

The plaguing thoughts have become incessant. She'll be chopping vegetables and imagine dropping the knife on little Iris below. She'll be walking down the hallway and imagine smashing her baby against the wall so that she crumples like an empty soda can.

This is because of her mother, she's sure of it. Her mother infected her with a poison, and Flora has to get the poison out. She won't be able to enjoy her baby until she does.

But she doesn't know how.

Flora wishes she knew someone like Belinda, her mother's "woo-woo" and "spiritual" friend who went to psychic fairs. If only Flora had a person like that she could call. Someone who wouldn't immediately stuff her in the car and drive her to the nearest psych ward. Someone who wouldn't immediately take away her baby.

"We're going to head back home after lunch," Esther says. She is packing her suitcase in the guest room as Flora sits nearby.

thank Christ

Flora is so tired of the watchful eyes, the looks of doubt, the thinly veiled questions.

"You guys have been amazing," Connor says, coming down the hall with Iris in his arms. "Thank you so much for everything."

Flora nods in agreement.

Truth is, she is envious. She, too, wants to get out of this house. Every day, the walls move closer, compacting the floor plan and restricting her breath. She is suffocating here. If she doesn't escape soon, the house will consume her, or it will force her to consume Iris. She remembers the cartoon child from her dream who ate baby Connor like a sub sandwich.

"I think I'll get out of the house today, too," she proclaims to the group.

Her dad, bagging up toiletries in the adjoining bathroom, smiles. "That's a great idea," he says.

Esther agrees. "A good sign, I think!"

Flora didn't anticipate the added bonus that wanting to get the hell out of this place would make her seem better to the others. Healthier, somehow.

Connor says, "You could take Iris to the library. They do a story-time thing for kids in the afternoon. I was looking into it."

Flora's heart sinks to her toes. She doesn't want to take Iris.

answer carefully this is a test

What would a good mother do? She would take her daughter to the library, of course. And anyway, it's a public place. Plenty of people around. They won't be alone.

Flora forces a smile. "Love that idea," she tells her husband.

"You and Iris haven't gotten much one-on-one time," Esther says.

Since when? Since Flora almost drowned the baby in the bathtub?

no that wasn't me I was trying to save her

"Want me to drive you?" Connor asks.

"No, no," Flora says, imagining the claustrophobia of a car ride with Connor. "I'd like to drive. It's an easy trip, all major roads that I'm sure have been cleared by now."

Connor smiles, and Flora's stomach fills with acid.

"You hear that?" Connor says to Iris, who is content in her father's arms. "You and Mommy are getting out!"

The car ride is torture. Flora blasts the radio in hopes of drowning out her growing urge to swerve the car into oncoming traffic. Her knuckles are white on the wheel. She doesn't let herself look in the rearview mirror, since the only time she did, she saw hollow shadows where her daughter's eyes should be. Connor never would have let her leave the house with their baby if he could see inside Flora's mind. If he could smell the rancid rot growing there.

The children's story-time hour is surprisingly well attended. Flora sits toward the back with Iris strapped to her chest in the carrier. The kids' section is carpeted in a colorful display of the solar system. The bookcases are stacked with vibrant spines, a stark contrast to the remainder of the library. A few small tables are scattered around, but, for the most part, this is an open space for children to roam and read and lounge.

Flora watches the other mothers arrive and settle on the ground and into chairs. Most of the children are toddlers, probably around three or four. Flora doesn't recognize anyone, but then, why would she? She has barely left the house since her baby was born, and she has few friends in the area as is, let alone the oh-so-coveted Mom Friends. Still, their presence is a comfort, a reminder that the world has continued to spin all these weeks.

"Hello, everyone," says a smiling woman in her forties. She wears a long, flowy dress and stark, high boots underneath. "We've got a good crowd today, don't we? I see lots of familiar faces." The woman's eyes scan the group, and Flora cringes at the thought that this lady is going to make the newbies speak up and introduce themselves. But instead, she waves energetically and moves her mouth in an exaggerated manner as she says, "And some new ones, too! Yay!" Flora sighs with relief.

well yeah what did you expect this isn't a goddamn AA meeting

The stylish reader is animated and enthusiastic, and the range of her character voices is admittedly worthy of a professional career. But by the time the librarian starts in on the second book, that familiar feeling of claustrophobia sets in. Maybe it wasn't the house, after all. Maybe it's Flora's own body that she needs so desperately to escape.

Flora wants to stick it out, mostly because she cannot afford to cause a scene, but the bookcases are suddenly closer and she wonders if they are on wheels, if a browsing customer has bumped them in her direction. She can't do this. She stands, tightening the carrier around her waist and reaching behind to clip it at her upper back. The stretch elicits an involuntary grunt far louder than she would have preferred, and the nearest mothers look slyly in her direction.

the eyes so many goddamn eyes on me all the time

The only way out of the space is through the crowd, so she steps between toddlers and babies and parents.

"Sorry," she whispers. "Oh, yep, oh, sorry, excuse me—"

A girl in a yellow jacket cries out when Flora steps on her hem. But Flora barrels on because the room is shrinking and her chest is tightening.

When she has made her way to the other side, she doesn't look back, doesn't bother to wave and say sorry with a sheepish grin. Instead, she hightails it to the bathroom, where she splashes her face with cool water. Iris protests when some of the water lands on her head, and Flora bounces in automatic response.

"Shhh," she sings, using a scratchy paper towel to dab her own face dry.

And then, Flora stops. She has caught her reflection in the mirror, and her body freezes in response to what she has seen there. No, it can't be...she leans closer to the mirror, her eyes only a few inches from the glass. And then it happens again. She blinks hard, keeping her eyes closed for a full ten seconds as a reset, and reopens them.

She waits. Stares. Almost thinks she was imagining it, but— there it is. Again. She's sure of it.

Her right eye is twitching.

40

Flora stands in the Paranormal and Supernatural section of the library. It's small and slightly hidden in its own corner behind the cookbooks and travel catalogues. Mixed in with the ghost stories are books about magic and witchcraft. She almost feels like she's breaking a rule by standing here; she keeps looking over her shoulder to see if anyone is watching.

She is terrified of her twitching eye. Of what it means. She needs answers *now*. Every twitch is like another tick of the clock. Time is running out.

Flora turns her attention to the books. Maybe they hold the clues she needs. There are three loosely packed shelves of spines that bear words like "divination" and "haunted" and "mythological." Her fingers feel the books, some old and ripped, others newer with a sleek finish. She lands on a collection of photographs, a large volume that looks like a coffee table tome. But when she opens it, she realizes only a very morbid human would have this book on display.

The photos are from the late 1800s and early 1900s. Flora gets stuck on a black-and-white picture that features a group of eight people, all staring straight at the camera. They wear an assortment of dark fabric robes with light-colored scarves or neck pieces. Every one of them wears the same pointed hat, like a cone on top of their heads, that is decorated with devil horns and the moon and stars. But the most haunting part of all is what they wear on their faces.

Every one of them sports a different mask, each more horrifying than the next. There's the plain white mask that covers the entire face, with only small slits for eyes and huge, dark, painted-on lips. Two of the masks feature bushy mustaches that look like bristles torn from a broom, obscuring and, in one case, disappearing the mouth completely. The worst one is a white mask with pockmarks, like it is half-melted, as if the person poured a bucket of hot wax on his head. Two thick, uneven eyebrows lay atop the eyes, which are cut large enough for the wearer's actual eyeballs to show through. And the mouth is upturned in a wide, gaping grin.

She thinks of her childhood sleep paralysis, the nights of torment lying in bed immovable. Her body tenses, as if it can right now feel the crushing weight of the haunting Night Hag. She has never seen the Night Hag's face, but she imagines it would probably look like this.

She flips through the pages and finds more of the same. There is little context for the photos, only the year in which they were taken and, in some cases, a location. Flora reads that people often dressed like ghouls on Halloween in order to trick the actual ghosts into thinking they were one of them, hoping they'd be spared. The thought tickles her spine.

"Looking for anything in particular?"

The voice startles Flora, and she drops the book. A hand reaches down and retrieves it for her. It belongs to a librarian she saw behind the reception desk earlier.

"Thanks," Flora says, returning the book to its spot on the shelf. She has seen enough of those photographs.

"Interesting section, isn't it?" the woman asks. She's a petite woman with gray hair and rich brown eyes.

"Uh, yeah..." Flora looks around, trying to decipher whether the children's story hour is over. How long has she been standing here?

"Okay, well, let me know if you need anything," the woman says and starts to walk away.

"Oh—" Flora stops her with her voice. "I was hoping to find something about birth tusks?" The woman stares at her blankly. "My dad, he got one at an Egyptian museum. It was supposed to ward off evil spirits or something? I mean, a long time ago, obviously."

The librarian thinks. "Do you know what time period?"

Flora wracks her brain. Her father mentioned that, didn't he? She chews her lip until she tastes blood. "Oh!" she exclaims. "Middle Kingdom?"

The librarian nods, looking toward the shelves and scanning the spines. She grabs a book about Middle Empire magic. "There might be something in here."

Flora smiles. "Thanks."

The woman walks away as Flora adjusts Iris, who has fallen asleep in the carrier with her neck at an awkward angle. Flora turns Iris's head, exposing her red cheek, warm from body heat, and the action is met with a loud protest. "Shhh," Flora coos as she rocks back and forth. She must admit that holding her baby feels right. Natural. She has missed this. Even if she has to continuously check that Iris hasn't suffocated in the folds of Flora's sweater.

Flora carries the book to a nearby table. She can't bring it home; Connor would have too many questions. She flips quickly through pages of figurines, bronze statuettes, carved bricks. There are passages on white magic versus black magic, descriptions of deities, photos of protective totems for tombs. Finally, she sees it: the apotropaic wand made from a hippo's tooth. A picture of a birth tusk, similar to hers but more curved, with a higher arch and sharper end. The caption says these were used to draw a circle around the area where a woman was to give birth or nurse her infant. Inscribed on the wand are nine magical figures, including Taweret, the goddess of childbirth. Her image is striking, even disturbing. She has the body of a woman with the giant head of a hippopotamus.

Flora's breath catches in her throat as she continues to read.

Taweret didn't only assist with birth. Apparently, she also helped with *rebirth*. She cleansed and purified the dead to aid in the process of their resurrection.

Flora pries her eyes from the page. She inspects her hands, the scrubbed fingertips, the dark under her nails. She feels her hair, brittle and stiff in its unbrushed state. She tastes the stale remnants of sickly-sweet coffee on her breath. Her eyelid spasms.

resurrection of the dead

So it's true: her mother is gaining more and more control of Flora's body. It's one thing to be tormented by thoughts and twisted ideas; it's another thing entirely to act on those thoughts. If Flora doesn't figure out how to purge herself of her mother, something terrible will happen to Iris.

no I'll kill myself before I let anything happen to her

And then what? Leave Iris motherless?

She looks again at the photos of the hippo goddess and arched birth tusk.

She has to find it. She has to find that thing and get it out of her house.

Flora is out the automatic sliding door of the library with a singu-lar focus and doesn't even feel the blast of cold air as she and Iris barrel toward the car.

But then—out of nowhere—a face in her face. Red and raw and peeling, reminiscent of those horrible images in the book, the masks and pointy hats. She can't help it, she screams right there in the library parking lot.

A voice responds to her outburst. "Oh my God! Are you *okay?*"

Flora steps back and assesses, the high-pitched voice squeal-ing with familiarity. And then she blinks and the world comes into focus.

Wanda. It's only Wanda.

"Your face," Flora says, pointing to Wanda's skin, horrified.

"Oh, I got a chemical peel! I'm just so tired of the *age spots,* you know?" When Flora doesn't respond, Wanda asks, "But, eek, does it really look that bad?" She laughs, likely expecting Flora to respond with some kind of *oh no you just startled me is all.*

But Flora does not. Instead, she stares and imagines wrap-ping her fingers around Wanda's neck, joining them in the back against the top of her spine, pressing until Wanda's eyes *POP* out of their sockets like a plushy toy.

Wanda shifts her weight between her feet, uncomfortable with the silence. "Seriously, though, are you okay? You don't look like yourself." She doesn't expand on Flora's haggard appearance. Her weight shifts again as she tries to fill the awkward silence. "Any bad clogs lately?" she asks in a congenial voice as she points to Flora's breasts. "Just because, last time, you know——"

oh God she thinks we're friends

"I stopped breastfeeding," Flora says. "We're using formula now."

Suddenly, Wanda's shoulders relax. "Ohh," she says, as if she has finally found the solution to a tough calculus equation. "My sister-in-law went through that. She got super sad when she stopped breastfeeding. Is that what's going on? Has the transition been rough?"

Flora looks at Wanda blankly. Then, without another word, she heads in the direction of the lot.

where did I park the car

She has to get home.

"Uh, okay?" Wanda says, her voice getting smaller as Flora walks farther away. "Bye, I guess?"

Flora raises her arm in response, something that resembles a wave. But really, she is batting away her nosy neighbor like she would a gnat in her ear. The last thing she needs is another pair of eyes on her.

weaning depression

term

1. depression that can occur after a lactating individual stops producing milk; a result of psychological stress and hormonal fluctuations

2. can we catch a fucking break already?!

41

Flora is losing time. Seconds. Minutes. Gone. She has begun to think of them as Dark Spots.

This morning, as she made her coffee and watched the machine whir and spit, she telepathically urged the brown liquid to taste normal. As if her daily ritual of a hot cup has now become a litmus test for her sanity. And when she did finally lift the mug to her lips, she was relieved to enjoy the taste of her coffee black.

But a bit later, Connor approached with a handful of empty sugar packets. "You put all these in your cup?"

Flora swallowed. She had no memory of that. She looked at her hands and rubbed her palms with her fingertips, as if trying to prove to herself that she had control over her own limbs.

Later, she retrieved Iris from her crib and found a small lovey on the mattress beside her, mere inches from her tiny nose. Flora knew she was the last one to put Iris into bed. She also knew she would never leave that blanket in the crib. How many times had she warned Connor about suffocation hazards?

But then, if she didn't put it there, who did?

The more time she loses to the Dark Spots, the more she

fears what she will do. Or, rather, what her mother will do with Flora's hands. Flora needs her body back. Her mother is latched to her brain like a leech, slowly sucking the good out of her and replacing it with a swirling, sinister matter.

That's when Flora realizes: she might not have a friend like Belinda, but maybe she doesn't need one. Maybe she can have the real deal—Belinda herself. If the lady really goes to psychic fairs like Jodi said, she won't run from Flora's wild claims. Right?

It's at least worth a try. Flora doesn't have any other ideas.

It is surprisingly easy to find Belinda's phone number. Flora has a first name, an address (her mother's same complex), and a rough age. With the combination of these factors, she finds her mother's friend quickly. The accessibility is both convenient and frightening.

She waits until Connor is on a walk with Iris to enter the number into her phone. With each ring, Flora's heart rate increases. But when an automated machine picks up, her chest sinks. What if this isn't the right number, after all? She has no way of knowing. She talks after the beep anyway.

"Belinda? Hi. Uh, I hope this is Belinda...my name is Flora. My mother was Jodi Martin, you guys lived together. Or, not *together* together but were neighbors? In the Breakwater Beach complex? I was hoping to talk with you about her. My mom. She—well—*please*. Please call me back. It's really important." She pauses, then repeats herself another three times and leaves her number. What a rambling mess. She might have just botched her one chance of getting to the truth.

Angry with herself, she scratches the back of her hand with her nails, which are growing more and more brittle by the day. Is that normal? They were so strong during pregnancy.

Before she knows it, she has drawn blood. She looks more closely and realizes the back of her hand is covered in scaly red patches. Her childhood eczema is returning. She inspects the other usual spots between her fingers, in the crease of her elbow, along the soft skin of her underarm. For now, it appears the rash is only on the back of her left hand.

She scratches it aggressively again, unable to stop herself. The itch goes deep, beneath the inflamed patches, down to her bones. It crawls beneath her skin and tickles her from the inside. She is desperate to dig it out.

The front door slams sometime later. When Connor announces his presence, Flora returns to herself. She stares at the knife in her hand, no recollection of how it got there.

Flora rips open the boxes the moment they arrive. As promised, her father sent Jodi's things as soon as he returned home. When Connor asks what they are, Flora shrugs.

"Oh, Dad mentioned he had some of Mom's old stuff, so I offered to look through it before it got thrown away."

He nods, and Flora hates how easy it is to lie to her husband. This is new territory for her. But the fibs slip out naturally, fluid and slimy like slugs that leave a bad taste in her mouth.

when this is all over I'll make it all right

This is what she tells herself to get through the days.

The first box is disorganized, like a junk bag at a garage sale. There are pieces of jewelry—necklaces and rings, mostly. There are many packs of developed film from various decades: baby pictures of Flora, photos from her parents' wedding, snapshots of birthdays and graduations and vacations. There are old cards and letters, as well as a couple of sketchbooks from when Jodi dabbled in art throughout the years.

And then Flora sees something familiar: the worn copy of *The*

Yellow Wallpaper. The same book she saw on the nightstand when her mother was here. And underneath the book is the small baby hat made of soft pink yarn. She has seen these items before, touched them with her own hands in her very own house, but how is that possible if they were in these boxes with her father hundreds of miles away?

Flora knows she is close to something, on the edge of discovery, but not yet seeing the whole picture. It is jumbled within the recesses of her own mind. Like her entire life is a dream that she has *just* forgotten. It's *right* there but slipping away with every deliberate effort to reach it.

She rips into the second box. This one is much lighter, and inside she is surprised to find a stack of beautiful handsewn children's dresses. The tiniest is floral patterned with a gathered neckline and no sleeves. One shoulder has a large red-ribbon bow. She fingers the delicate fabrics. Each dress is progressively larger, as if there is one for every year of a child's life. Ten in total. The last one is Flora's favorite. It's a lightweight dress with a faux button placket featuring giant baby-blue buttons. The sleeves are short and puffed, and the pattern is a plaid delicately woven of blues, purples, yellows, and reds.

Flora can't begin to imagine the story behind these dresses. She wonders if her mother made them, but then, she never knew her mom to be a sewer. She never once saw her mend a pair of socks, let alone handcraft an entire dress. Even Flora's Halloween costumes were sewn by her dad, because her mom always claimed he was "so much better at those things."

So if her mother didn't make these, who did?

Flora looks back to the book, the hat, the dresses. Although her hands are full of her mother's things, she feels more disconnected from her than ever. There is so much Flora doesn't understand. A chill climbs up her arms and makes the hairs stand on end. She wonders if she ever really knew her mother at all.

Flora's eyes pop open. That deafening noise again: metal on metal, gears clashing. Like hot tires skidding to a desperate stop on cement.

again it's happening again

Sleep paralysis.

It starts the same as always. Her arms glued to her sides, her chest taut, like plastic wrap pulled over a container so tight that it's a fraction of a moment from ripping. Her breathing is shallow; if she tries to inhale deeply, it catches in the muscle under her heart. No part of her body will move, and she realizes that only her left eye is slowly adjusting to the dark. The right eye is blurry.

She braces herself for the heavy weight of the Night Hag, but it doesn't come.

And then she hears footsteps.

THUD. THUD. THUD.

They are heavy and deliberate. Up the stairs. They get louder as they get closer. The Night Hag is coming. Taking her time.

Beside Flora, Connor sleeps, oblivious.

THUD. THUD. THUD.

Down the hallway now.

The footsteps stop right at the moment they would be in front of the nursery. A pause. Watching Iris sleep.

Flora tries to scream, but her lips are glued to one another. Or maybe she doesn't have a mouth at all. Just smooth skin from the bottom of her nose to her chin.

THUD. THUD. THUD.

The footsteps start again. The Night Hag is coming for her

now. Flora wants to warn Connor, who continues to snore beside her. But, of course, she cannot. She is only a sack of bones and useless muscle, like overworked elastic.

The footsteps get closer. They are in her room. They approach the bed. The Night Hag is only feet away now, though Flora can't turn her head to look.

THUD. THUD.

The Night Hag stops right beside her. Flora knows she is being watched, can feel the gaze ravaging her body, filling her up with shame and filth.

Flora's skin sizzles. It starts at the back of her left hand and travels up her arm, first to her elbow, then to her shoulder. A trail of gasoline lit by a match. She cannot react to the pain, but she can feel it. The worst of both worlds.

It's there again, that deafening gear sound, metal on metal and the echoes of screaming souls.

Just as the familiar heavy weight lands on her body and the sound of rushing water fills her ears, a flicker of movement catches her one good eye. A shadow on the wall. The shadow grows and grows, until it is as tall as the ceiling. Like a shadow puppet made from a child's hands. The creature has long legs and a ginormous head. It's not quite human. It has the head of a hippopotamus.

Taweret

The hippo opens its giant mouth and sucks in air. Wind whips Flora's hair against her cheeks as she lies still, paralyzed. The weight on her chest quickly dissipates, as if the shadow has sucked the Night Hag off Flora. The sucking sound gets louder and louder until *WHAP!*

The room is back to normal. Flora's body buzzes with circulating blood. She wiggles her fingers and toes.

On the monitor, Iris sleeps, oblivious.

42

Flora's eczema has spread. It rears its angry scales up from her hand all the way to her shoulder. The exact trail of fire brought on by the Night Hag's visit last night. Her skin is red, so red. Connor is shocked when he sees it, but she assures him she is used to it. She dealt with skin issues all the time as a kid. Of course, she does not tell him this is much, much worse.

Iris is particularly fussy after waking, and Flora soon realizes it's because she has her first cold. Green mucus leaks from her tiny nostrils and even the inner corners of her eyes. The small nasal cavity is so backed up that the gunk is forced to ooze out elsewhere.

Flora can't help but worry that this sudden illness is connected to last night's events. If so, she fears she is officially out of time.

Mercifully, the pediatrician is able to see Iris at midday. Flora convinces Connor to take the baby, claiming she will use the time to nap after a rough night of sleep—but, of course, she has other plans.

Together, they get Iris ready for her appointment. Flora snaps the baby into a soft pair of corduroy overalls as her husband bends down to retrieve something he dropped under the crib.

When he reappears, his face is white. "What the fuck is this?" he asks.

Flora turns to find her husband holding the birth tusk.

"Where was that?" she asks, grabbing it from him, turning it over in her hands to confirm it is real.

"Taped to the underside of Iris's crib. What the hell is it?"

Her mind races. How did it get there? When?

another Dark Spot

"A what? What dark spot?" he asks.

She looks at him, confused. Did she say that out loud?

Her fingers graze the carvings, including the hippo-goddess Taweret. A flash of the woman's shadow figure on the wall of her bedroom plays behind her eyes.

"My dad bought this after I was born," she tells him.

"Okay," Connor says dubiously. "But what *is* it? And why did you tape it to Iris's crib?"

"I didn't," she says. "I didn't put it there."

Connor frowns and raises an eyebrow. "Flo," he says, "who else would have put it there? Don't lie to me. Just tell me what it is."

"I..." She doesn't know where to begin. "It's just a good-luck charm, kinda. Like a rabbit's foot or four-leaf clover."

Suddenly, she has the urge to replace it under the crib. Maybe it was the tusk that prevented Iris from suffocating on the lovey. Maybe the tusk deterred the Night Hag from entering Iris's room. Maybe it has kept her safe this whole time.

Flora shakes her head. That's not right. Isn't it the birth tusk that brought her mother here and put them in danger to begin with? But then her mother tried to destroy it and it burned her feet...Flora is so confused.

"This thing is creepy," Connor says, grabbing the tusk out of Flora's grip. "I don't want it under Iris's crib. I don't even think we should have it in the house."

Hours ago, she would have agreed with him. But now she doesn't know. The events of the past few weeks swim in her brain. She no longer understands what is bad and what is good.

Connor continues. "A guy in the field had a bunch of weird shit like this, and he had something going on up there, you know? Something not right about him."

Flora nods, her mouth slightly open. She wonders if it was that guy's "weird shit" that kept the soldiers safe. But she does not say this out loud, because Connor will think she is sick in the head, too.

they want to take your baby away

Flora gently retrieves the tusk from Connor's grasp. "I'll give it back to Dad, okay?"

Her husband eyes her closely, and she wants to smack his gaze away.

"You should get going to Iris's appointment," she says.

After they have left, Flora wraps the birth tusk in a pair of socks and hides it in the back of a drawer. She spends some time pacing the perimeter of the house, roaming the halls like a ghost.

Hot water heats on the stove. Flora gathers Iris's bottles and pacifiers, compelled to sanitize them all in the wake of the baby's runny nose, perhaps afraid that her own sickness is spreading to Iris. When bubbles spring to the surface of the pot, Flora carefully places the items inside and watches as they bob around.

The boiling water emits a *hissss* sound that bores into Flora's temples. She steps away, but the sound only gets louder. Maybe it isn't coming from the pot, after all. She squints, as if that could somehow help her hear better, and walks toward the front door.

The hissing is coming from upstairs. Running water. Did she leave on a faucet?

Her feet carry her up the steps. Steam escapes from under the bathroom door. When she opens it, she finds the shower running at full pressure. The room is like a sauna, warm and inviting. No hint of the terror that has plagued it since her mother left.

Flora disrobes and steps into the water, letting it pelt her back and arms. Drops stream down her body, tracing the lines of her flesh. She closes her eyes and feels the heat and sting and electricity through her muscles. Her rash lights a fire under her skin, but she welcomes the pain. After pain comes healing.

A small hand presses on her back. Before Flora even looks, she smiles, knowing that her friend has finally returned.

"Zephie," she says, relieved. "Where have you been?"

But when she looks at Zephie, the girl is not smiling.

"I'm sorry," Zephie says. "But this was the only way."

"What do you mean?" Flora asks.

"We have to keep Iris safe. I didn't want to hurt you, but it's the only way," the girl repeats.

"Hurt me how?"

"Maybe I *am* bad," Zephie says. "Maybe there *is* bad inside me."

"What are you talking about?" Flora asks.

But then she hears something. A siren? She grapples with the shower curtain and when it finally opens, she is accosted by high-pitched beeps. She winces and brings her hands to her ears.

Someone is there. Standing just on the other side of the tub. A man. A stranger. He wears a heavy coat, a large hat, and giant boots. The image is familiar.

"Ma'am?" he says. "Ma'am, we need to get you out of the house."

He hands her a towel and guides her out of the shower. She walks barefoot into the hallway and a foul smell hits her nostrils with an angry slap. Burning plastic.

the bottles boiling on the stove

but I only just left them only just got in the shower

The smoke is thick downstairs, and it coats her insides when she breathes.

Connor is outside talking to one of the firemen. When he sees Flora, he breaks down. "Oh, thank God," he says. "Thank God."

Didn't he just leave for Iris's appointment? Flora's brain is Swiss cheese. So many holes in her timeline.

She sits on the grass, naked under her towel. The firefighter tells Connor that they arrived before too much damage occurred. "It could have been much worse," the man says. His large mustache dances when he speaks. "You guys got very lucky today. Send that neighbor of yours a nice thank-you basket." He nods toward the street, where Wanda throws up a little wave.

fucking Wanda Jesus Christ

"She saw the smoke and called," Connor tells Flora. "Said she was worried after bumping into you the other day—"

"So you're saying—*Wanda* saved my life?" Flora laughs. She laughs and laughs until her left side cramps.

The fireman sees Connor's concerned expression. "Your wife is just in shock," the man assures him.

Later, when the house is properly quiet again, and the beeping machines have been silenced, and the red and blue lights have been extinguished, Connor comes to Flora, a ball of energy.

"What the hell happened?" he asks.

Flora squints. She hits the side of her head, like she's smacking a mosquito, but really she's trying to jostle the gears back in order.

"The bottles," she says. "I was sanitizing the bottles."

"Yeah, I get it," he says. "And I might even understand walking away and getting distracted. But the smoke! You didn't smell the smoke? You didn't hear the alarms? They must have been going off for...Jesus, I don't know, how long were you in that shower?"

"I'm not sure," Flora admits. Her skin is still pruned and raw from the pelting water. She remembers Zephie's hand on her back. The little girl's apology.

Zephie wanted to burn the house down

Zephie was trying to kill me

Connor sucks on the scar above his lip. Flora wonders, not for the first time, what trauma he endured in his mother's womb to warrant the lifetime tattoo.

"What if Iris had been home? What if—?" He can't bring himself to say more.

"That would never happen," she says. Zephie wouldn't have done it with Iris in the house. Zephie thinks Flora is the threat, so she was burning the house down to *help* Iris. To save her.

There it is again. That same refrain.

I wasn't trying to kill her I was trying to save her

"You shouldn't have moved the birth tusk," Flora says.

"Huh? What is going *on* with you?" he asks. "You have to get your shit together."

Flora does not like his tone of voice. This is not her husband. He does not speak to her like this. But then, maybe she has never seen him truly afraid.

"What can I do, Flo?" he asks, his voice softening but panicked. "I did the night feeds, I tried giving you breaks during the day. What else can I do? Tell me, really. Tell me, and I'll do it."

Her phone vibrates in her pocket. It's an unknown number, but she recognizes it immediately. This is bad timing. The worst timing. But she has to answer it. She holds up a finger to Connor's face and walks out the front door with her phone. Her feet carry her farther and farther from the house, despite her husband's frantic protests, which grow dimmer with each step.

43

I t sounds crazy, I know," Flora tells Belinda on the phone. She has laid it all out: her mother's visit, the tusk, the rash and eye twitch and beetles and Dark Spots. She even told Belinda that her imaginary friend tried to kill her.

Belinda is silent for a long moment, but Flora can hear her breathing and knows she is still on the line. "I'm sorry to hear all that," Belinda finally says, "but I'm not sure why you're calling me. I don't know how I can help."

Flora is in the woods. The sun warms the air and the ground; here under the trees, the snow is turning to ice. She slips and catches herself on a nearby tree trunk. The near fall skyrockets her heart rate.

"I need to talk to someone who knew my mom," she says. She looks up at the branches above, which weave a netted pattern in the sky. "Someone who won't think I'm totally nuts. Mom said you're spiritual, so I thought…" Her phone vibrates in her hand, and she pulls it away briefly to see that Connor is calling. She presses "ignore." "Or maybe you would know something about her, something from the last few years that might help me make sense of all this."

"I wish I did," Belinda says.

"Did you really go to psychic fairs together?"

"A few times," Belinda says.

"My mom never believed that stuff. How did you get her into it?" Flora asks.

"*She* got *me* into it," Belinda answers, much to Flora's surprise. "It all started because she wanted to reach someone on the other side."

Flora scrunches her eyebrows together and furiously itches the back of her inflamed hand. "What do you mean? Like...a dead person?"

"That's right," Belinda says.

"Who?" Flora asks quickly.

Belinda breathes into the phone. "She never told me." Disappointment or maybe regret laces her tone. "Your mother was a secretive person. We spent a lot of time together, yes, but it still felt like she was always holding something back."

"Yeah." Flora sighs. This is the first thing Belinda has said about Flora's mother that makes any sense.

Her phone vibrates. She again presses "ignore."

"I got the sense it was someone from her childhood," Belinda says. "A sibling, maybe. A sister. Did your mother lose a sister?"

Flora chews her lip. "No," she says, then quickly adds, "Well, not that I know of, anyway."

She thinks of the box of dresses, handmade with so much love. Maybe they belonged to an aunt Flora never knew she had. If the girl died when she was ten, that would explain the number of dresses. She just can't believe her mother wouldn't have told her.

actually I can believe it I just don't want to

Flora tries to picture her mother contacting the dead. A

cartoonish image pops into her mind of Jodi staring into a crystal ball. "So when you went to these fairs, she would ask the psychic to make contact?"

"At first," Belinda replies, "but eventually we learned how to do it on our own."

"Like a séance?" Flora's voice explodes in disbelief.

"Yes, and we did it," Belinda says somewhat defensively. "We never reached your mom's contact, but we reached mine."

Flora's phone vibrates again, this time with a text from Connor. *We need to talk, I'm gonna stay with friends back home for a bit. Give you a break. I'll be taking Iris.*

Flora's heart detonates, every piece of shrapnel slicing her insides.

"You need to come here," she says to Belinda before she has even thought about the words. "You need to come and do a séance. To talk to my mom."

"In Vermont?" Belinda asks.

"Yes, this must be—this makes sense now—why she mentioned you to me, why she mentioned the psychic fairs. You're the only one who can help—"

"Flora..." Belinda takes a deep breath, and Flora can tell that Belinda does not understand the urgency of the situation.

"Listen," Flora says, "I'm worried. About what I might do— what *she* might do *through* me. My daughter, she's so little." Flora tries to steady her voice. "Please, please, you have to come tonight. He's taking my baby."

"Who is taking your baby?"

"My husband," Flora says, unable to catch her breath, "he's taking her away. I need you to come now. I don't have time, I—" She cannot hold it in anymore; the tears begin to fall. "Oh God, it's all happening now."

"I can't come to Vermont tonight," Belinda says, and Flora crumples. Of course she can't expect a stranger to hop on a plane in a matter of hours to maybe-kinda wrangle a dead spirit.

But she has to try. For her daughter, she has to try. Because the moment she loses her, she loses everything. She loses her will to live.

"Please," Flora says, "if you've made contact with the dead before, you have to come here and try. You have to try to talk to my mother. To figure out what she wants. To force her to leave us alone. If you don't, my daughter...She is going to hurt my daughter. I know she is." Her voice drops impossibly low. "My mother wants to kill her. She wants her *dead*."

A very long silence hangs in the air, and Flora can suddenly hear a *whooshing* around her, as if she is attuned to the world's blood rushing in its veins all around her. Finally, she hears Belinda's lips part.

"Okay," the woman says, her voice small.

Flora sucks in so much air that her chest might pop.

"Okay," she replies.

44

When Flora walks through the front door, she is met with stark silence, and a fear ignites in her gut.

Connor left he's already gone he already took her away

Flora knows, just knows in her bones, that the only thing more dangerous for Iris than being *with* Flora is being *without* Flora. The thing set out to destroy Iris is also the only thing that can keep her safe. Flora is the only one who understands what is going on, the only one who knows what danger Iris is in. If Connor leaves here with the baby, Flora's mother will find some other way—and Flora won't be there to protect her daughter.

So, *no*. He cannot take her.

But he hasn't yet. He is here, at the top of the stairs.

"Iris and I leave tomorrow," he says. "Gives me time to pack."

"Connor, please."

He walks down the steps. "What do you want me to say?"

"Please," Flora repeats, her voice impossibly small, "don't take her."

"She's my daughter, too. It's not like I'm kidnapping her." He comes closer to her, and something in his stance softens. "I tried

224

talking, Flo. I tried that. But it seems like you don't know what you need. So I don't know how to help you. You have to figure this out."

She leans all her weight against the railing. "But why do I have to figure it out alone?"

"Don't put that on me," he says, his softness stiffening again. "I have to protect Iris."

"What do you think *I'm* doing?!"

He explodes back in her direction. "You almost burnt the house down today!"

"I know, but *listen,* I talked to Belinda—"

"Belinda?" Connor asks, and his expression is tired, so tired.

"She was my mom's friend, that's who called me just now. She's going to come here, to Vermont. She can do a—"

"I don't have a clue what you're talking about." His eyes are cold. "And honestly, I can't do this right now, Flora," Connor says. He rarely calls her by her full name. "I'm exhausted. It's been a crazy long day. Oh, Iris is fine, by the way." Flora tilts her head in confusion. "I had to take her to the doctor, remember?"

Flora had forgotten. How could she have forgotten?

when this is all over I'll make it all right

Connor shakes his head, heavy with disappointment. "I'm going to sleep in the guest room tonight," he says as he heads back up the steps. "I'll handle the night shifts." He doesn't turn to look at her again before disappearing from view down the hallway.

Flora books an outrageously expensive last-minute flight for Belinda—yet another thing she dreads having to explain to Connor—and then calls her dad. He *must* know who her mother was trying to contact through those séances. And that has to

be important. If her mom was seeking connection with someone, maybe she still is. If Flora can understand what her mother
wanted in life, it might help her to understand what she is now
seeking in death.

But her dad doesn't answer.

The house is quiet, but Flora's inner world is blaring. She's
unable to eat, subsisting alone on the energy generated by her
anxiety. Her eye twitch has worsened, and a white, pimple-like
bump has appeared on the underside of her lid, right at the lash
line. Every time she blinks, it aches, like tapping on a bruise.
Her eczema burns, and she isn't sure it is even eczema, after all.
Four large, dome-like blisters have sprouted on her underarm,
see-through and full of viscous liquid. Smaller dots mark a trail
from there up to her neck, a map of future blister constellations.

She just needs to make it to tomorrow morning, when
Belinda arrives.

She hides herself in a baggy sweatshirt and returns to the
boxes her father sent. Flora runs her hands once again over the
dresses, willing them to speak to her. She pulls them out one by
one, trying to imagine their importance to her mother. Trying to
imagine the body that was meant to fill them.

Then, in the pocket of the second-to-largest one, she feels
something. A piece of paper. It crinkles under her touch, and she
delicately pulls it from the fragile pocket. When she unfolds it,
she sees it is the sewing pattern for the dress she's holding.

There are a few handwritten notes on the instructions.
Phrases like *shoulder line* and *center back*. Some arrows drawn in
the margins. These notes mean nothing to Flora except for one
particular detail: they are most definitely written in her mother's handwriting. Which means it *was* her mother who made
these dresses. Were they some kind of tribute to her mom's dead

sister? The idea makes Flora sad. That her mother put so much time into something, so much care, only to stow it away in a box to never be seen.

She lays the dresses on the ground, side by side, from smallest to largest. None of the others have patterns with them that she can find, but she does another sweep to be sure. And that's when something else catches her eye. Just on the inside hem of the smallest dress: tiny embroidered letters. In the same color as the dress's fabric so it blends in. A name, no larger than a quarter inch high. Flora's heart catches. She lifts the second dress, running her fingers along the hem, and finds the same name again. She lifts every hem of every dress and finds the same hidden name lovingly sewn on each one: *Zephyr.*

The room spins. Flora doesn't know how to make sense of this. She thinks of Zephie and tries to remember how she came up with that name for her imaginary friend. But of course, she can't remember; she was too young. Did her mother give her the idea? Plant the name in her mind for some reason? It would be strange, surely, to think Jodi would suggest her dead sister's name as the name for Flora's imaginary friend. But then, Flora rarely understood her mother's motivations.

She pulls out her phone and searches under her mother's maiden name. *Zephyr Martin death certificate.* The name is unique enough that, mercifully, she doesn't have a lot to sift through. She clicks around on various ancestry sites, just shy of coughing over $9.99 to "read more," but none of the results are relevant. Flora frowns.

And then a devastating thought comes to her.

Maybe the person Jodi was trying to reach wasn't her sister at all. Maybe Jodi really did sew these dresses for a child. A child she lost. Could she have lost a baby before Flora?

She looks again at the hand-stitched dresses and pictures her mother choosing a pattern, shopping for threads, and sitting down to assemble a new dress for her dead child. A dress that would never be worn. Maybe she did it every year on what would have been the little girl's birthday. Or perhaps the anniversary of her death. And when she was done, she packed it carefully into this box, away with the others, hiding not only the clothes but also her love for sewing, preserving that hobby only for the little girl she lost.

As a mother now herself, Flora can barely entertain the thought that her parents could have been harboring such heavy grief for so long.

This time, Flora enters her own maiden name in the search bar. *Zephyr Graham death certificate.*

And there it is. Within a few clicks and a couple of long loading bars, Flora's world comes into focus. Zephyr Graham. Parents: Jodi and Michael Graham. Age at death: six weeks.

The same age Iris is now.

But the most shocking piece of all is Zephyr's birth date.

Flora takes breath in through her teeth and clutches the muscles around her heart, afraid they might seize or spasm. She massages her chest, as if she could massage the very hurt now loosening and running wild within her.

Zephyr had Flora's same birthday. Which means Zephyr was Flora's twin sister.

Flora drives thirty miles per hour over the speed limit. It's almost midnight, and the roads are nearly empty. Her dad's house is normally a three-hour drive, but she bets she can do it in two.

She has taken the family car. Iris's empty car seat is in the back. This is by design: Connor won't be able to leave the house with the baby until Flora returns. He was sleeping when she left, but she knows to expect a scathing call when he realizes that she and the car are gone.

when this is all over I'll make it all right

As she drives, her mind travels great distances to imagine how her twin sister might have died. A sickness: some kind of rare infant disease. An accident: a fall from the changing table that resulted in instant, painless death. An allergy: a routine vaccine or antibiotic that shut down her organs.

Flora is not entirely surprised that her mother kept such a secret from her. Her mother always had a private life, one into which Flora was never welcomed. It was like Jodi had given something up to be a mother, and she was just waiting for the moment to reclaim what she had left behind. As a result, there was a hole in Jodi—one that Flora spent her life trying to guess the shape of in order to fit herself into it. She never succeeded, of course.

No, her mother having a secret is not a shock. In fact, her mother probably had many more. But her father is another thing entirely. The idea that he lied to Flora for her entire life is enough to slice the foundation out from under her world. It's enough to brew a storm of rage within her, and it's that anger that presses her foot even harder onto the gas pedal now, nudging the needle of the speedometer up and up and up.

When she arrives, she parks haphazardly in the driveway, barely turning off the car before running toward the front door, setting off a handful of motion-detector lights in the process. The perimeter of her father's house lights up to announce her arrival. A neighbor's dog barks at the sudden middle-of-the-night commotion.

229

Flora bangs the door with both fists, and it is only now she realizes she is crying. The banging becomes cathartic, echoing down the street, under doorframes, through open windows. A light flicks on from the upper floor of her dad's house. Then another near the staircase. She maps his movements with the flow of electricity.

When the door finally opens, Flora is still leaning her weight against it, banging with a force she didn't know she had, and she loses her balance and falls into the house. Her father's face is a portrait of confusion and worry. He reaches a hand toward her, but she smacks it away. Her tears are fierce and taste sour in her mouth.

"I know," she says. "I *know.*" Then, wielding the words like a sharp knife, she says, "About Zephyr."

He backs up as if he has been shot in the chest, and sits on the bottom of the nearby staircase. He leans forward, digging his elbows into his knees and rubbing his eyes with fervor. His voice is hollow.

"I figured this was coming. When I sent those boxes...maybe I wanted you to know."

"Tell me," Flora says. She's not begging. She's demanding. "Tell me what happened."

Her father looks up—a different man entirely, a face she has never seen—and nods.

PART
4

45

Michael met Jodi when they were both twenty-seven years old. He had just secured his first "real" job as an electronics engineer at an aerospace technology company.

"I only know what half those words mean," Jodi said. They were at a bar not far from Michael's apartment, one he frequented often with friends. But he had never seen Jodi there before.

Michael laughed. "Basically, I play with circuit boards and stuff."

"I have a feeling it's slightly more complicated than that." Jodi smiled and sipped her drink, a vodka soda with two limes.

"Only slightly." Michael winked. He bought her next drink. And every drink thereafter; the two were inseparable after that night.

They were married at the courthouse. Jodi wore a simple but elegant white linen-blend dress with her favorite pair of Converse. Her nails were painted bright blue. Michael could only imagine what his prim mother would have said; he was quite certain she'd have been horrified by the whole affair. But she had died of lung cancer when Michael was seventeen, so she wasn't around to voice an opinion. Michael's father had been distant in more ways than one—he sent his regards from Singapore, where he had relocated years prior.

Jodi's mother was very much alive, but Jodi had not invited her. Michael had only met her twice, neither occasion being one he cherished. Jodi's mother was a textbook narcissist who would never be honest enough with a therapist to get any real help. And Jodi's father died tragically young in a helicopter crash.

So there they were, just the two of them. They could have invited a few friends, of course, but they decided this was more romantic. An "elopement." They paid for a random witness at the courthouse—an elderly woman with the kindest smile Michael had ever seen—and took their vows in front of a large stained-glass window that painted the incoming sunlight blue and purple.

After the ceremony, they walked the grounds of the courthouse together, slowly taking in the lush greenery and perfectly landscaped flowers. Bumblebees and ladybugs danced around them.

They spent the first years of their marriage enjoying each other's company. Neither was in a rush to have children, though they both were adamant that they did, eventually, want to be parents. Those early years were spent reading to one another, traveling to both exotic and not-so-exotic locations, working hours that only a twentysomething would agree to work, and drinking beers on the roof of their apartment building in the sweltering days of summer.

They had trouble getting pregnant. They tried for three years before each checking with doctors. But they were both handed clean bills of health.

"You're too focused on it," one doctor had said. "Try to relax and forget about it."

Jodi had, admittedly, blown up at him, telling him that was the worst medical advice she had ever received.

But finally, a year and a half later, she got pregnant.

And that's when the real trouble began.

Michael didn't know how to help her. It wasn't that Jodi was overly miserable throughout pregnancy; it was just that she got every symptom in the book. Each trimester brought a new smorgasbord of side effects. Fatigue, migraines, leg cramps, insomnia, night sweats, carpal tunnel in both wrists, heartburn, swelling, nausea. Michael couldn't keep track of all her ailments. He just knew at any given time at least three parts of her body were probably hurting.

Still, they were both overjoyed. Even at that first ultrasound, when they discovered they were having twins, Michael was tingly with excitement. A small part of his brain acknowledged that this would make things doubly hard, but the bigger part, the louder part, said things would be doubly wonderful.

Jodi spent most evenings sewing baby clothes like hats and mittens. One night, she gasped excitedly with an internal epiphany.

"The names!" she said. "I've got them!"

Michael joined her on the couch, fiddling her soft craft yarn with his fingertips. "Lay 'em on me," he said.

"In college I took this art history class and, God, I remember nothing. *Except*—we learned about a painting called *Flora and the Zephyrs*. I always thought it'd be a cool band name. Don't you think?"

He shrugged. "Sure…"

"Well, unless we're going to start a band in this lifetime, I think we should commandeer the names for the girls. Flora and Zephyr."

"Zephyr? That's not weird?"

"It's a little weird, but it could be cute. *Zephie.*" She smiled. "I love it. It's unique."

Michael wasn't sold, but he saw the joy in his wife's eyes. Her excitement was infectious. And soon, he loved the names as much as she did.

"Flora and Zephie," he agreed, trying them out on his tongue.

Jodi was scheduled to be induced, but she naturally went into labor the day before. Michael was grateful that, unlike the pregnancy, the labor went smoothly, with no complications. Even so, it was difficult for him to watch. Not because he was queasy, but because he wished, with every pained moan that Jodi emitted, he could take her place. He wanted a button that would transfer the pain to him. It was too difficult to watch the person he loved struggle to that degree.

"Not as difficult as giving birth," Jodi had retorted when he later shared this feeling with her. And, well, he couldn't argue with that.

Flora and Zephie had a way of finding one another. Even in the womb, at every ultrasound, the techs commented on how the twins were intertwined, always holding each other. Out in the world, if one cried, the other cried in response. It felt more natural to say they were two pieces of the same person rather than two separate entities. Michael didn't know if that would change as they got older, but he found comfort and delight in their intense connection.

At first, Jodi said she was sad to no longer be pregnant, which made absolutely no sense to Michael, who knew how hard those months had been for her. But she insisted: she missed feeling the babies kick and wrestle within her; she missed knowing that when she took a bite of food it was nourishing them as well; she missed the incessant hiccups, even if they kept her up at night.

Michael had to return to work soon after the birth. He had quickly climbed the ranks at the aerospace company and was now responsible for a group of eight engineers. The team couldn't afford for him to be away. And so, just a week and a half after the twins arrived, he went back to work full-time.

In the hours that he was home, Jodi holed herself up in bed. Michael figured she was tired; the girls needed to eat every few hours at night, and they struggled to fall back asleep once awake. But as the weeks progressed, he saw less and less of his wife. She was there, of course, going through the motions, but she wasn't really *there*. He was watching her slip away.

One night, he came home from work to find Jodi in the kitchen. She was staring into the refrigerator, the harsh light yellowing her skin, and speaking just under her breath.

"Who are you talking to?" Michael asked.

Jodi looked at him with a blank expression. He wasn't sure if she even saw him or if she was looking through to the wall behind.

"I was talking to you," she said. "Do you want something to eat?"

But Jodi had not been talking to Michael. He knew that.

Two days later, Jodi and Michael were getting into bed at the same time—a rare occurrence those days—and she confided in him.

"I think there's something wrong with the girls," she said.

Michael sat up, concerned. "What do you mean? Are they sick?"

"No, I mean…" Her eyes looked faraway, that same emptiness he had seen in the kitchen. "I think there's something *in* them. I think they may not be *good*."

"They're babies," he said. "They're only six weeks old. What could possibly be *bad* about them?"

He knew right then he had made a mistake. Jodi rolled over and mumbled something about getting thirty minutes of sleep before needing to feed. He wanted to touch her softly, to pull her shoulder and bring her face to his, to comfort her and assure her that their babies were the most perfect creatures he had ever seen in his life.

But he didn't say any of those things. Instead, he rolled over, too, his back now almost touching hers, and he went to sleep.

The next morning, Michael woke to an empty bed. That was not unusual; Jodi was typically up with the twins, nursing them in their room or making herself a small breakfast while they lay in the bassinets downstairs.

But as he rose and wiped the crust from his eyes, he heard a strange noise. It sounded like a foghorn. The more he brought his mind to the present moment, and the further he got from sleep, the louder the sound grew. And finally, he placed it. Jodi was crying.

Not just crying. *Howling.*

He flew out of their room, still in boxers and a light tee, and ran down the hall.

"Jodi?" he called out. "Jodi, where are you?"

The carpet squished beneath his feet as he approached the

bathroom. *This doesn't feel right,* he thought. *Why is the carpet so wet?* Michael looked down to see that the carpet was soaked near the door.

Jodi's moans were loud, so impossibly loud. And primal. Michael had never heard anything like it. He was reminded of a video he saw once of a mother elephant standing over her dead baby, her trunk braying to the sky, her cries desperate and fierce. There was something like that in Jodi's voice now. Something born of instinct.

Michael was terrified.

He beat on the door, begging Jodi to unlock it. She didn't respond, and he wondered if she even noticed he was there. Finally, he kicked hard enough right by the doorknob that the door gave in, swinging open to reveal the flooded bathroom.

Jodi was holding one of the twins—Michael couldn't see which one—and rocking her body back and forth. The tub was overflowing, water still pouring from the spigot and escaping quickly over the edge.

"Jodi," he said, "give her to me! Give her to me!"

It was Zephie. He held her in his arms and knew instantly that she was gone.

Before he could process it, his brain went into high alert. "Flora," he yelled. "Where is Flora?"

Jodi didn't answer, and Michael ran out of the room, toward the nursery, convinced that Flora must be gone, too.

He found her in the crib, hidden in the loose folds of a blanket—*didn't Jodi say to never put this in the crib?*—and fumbled one-handed with the fabric to find Flora's face. Her eyes were open. She was alive.

He held both of his girls, one here and the other very far away, and wept. The weeping turned to sobs turned to convulsions turned to dry heaving.

DEAREST

It was an accident.

That was the official determination. After all, even toddlers can drown in only an inch of water. Sure, there were judgments. Jodi should have been bathing her in the sink, not the tub. She shouldn't have turned her back for even a second. She should have tried baby CPR. She should have done any one thing differently that morning so that they could still have two baby girls instead of only one.

Michael helped steer the story with investigators. He knew his wife couldn't have done this on purpose. And he also knew that his remaining daughter would not benefit from a mother in prison.

So he backed up her version of events and edited out some of the less convenient parts: Jodi feeling sad, losing sleep, hearing voices, talking to thin air. The picture he painted for the police was much more traditional. Yes, they were both tired, but that was normal with a new baby—and especially normal with twins. But in general, they were managing well. Spirits were high. Until, of course, this horrible, tragic accident.

Michael always wondered, though. Of course he wondered. He was plagued by dreams for years. In them, Jodi was dressed as a nun and baptizing Zephie, trying to get the *bad* out. But she was never satisfied, never felt Zephie had been fully cleaned, and was too earnest in her attempt so that she eventually drowned her. Sometimes, Zephie died very quickly. Other times, in the worst dreams, it took many dunks in the holy water. And all the while, Michael was stuck on the other side of a large piece of never-ending glass. No matter how far he ran, there was never an opening. It was like he was stuck in a parallel dimension.

And he felt like this in his real life sometimes, too. He wanted to be there for Jodi in her grief, but he couldn't even process his own.

One morning shortly after, Michael found Jodi staring at her hands. She admitted her vision was blurring. She mumbled to herself, slightly slurring her words. Afraid she was having some kind of stroke, he drove her to the hospital. The routine checks returned nothing; still, they were concerned enough to suggest she check in to the psych ward. She stayed for ten days, and for ten days Michael worried that he might have to walk down the rest of his parenthood path alone. He feared his wife was gone for good.

But her time in the hospital proved to be a reset. She had either begun to heal or had learned to construct a lifelike mask that carried her sadness through the world undetected. In any case, she slowly returned.

But Michael felt further from himself than he ever had. And as hard as it was to admit, he didn't know if he loved his wife anymore.

He didn't know if he, in fact, hated her.

Did Jodi kill Zephie intentionally?

That was the question always at the center of Michael's existence. It was behind everything he did. He spent hours replaying those memories from before Zephie's death, the moments in the kitchen and in bed when Jodi had not been herself.

He wondered about Flora, too. The blanket in her crib. Had Jodi started with Flora, then moved on to Zephie? Maybe she thought she had finished the job, thought she had suffocated the first baby—but, mercifully, she had been wrong.

He didn't let himself venture down this rabbit hole often. What difference would it make? Flora was alive.

Michael knew that this was, at least in part, his fault as well. Because he had done nothing, had said nothing. If he had only talked to Jodi, asked her questions, called the hospital. If he had insisted she get more sleep, had hired a nanny to help, had reached out to her mom even if Jodi would have hated it. If, if, if. The ifs absolutely consumed him. They crawled within his veins and slid in and out of his heart like a knife.

Each of them was slowly dying in their own way. And yet— they still had a child to raise. Still had one perfect daughter who needed her parents.

And who needed protecting.

He took Flora with him to Pennsylvania. He had a two-day work conference and arranged for childcare in the city through his company. Jodi was grateful for the break. Neither of them said the truth out loud: that Michael was taking Flora with him because he could not trust Jodi with her at home alone.

Michael was leaving the last team event—a museum visit— when he saw the woman selling trinkets. She locked eyes with him and held up the birth tusk.

"You need this," she said. "For the little flower."

The little flower. *Flora.*

The woman told him about the birth tusk. She told him to wrap a single strand of Jodi's hair around the tooth to connect it to her. She told him to attach it to the underside of Flora's crib. And in a world that now felt so out of Michael's control, he was happy to oblige. He was happy to have some direction. He was happy to do something, *anything.*

He kept the birth tusk safely in his pocket until he arrived back home. That same night, he plucked a fresh hair from Jodi's scalp as she slept, wrapped the tooth, and said a little prayer. He didn't know if any of it would work. But he knew it couldn't hurt.

It was easier for both of them if they never talked about it. They moved to New Jersey, where no one knew they'd ever had another daughter. And eventually, they believed this narrative, too. It was astonishingly simple, actually, to erase the six short weeks of Zephie's existence.

Michael was, of course, in charge of bath time moving forward. This wasn't something they ever needed to discuss; it was a routine they fell into naturally. He did it for years, until Flora was old enough to shower on her own, at which point Jodi felt comfortable lending a hand when needed. The rushing, moving water did not hold the threat of still water that unraveled her every time.

He worried he should have been honest with the investigators. Even after Jodi's mood improved with the medication, he avoided leaving her alone with Flora. And perhaps this, too, was a mistake; perhaps he was sending his wife the very message that she needed to dispel—the message that she could not be trusted.

He was wary for years. But then his own wariness was overshadowed by Jodi's. It became clear that no matter how much time passed or how many pills she swallowed, she would never fully allow herself to connect with Flora. A fear lived inside her. A fear of herself. And Michael could see the tragedy in this. Jodi had an opportunity to form a bond with her remaining daughter, but she ended up losing Flora, too, because she prohibited herself from getting too close. Maybe she worried she would hurt Flora. Maybe she worried she couldn't withstand the death of another child, no matter how that death occurred, so it was easier to keep her distance. Whatever the reason, she self-sabotaged, missing all the best parts of motherhood.

Every year they'd go to the Outer Banks for a weeklong vacation. It often felt more like a father-daughter getaway than a family one. Jodi would disappear for hours at a time, communing with the sea. Flora grew up thinking her mother loved the water. The truth was, Jodi couldn't trust herself to be around it and her only living daughter at the same time. Michael tried to convince her this was rubbish; enough time had passed; she needed to live in the present and stop punishing herself. And stop punishing her daughter, who spent those vacations wondering why she wasn't good enough, why her mother didn't like her.

He could never convince Jodi, though. He could never make a compelling enough argument to encourage her to open up to her little girl. And so, eventually, he stopped trying. He became the referee for the two female opposing teams in his home and counted the years until he could leave.

Because Michael and Jodi never spoke about Zephie, he assumed his wife's heart had hardened against the past. He assumed she got through by going numb, being cold, not caring.

It wasn't until decades later, when Jodi died, and Michael was cleaning out her condo, that he discovered the dresses that his wife had so lovingly handcrafted over the years in remembrance of their baby. And the sadness crept back in, not so much for him losing a daughter, but for the fact that losing a daughter had meant losing his wife, too. All those years together, but each of them was suffering alone. All those years together, and, by the end, they barely knew each other at all.

46

Flora has listened to her father's story in silence, her heartbeat steadying but still strong, pushing against the hard cavity of her chest in search of an escape route. She cannot fathom how her father has kept this from her.

"How?" Flora asks. "How could you not tell me?"

He shakes his head. "You were so young..."

"And then I grew up. You had thirty-two years to tell me this," she spits.

"It didn't feel like my story to tell," he says.

Flora throws up her hands. "Bullshit! Zephie was your daughter, too."

"I was trying to protect you—"

"You were protecting *yourself*," she says.

He sits with this a moment, swallowing whatever other excuse he might have had on deck. And then he is crying. Soft but strong, nearly silent sobs. Flora can count on one hand the number of times she has seen her father cry.

"I was ashamed," he finally admits. "I was so ashamed." He clears his throat and leans his head back to direct the tears back into his eyes, as if he could rewind time and stop them from ever falling.

"Why?" Flora asks, her voice still biting but her body softening. "*She's* the one who should have been in jail."

"Maybe," he says, his shoulders sagging. "Truth is, we don't know what happened in that bathroom. We never will. Because I wasn't there. And I should have been."

"Dad, you can't——"

"No, Flora," he says, his voice stronger now, his chest puffing out with authority. "I should have done more. Should have done *anything*. I knew she was struggling, but I didn't want it to be true. I didn't want that to be our story." He bites the knuckles of his right hand, and Flora wonders if this is to stop himself from punching the wall beside him. "But our story turned out so much worse."

Flora remembers her mother's admission about how lonely that time had been. She remembers her mom's comment that Michael had not been there for her the way he was always there for Flora. Now knowing the truth in those words, Flora wonders what else her mother told her over the years that Flora dismissed as exaggeration or pity bait. What other moments of connection did Flora unknowingly bat away? The familiar heaviness of guilt sets in.

Then another realization dawns on her.

"I told you," she says. "I told you about my imaginary friend. That her name was Zephie. You didn't think that was *weird*?"

"No," he says, a brightness sneaking into his eyes, curling the edges of his lips upward in a slight smile. "No, not at all." His voice is suddenly light and full of hope. "When you told me that, it was the most comforting thing to happen to me since her death. I knew then that she was still with us."

Flora shakes her head. "What are you talking about? You think—you think she wasn't an imaginary friend? You think she was some kind of *ghost*?"

Her words are laced with doubt, but even as she says them, she knows they are true. Flora always thought Zephie looked just like her, but when she inspects her memories, she sees the subtle differences of a twin: Zephie's left incisor that jutted forward, the cowlick at her hairline an inch from her middle part, her eyes beautifully flecked with gold.

But that's impossible, isn't it?

Flora shakes her head again. "I probably just internalized her name or something, when I was a baby..." Her voice trails off, the words not even convincing to her.

Her twin sister hadn't left her. She had stuck around for as long as Flora had allowed.

Her dad looks to her. "Maybe I should have told you then. But part of me thought you already knew. That you *had* to know. Your sister was with you."

Flora's heart aches. She is a cauldron of emotions. Anger, surprise, devastation. She feels unmoored, as if her father has pulled up the anchor of who she is and has set her boat free in the middle of the ocean. Suddenly, the world around her presents a narrative that is not her own. When one thing is painted a lie, everything else takes on a similar hue.

Her father holds out his arms, and Flora crawls into them like a small child. "I'm sorry," he says. "I'm so, so sorry."

"Me, too," she says.

And she *is* sorry. She is sorry for Zephie, who Flora knew was always something more but never allowed herself to believe. She is sorry for her father, who carried this burden alone so unnecessarily for so long. And she is sorry for her mother. Because no matter what happened in that bathroom, her mother had to live with the consequences. She spent her life in prison, after all. A prison of her own making.

Flora pulls away from her father just enough that she can make eye contact. "I'm afraid, Dad," she says. "I'm afraid she's trying to do it again."

"What do you mean?" he asks. "Who?"

Flora decides to lay it all out for him. No more secrets. She has seen the destruction that lies leave in their wake.

"Mom was at my house last week," she begins.

47

Her dad believes her. He *believes* her. He didn't call her crazy. He packed himself into the car and agreed to ride with her to fetch Belinda.

Even if he is only *choosing* to believe her, something cracked open within him last night. His confession about Zephie crumbled decades-old walls around his heart. And Flora knows that he will do anything to protect Iris—he would never forgive himself for making the same mistake twice.

Flora drives fast this time, too, but not out of anger. Now she is giddy with hope. She isn't going at this alone. It finally seems like she and Iris might have a chance. Flora will not live the rerun of her mother's life; she will not waste the years avoiding her daughter out of fear. Because she knows now: She is *not* a bad mother. This isn't her. At least, this isn't *all* her. She is not to blame. She can make this right.

"I think that's Belinda," Flora says when they arrive at the airport. She points to a woman at the curb's edge leaning on her suitcase. Belinda wears a soft linen-blend knee-length black shirt over a pair of dark jeans. Tall boots kiss the bottoms of her knees, and her hair falls in thick waves past her shoulders, graying at the roots. Her delicate jewelry is made of colorful stones and thin silver. Her waist is slim but her hips balloon out as if she is wearing a small inner tube around her gut.

"You look so much like your mother," Belinda says when she sees Flora.

"Really?" Flora is surprised. "I never thought so…"

Her dad pipes up from the back seat. "Oh, yes, you definitely do," he says. Something he has never told her before.

The three make introductions, pack Belinda's suitcase into the trunk, and set out on the road. Flora feels a bit like she's driving a demented clown car: a new, emotionally vulnerable version of her father in the back; Belinda, a stranger who talked to dead people with Flora's mom, in the passenger seat; and, most likely, floating around somewhere in here, the spirits of her dead sister and mother.

Flora catches Belinda up to speed on everything she learned in the last few hours. Her dad contributes when relevant. At one point, Belinda's eyes drift upward as she nods slowly, assembling puzzle pieces in her mind.

She asks Flora, "Zephie appeared to you when?"

"Oh, I must have been two?" Flora guesses.

"No," Belinda says, "I mean when did she first appear to you recently?"

Flora thinks. She remembers the voice in the monitor, Zephie holding her hand, the trail of beetles. "The same day I reached out to Mom."

Belinda nods, as if she had been expecting this answer. "And the last time you saw her was in the bathroom? When you stabbed your mother with the tusk?"

Flora sees her father wince in the rearview mirror. She grips the wheel more tightly. "Well, I saw her for just a second in the shower the other day. When she tried to burn the house down."

"Yes, that's right. She lured you to the tub. The same bathtub." Belinda sucks on her incisor with her tongue, nodding to herself. "I wonder if they are connected somehow. Your mother's spirit and Zephie's. Zephie appeared first, then you contacted your mother shortly after. When you stabbed your mother's form with the tusk, Zephie, too, disappeared."

"So what does that mean?"

"It means, perhaps, that if we have trouble connecting with your mother, we might have another pathway through Zephie. It's a good thing."

Suddenly nauseous, Flora rolls down the window. She doesn't like the idea of using Zephie to get to her mother. It feels dangerous or cruel.

Belinda's face goes slack, a heaviness setting in. "That must be who she was trying to reach. I had no idea…"

Her father leans in from the back seat. "So are we really going to have some kind of séance?"

Belinda turns toward him and nods. "It's a scary idea, I know. I thought so at first, too."

"Flora says you've done it before? That it worked for you?" he asks.

"My son." Belinda nods. "He was very sick when he died." For the first time since she got into the car, her gaze retreats out the window. "It was nice to know that he is no longer in pain. Comforting."

Flora slowly passes a cyclist, who is illuminated by the early morning light that greets the quiet backcountry road. A month ago, she would have doubted Belinda's story. She would have chalked it up to some kind of mental placebo effect: an elaborate form of self-therapy for a grieving mother. But now, just a few weeks later, having gone through what she has gone through, she is more inclined to believe Belinda.

Or maybe, like her father, she *wants* to believe her. *Needs* to.

Belinda continues. "You know, it's even more unusual to me that Jodi never told me about the daughter she lost. She knew my son had passed. We had that in common. Why wouldn't she have shared?"

Flora echoes her father's words from years ago. "My mother's sadness was all her own. That's all she'd let it be." She makes eye contact with her dad in the rearview, one corner of his mouth turning upward in sad acknowledgment.

Then he asks Belinda another question. "Why is this all happening?"

Belinda sighs. "I suspect there is some 'unfinished business,' as they say. Between Flora and her mother." Then, to Flora, she adds, "Or maybe some problem of your mother's that she thinks you can help solve."

Flora loosens her grip on the wheel, which she had inadvertently tightened again. She stretches her fingers long and sees that they are shaking. She takes a deep breath in an attempt to steady herself. They are on a narrow two-lane road flanked by ditches.

"Is there anything you want to tell her?" Belinda asks.

"Yeah, 'leave us the fuck alone,'" Flora says.

Her father raises an eyebrow.

Belinda is struck by another thought. "You said the tusk burned her. You still have it?" she asks.

Flora nods.

"Good," Belinda continues. "I think that tusk is the only thing that can destroy her."

Flora thinks about this duality that keeps coming up for

her—this notion that creator and destroyer are one. The tusk, the very thing that facilitated her mother's return, is also the only thing that can get rid of her.

"You want to destroy her?" Flora's father asks, eyes wide.

"Dad..." Flora says, making eye contact in the rearview. "What choice do we have?"

"Right," he says, looking down. "You're right, of course."

Belinda looks to them both, sad. "I know on some level it probably feels like a betrayal. But this thing is clearly not your mother. It is only the worst parts of her. It's like this broken part of Jodi was awakened when you had a baby, and that broken part of her—that's the part that wants to hurt Iris."

"She couldn't have her daughter, so she doesn't want me to have mine," Flora says, realizing the truth of the words as she says them.

Belinda nods. "I think so. The worst parts of her want you to suffer as badly as she did. But again: that *thing* is not her. It's not Jodi."

Her dad agrees from the back seat. "You're right. Jodi wouldn't want this. Never."

Flora's eyes remain fixed on the road but glaze over in a glassy stare as she thinks. The spirit of her mother is hurting, and it only knows how to exist by hurting others the same way. It's a childish motivation: something a toddler would do. Flora thinks of all the times she had to parent her own mother in life. Perhaps she should not be shocked that she will need to parent her mother in death, too.

48

W hat the hell is going on, Flo?" Connor says when Flora finally arrives at the house. He holds an empty bottle in his hands, and Iris swings happily nearby. "You stole the car and turned off your phone? I've been trying to reach you for hours!"

Flora thinks about correcting him—she can't technically *steal* her own car, and her phone *died*—but before she can respond, Belinda and her father appear in the doorway behind her.

"Hey, Connor," her dad says.

Connor keeps his eyes trained on Flora. "What's going on?" he repeats. Then, pointing to Belinda, he asks, "Who is this woman?"

"She knew my mom," Flora says.

Connor's eyes narrow. "Okay, and you drove in the middle of the night to pick her up, why?"

"Things have been *happening,* Connor, things that are *scaring* me—"

"So let's call the police," he says.

"The police?" Flora's voice is louder than she intends, more shrill than she would like. "The police can't help us!"

"But some stranger can?" He waves his arm in Belinda's general direction.

"Connor," Flora says, trying desperately to calm her voice, "I'm being...stalked." This feels like a safer word than "possessed" or "haunted." A way to ease him into the conversation.

But Connor has no intention of talking things out. "I'm calling the police," he says, reaching for his phone. "You can explain everything to them——"

"No police!" Flora's voice booms. "They'll take my baby away!"

The anger in her voice is biting, and when she yells, her right eye *POPS!* The pimple-like bump on her lash line finally bursts, and a white substance dribbles down her cheek. When she tries to open that eye, the lashes half stick together with gunk. She holds her hand an inch from her face and waves it back and forth. She can barely see out of her right eye now. It's all blurry.

Connor's own eyes go wide in response. "What the fuck..."

Flora looks to Belinda, who understands immediately, her expression laced with fear. "We need to do this as soon as possible," Belinda says. "Where should I set up?"

Flora points toward the living room, and her father leads Belinda into the house with her suitcase. Connor watches, his mouth hanging open like a dead fish.

"Set up for what?" he asks. He watches as Belinda pulls items out of her bag: a large black candle, a worn journal, a white pyramid-shaped crystal. "Flo..." he says, turning to his wife with pleading eyes.

"Listen," Flora says, taking a step toward him. "It's my mom. It's my mom who has been stalking me. She's trying to hurt Iris. This is what we need to do now." She gestures toward Belinda, who is setting items on the coffee table.

"Just to be clear," Connor says, "you're talking about your *dead* mother. You're saying that your dead mother is trying to hurt Iris."

Flora barrels on. "Belinda has done this before. She talked to her son—he died and she *talked* to him—and now we are going to reach out to my mom, to find out what she wants so that she will leave us alone—"

"Oh my *God*," Connor says. "You've lost it. You've totally lost it."

Belinda ignores him and asks Flora, "Do you have something of your mother's we can use? We should get something of Zephie's, too."

"Who is Zephie?" Connor asks. But just as Flora opens her mouth to respond, he stops her. "Actually, I don't want to know. This is insane. I'm leaving."

Flora's dad speaks up from the living room, leveling his gaze with Connor's. "You're not leaving," he says. "Flora is in trouble. Your daughter is in danger. And Belinda is here to help. So we are going to do what she tells us."

"The fuck I am," Connor says, unstrapping Iris from the bouncer.

"Where are you going?" Flora asks, panicked. "Where are you taking her?"

"Back home, like I told you." He hoists the baby into his arms and grabs the diaper bag. "I'm not staying under the same roof as this bullshit."

He looks again toward the living room, where Belinda has surrounded the coffee table with chairs. As he opens the door, Iris begins to protest.

"She doesn't want to leave me," Flora says. "See? She's crying. Please. She needs her mother, Connor."

"She doesn't need this version of her mother."

"You don't get it—if you take her, my mom will just find another way. You're putting her in more danger, you don't know how to—"

Connor slams the door behind him. Flora crumples to the floor. Heaving sobs pull her chest closer and closer to the ground, until she wishes she could just melt into it entirely, surrendering her body to the earth.

you were right Mom

everyone wants to take my baby

But no. Fuck that. She won't let them. She won't let *anyone* take Iris.

Including her mother.

Flora turns to the living room. She grabs two small items from the box her father sent: a Polaroid and her mom's wedding ring. Then she spots the small baby hat in the bottom of the box. The one she initially found in her mother's suitcase, then again here. She realizes now that her mom must have made it for Zephie.

Flora brings these things to the table. Goose bumps sprout on her arms and sting the rash that continues to spread. She can't see the blisters under her sweatshirt, but she can feel that they are fuller, can feel the risk of their popping with every brush of the shirt's fabric. One is growing just beneath the collar line, and more are sprouting on her upper back now, too.

Her mother is just under the surface. It's time.

"How do we start?" she asks.

49

Just as Belinda is about to read a prayer from her journal, the front door opens. A cold blast of air shoots through the room.

"The car won't start," Connor grumbles. Iris still crying.

she won't let you leave with the baby

Flora pops up from the table. "See? This is happening, Connor. This is real."

"What's real?" His eyes slant in the way that has become so familiar to her. The look of doubt and condescension.

"The car won't start," Flora says, "because *she* won't let you leave. You should be here for this. Iris should be here for this."

Connor's head falls backward in an exaggerated gesture. "The car won't start, Flora, because something is wrong with the engine or the battery. It's not because the spirit of your dead mother is willing me to stay."

He looks to the others, who say nothing in response. "Really?" he asks them. "You all believe that? You all believe that some ghost is holding me here? That some ghost is responsible for a bad alternator?"

"We do not know what we do not know," Belinda says, and Connor immediately rolls his eyes.

"Okay," he says, "sure. Can't argue with that." He pulls out his phone. "I'm calling a cab."

Iris cries in his arms.

"She needs to eat," Flora says. "I can feed her."

Because even though the blisters are burning and her eye is blurry and swollen and she is running out of time, a thought has come to her suddenly. This might be the last time she sees her daughter. What if the séance doesn't work? What if she can't rid her body of her mother? If that's the case, it's all over for her. And so she wants one more moment with her baby.

"Fine," Connor says. "But stay here where I can see you both."

Iris fits just so in Flora's arms. She was custom built for this embrace. Flora smells the top of her head, filling her nostrils with the newborn scent. She begins to prep Iris's bottle when she hears her father's voice from his designated spot at the coffee table.

"You should stay, Connor," he says. Connor looks up at him, about to protest, when he sees Michael staring intently into the flame of the black candle on the low table. "Don't make the mistake I made. Don't walk away." He looks up at Connor, his eyes determined but also kind and understanding. "You see it. I know you see it. Your wife slipping away little by little. Every day there is less and less of her left. And you don't know why. It scares you, so you push her away. You push it all away because you don't have the answers. And you don't know what that means about who *you* are if this is something you can't solve." He looks at his own hands, inspecting the lines and wrinkles as if searching for some hidden message. "But if you walk out that door...*then* you will know who you really are. And you will struggle to live with that man for the rest of your life." He looks up again. "Trust me. I struggle every day."

The air is thick. A single tear paints Flora's cheek. Her father's pain is palpable. She instinctively holds Iris tighter.

Flora wonders, not for the first time, if her family would be better off without her. She could leave right now, and all their problems would be solved. She imagines kissing her daughter goodbye, then escaping her body, floating above it, looking down at her house from the frigid sky, higher and higher until the roof of her home is just a speck, until her problems and shortcomings and failures are too small to be seen.

Too small to have ever existed at all.

Flora feels Iris's chest rise and fall as her tiny lungs fill with air. Flora's own breath adjusts in response, calming as it matches Iris's rhythm. And she resolves to keep going. Because as long as this tiny human exists in the world, Flora knows it's a place worth fighting for.

She reaches for the bottle she prepped, now warm and ready. But when she brings it closer, her nose crinkles. It stinks of fermentation.

"Oh God," Flora says. "The formula must have gone bad."

Connor looks over and latches on to the distraction. "I'll open a new can," he says. Flora thinks maybe her father's words have resonated with her husband. Connor is rarely speechless.

When he has finished preparing a new bottle, he unscrews the top and sniffs to confirm that it's good. "Smells okay," he says.

He hands the bottle to Flora. And as he does, the very second Flora's fingers touch the outside of the bottle, the milk curdles. Chunks float around like a soupy cottage cheese. The color even shifts from a translucent white to a stained yellow. When she screws off the nipple again, a strong whiff of sour urine punches her nose.

oh my God I can't feed my baby I can't feed my own baby

"What the hell..." Connor stares.

Flora looks at him, scared. "We're out of time," she says.

He pries his eyes from the curdled milk to look at his wife. And finally, he says, "All right. Tell me what to do."

50

After Connor situates Iris in the crib upstairs, the group settles around the coffee table in the living room, everyone close enough that their fingers touch. Each of them holds a mirror. Belinda brought her own, and the others found some around the house.

"It's called 'scrying,'" Belinda explains to the group. "If we manage to make contact, it will be through the reflection. And that is how it must remain. In the mirror only."

"What do you mean?" Michael asks.

When Flora looks over to her father, who sits to her left, black spots dance over his face. She cannot blink them away; the vision in her right eye is almost completely gone.

"If someone appears in your mirror," Belinda replies, "you should only look at them through the glass. Don't turn around."

"Why?" Connor asks. "What happens if we turn around?"

Belinda frowns. "I'm not sure, honestly."

"Jesus," Connor says, "are you sure you know what you're doing?"

Flora stares at the large black candle in the center of the table, mesmerized by its flame. On one side of the candle is Zephie's baby hat. On the other lies her mother's wedding ring atop the Polaroid. In the picture, Jodi smiles with her feet in the ocean and arms outstretched toward the sun.

"Connor," Flora says, "please. Let's just do what Belinda tells us."

The soft candlelight reflects off her husband's face and carves deep dark spots under his eyes. Or maybe he is just that tired. Maybe Flora has done that to him.

He holds up his hands in surrender.

"So keep your focus on the mirror," Belinda continues. "That's where Jodi will reveal herself." Belinda then presses her hand against her jeans pocket and nods a confirmation to Flora.

the birth tusk

Flora retrieved it from the back of her drawer and gave it to Belinda. They don't want it on display for Jodi, as it might deter her from showing up, but they do need it close. Within reach. And Flora doesn't trust herself with it. What if she doesn't have the strength to use it when the time comes?

Belinda places her mirror in her lap and holds her journal. She flips to a page toward the middle and begins reading a prayer.

"To our Spirit Guides," she begins, "our Guardian Angels, our Ancestors. We approach you humbly in this moment. We seek your guidance. We seek to connect..."

As Belinda talks, Flora watches the flame of the candle. It flickers normally, the very tip turning black and emitting a thin, wispy smoke that detaches from the flame and immediately dissipates.

Flora holds up her own mirror, the nondescript black one she keeps in the bathroom for when she needs to tweeze her eyebrows. She barely recognizes the woman who returns her gaze. New wrinkles have sprouted beside her eyes, new cracks in her lips. She looks years older. Even the color of her eyes has dimmed.

"Jodi?" Belinda asks, her voice returning to a more conversational tone after the conclusion of the opening prayer. "Jodi, if you're here with us, can you please give us a sign?"

Flora's gaze travels around the circle. With her good eye, she sees her father staring intently into his mirror. Connor watches Belinda carefully, like a lion ready to pounce. Belinda holds her mirror between her hands and speaks into it, as if chatting with her own reflection.

"Jodi?" she asks again. "We would love to hear from you. We've brought you some things. Did you see that Flora found Zephie's hat?"

Suddenly, Flora's rash is on fire. "Ah!" she cries out. The rash eats its way through her skin, expanding yet another inch down her back.

Connor reaches for her, but she doesn't want to break the circle. "I'm fine," she manages to eke out, though the pain shoots down her spine all the way to her ankles.

"Is that you, Jodi?" Belinda asks. "Can you hear us?"

Another blaze of pain, this time in an upward motion, running between Flora's shoulders and wrapping around her neck like thin fingers. She can't help it; she rips off her sweatshirt, and her father gasps in horror at what he sees. Bright red welts and swollen, oozing blisters. A red-hot imprint of a hand around her throat.

"My God, Flora, what is happening to you?" he asks.

"You're hurting her!" Connor shouts to Belinda.

Belinda looks to Flora to gauge the situation.

"It's okay," Flora says. She turns to her husband and assures him, "I'm okay. We can't stop now. We have to finish this."

But she doesn't know if she believes her own words. This might have been a mistake. She has a strong urge to stand, to break the circle and smash her mirror. But then she remembers the curdled milk, and her blood boils hotter than her rotting skin. She will not let this *thing* keep her from her daughter.

"Jodi, my friend," Belinda says, gentle but firm, "hurting Flora will not get you what you need. What is it that you want? Let us help you."

A draft travels through the room. Has a door opened somewhere? Ice cold slinks up Flora's spine and even to the roots of her teeth.

To her left, her father pulls his feet in close, making himself small in his chair. He looks at the ground around him, as if it's suddenly covered in lava. Flora cannot see what he sees, but she can tell he is frightened. When she comes back to her own mirror, she notices that her right eye now has a glassy white pupil.

"My legs!" Connor shouts. "My legs are gone!"

Connor is wrong. Flora can see his legs. But Jodi must be playing some mind trick on him, because he is convinced they are not there. His face is white with panic.

"Connor," Belinda says, "your legs are there, I assure you. Everyone, keep your eyes on your mirrors." There is a new desperation in Belinda's voice, like she is grasping for some sense of control.

"Oh my God!" Connor keeps shouting. "What the fuck happened to my legs?"

He grabs at his pants, pulling them up from the ankle to his upper thigh, seemingly unsatisfied with whatever he finds there. He looks around frantically, dropping the mirror to the floor, and grabs the black candle from the center of the circle. Without hesitation, he flips it over and guides the hot wax to drip onto his bare knee.

"Connor, don't—" Flora shouts.

"I don't feel it," he says, looking up at them with wide, child-like eyes. "I can't feel it. I can't feel it at all. Do you hear me?"

Frantic, he lowers the candle—Flora and Belinda both shouting for him to stop—and burns the wick straight into his skin, stamping out the flame. His flesh sizzles.

"I feel nothing," he says. "Nothing!" He laughs, then cries, hysterical, trying to stand from the chair but convinced he cannot move.

"What's happening?" Flora asks Belinda. "Is this normal?"

Belinda shakes her head, clearly out of her depth, eyes unblinking. "I—don't know—I've never—"

"It's rising," Michael says, still staring at the floor around him, preoccupied with his own hallucination. "I can't—" His hands come to his chest and throat. He lifts his chin high, as if trying to keep his nose above water. "I can't breathe."

"Belinda," Flora says, "what do we do?"

Belinda stares dumbly at Flora. "I don't know. Maybe we shouldn't have...Making contact with an evil spirit seems to be something else entirely..."

Beside her, Michael gasps for air. Across the table, Connor continues to panic, twisting and writhing in his chair.

Flora reaches into the center of the table and grabs the baby hat.

help me Zephie what do I do

Flora stares into her mirror, squeezing the hat between her fingers, chanting Zephie's name in her head like a prayer. The room is dark, the cold undeniable now. The stench of spoiled milk fills her nostrils.

But Flora will not be distracted. She leans in close to her mirror, her nose almost touching the glass, then pulls away, like she's looking at one of those Magic Eye illusions. And as she does, finally, mercifully, the shape of a girl takes form.

there you are

Zephie looks healthy. Her hair is in French-braided pigtails, and she wears a soft cotton romper. She lifts her hand to wave, and a slight smile spreads across her lips.

"Zephie," Flora says, "Zephie, we need your help. We need—"

But before she can say more, Jodi appears in the mirror, too, just behind Zephie. She is sickly thin and pale and barely resembles the mother Flora once knew. Her bony hands reach toward Zephie's throat, but Zephie does not sense her approaching.

"Zephie!" Flora warns. "Watch out, Mom's there, behind you, she's—"

"Flora, wait," Belinda says, reaching across the circle toward Flora.

But it's too late. Flora is already turning toward Zephie, desperate to stop her mother from hurting the little girl. "Don't touch her!"

"Don't turn around!" Belinda yells, but Flora has already done it and now stares into the space where Zephie should be. All she sees, though, is a growing, moving hole of darkness—a living shadow.

"It was a *trick*!" Belinda moans. "That wasn't Zephie!"

Flora hears it again, the deafening sound of metal gears clashing. Her body is pushed backward with force, landing flat on the couch, and immediately paralyzed. Everything else—Belinda's muttering, her father's gasping, Connor's panicked cries—is suddenly very far away.

The shadow moves closer, its edges undefined, its movements jerky and inhuman.

the Night Hag
she is here

The figure glides toward Flora. It does not walk, does not move around furniture. It follows a straight trajectory to Flora, and then the familiar weight on her torso, the familiar crushing of her organs. More intense than ever before. One of her ribs *SNAPPPPS*.

The figure leans in, bringing its face an inch from Flora's, and Flora finally sees: the Night Hag is her mother. Or a *version* of her mother. Like a Victorian painting that only resembles the likeness.

This is not surprising. In fact, Flora feels as though she has always known this. She has been here many times before. And now she understands why. Maybe this is what dying is like; maybe, on the way out, the world, for the briefest of blips, makes sense.

Flora knows now that the very first time she was here— the first time she was ever suffocated under the weight of her mother—she was a six-week-old baby. She was wrapped tight in her swaddle, unable to move, when her mother approached the crib with a blanket. And when her mother thought the deed was done, Flora heard the rush of running water from the nearby bathroom. She sensed the empty space beside her where Zephie had been. Flora's tiny little body knew that her sister was in trouble. And there was nothing she could do.

Now, all these years later, the Night Hag smiles grimly at Flora. Her teeth are impossibly crooked, and each sports a tiny hole in the center, as if they are rotting from the inside out. Her eyes are hollow, and she wears a mask like the ones Flora saw in that library book. It is white with sunken pockets and large cutouts around the eyes and mouth. The space where her nose should be is flat, like nothing is there. Below that is the broomstick mustache. Flora feels it scrape against her own chin, scratchy and unforgiving.

Her mother the Night Hag opens her mouth wider, as if to speak, but the mouth keeps opening, wide, wide, wide, the jaw unhinging, and Flora stares into the dark, empty throat, unable to move. Spindly, dirty fingers find their way toward Flora's mouth, gumming around inside, and Flora is reminded of doing this very thing to Iris when she saw the beetles. Flora tries to bite down, but she cannot. The fingers taste like sour sweat and rubbing alcohol. Flora's mouth spreads wider and wider as the fingers pull her lips apart, stretching them beyond repair. They finally rip at the corners, and she tastes blood on her tongue. She tries to scream, but when she can't, her demented mother screams instead—as if Flora is speaking through her—and when her mother leans her head back, howling to the sky, it is not really a scream that comes out but, rather, the loud wail of a baby.

That cry is Zephie's cry. Flora is six weeks old again, tight in her swaddle, staring at the world from the bottom of a crib. She hears her sister, *feels* her pain and fear. Flora's own baby muscles tighten in response.

I remember everything

Adult Flora lies immobilized, just as she did the morning of Zephie's death, and watches as her mother's body evaporates from the feet up, as if it were only ever made of mist. And then, with only her head and arms left, her dirty fingers pull and pull until she fits all of what remains of her inside Flora's mouth. She crawls down Flora's throat, igniting a jolt through her spine, firing up the blisters and rash on her back.

And once again, Flora can move her limbs—the marionette to her mother's ghost.

51

Flora no longer thinks of herself as Flora. Nor does she think of herself as Jodi. She is simply: the Mother.

The Mother's first order of business is to gather supplies. She swings her legs off the couch and stands.

"Flora?" It's Connor's voice. He sits in his chair, his legs dead-weights beneath him. "Flora, what just happened?" His eyes are wide with horror.

The Mother's feet move stiffly across the floor, *thump thump thump,* slowly and deliberately toward the garage. Her movements are stilted, like a foal learning to walk with bricks for feet. Behind her, Michael lies unconscious in his chair. Belinda is gone.

A small, sunken voice bubbles up from within the Mother.

please stop you have to stop

But the Mother is not bothered by it. This body is merely a means to an end. She owes it nothing.

When she reaches the garage door, she pushes it open and steps onto the landing of the stairs. Suddenly, she is propelled forward, pushed from behind, and she tumbles down the stairs, landing with a *THUD* on the cement floor below. The Mother has a singular focus and is unfazed by sensation, but even while drowning under the surface of consciousness, Flora feels the *crack splat splice* of her right leg. Pain shoots up to her hip, through her spine, electrifying.

The Mother uses her hands to twist her torso, and Flora feels a broken rib poke around her insides, its jagged edge like a knife on her lungs. Belinda stands in the doorway, a dazed look in her eyes, her hands still outstretched from the push that sent the Mother reeling.

run Belinda run get out of here

But Belinda's focus is on the Mother's leg, where something thick and round pokes out from beneath the skin of her calf. It looks like one of those stuffed bones they make as treats for dogs.

"Flora, I'm sorry," Belinda says, "I didn't mean—"

Flora's consciousness fights for power. She struggles, pushing against the Mother like a face pressing into a latex wall. She wants to tell Belinda that this is not her, that Belinda is not safe here, that the Mother does not feel pain, she will retaliate—

THWACK

—Flora watches as her own hands swing a shovel into the side of Belinda's head. The woman crumples to the floor, a single drop of blood running down her temple.

The Mother stands above the fallen woman, effortlessly bearing weight on her newly broken leg. A moment later, Flora wakes up to this pain and wishes she were dead, wishes the Mother would end this thing.

She scans the garage with her one good eye. She limps over to the tall shelf unit. With each heavy step, *thump thump thump,* the bones in the broken leg shift like unset jelly in a mold of skin. The Mother runs her fingers over the boxes on the shelf until she finds a coil of thick rope. She grips it tightly and pulls it from its spot.

The Mother turns back toward the main house. She steps over Belinda's unconscious body on the way but lands *crack* on two of Belinda's fingers. The bones crunch beneath her weight like salt beneath a tire. The Mother does not stop.

Flora wills her hands to reach for Belinda's pocket as she passes,

the birth tusk if I could just get the birth tusk

but she is no longer in control of her limbs. The signals her brain sends are stamped out before they arrive.

The Mother walks slowly back through the living room. Flora tries to turn her head, tries to look toward Connor or Michael, tries to send them some kind of signal. She can just barely hear Connor's voice, something about *what did you do what did you do*. But the Mother has a singular focus, and Flora is unable to deter her. When she reaches the bottom of the stairs, she looks up.

no God no not the stairs don't go upstairs

The Mother hooks the thick coil of rope loosely around her neck to free up her hands. With her right hand on the railing, she starts her journey up.

ayyyyyeeeeeeeeeee

The first step on her bad leg sends her hip completely out of alignment. A loud *pop* accompanies the movement.

ooooommmmmmppphhhhhh

The third step, again on her bad leg, jostles the hip joint back into place before dislocating it again with the weight shift.

The steps are slow and deliberate, the Mother oblivious to the pain. Each step tears and splinters and cracks the leg a little more. And each one also brings her closer to Iris, the only thing that keeps Flora alert enough to withstand the torture.

Finally upstairs, she labors down the hallway

not the nursery stay away from the nursery

and into the bathroom. Her bad leg gives out completely, hanging loosely from the hip joint. The Mother leans against the wall, hopping on her left foot and dragging the right behind her, using the wall as both a guide and a crutch.

In the bathroom, the Mother removes the rope from around her neck and places it on the countertop. She stands square in front of the mirror and stares at her reflection. The face is blurry, as if the mirror is foggy. Flora witnesses her right hand rise toward her face and cover her bad eye—and that's when the reflection comes into focus.

Flora's good eye is her own, but her nose and cheeks are Jodi's, smaller and birdlike. Her lips are torn at the corners, like she licked a knife and sliced both sides, and drool drips down her chin.

Flora feels her mouth curl upward in a smile, the cracked parts igniting as the lips stretch wide. But in the mirror, her expression does not change. Her mouth does not move.

Until suddenly, the reflection morphs rapidly—the image flickering like a TV on the fritz—and lands on a new face: Zephie. She's there, frantic, as if she has been trying to get through, and shouts, "Get out!"

The two words fly out of the mirror and smack the Mother in the face. The house rocks like an earthquake.

Flora's back ignites. The rash lights up and glows like a starter log on a rekindled fire. Zephie's appearance has angered the Mother. She turns quickly away from the mirror, away from Zephie, and toward the bathtub. Flora watches as her own hands reach for the spigot and turn on the water. She locks the drain. The bath begins to fill.

no no no no

There's a knock on the door. "Flora?" It's her father.

For a moment, the Mother has stepped into a memory. Michael's voice tugs at something primal within her, traveling her consciousness through space and time to another bathroom, another bathtub, another infant.

Flora wants to scream for him to run, grab Iris and get away from here, get away from *her*. But instead, she watches as her hands open the door to reveal his kind face.

"Flora," he says, "what are you doing?" Then he spots the bone protruding from her skin. "Jesus, your leg." The sight of it straightens his spine, a shock to his nervous system.

Her mouth curves into another smile, and she watches helplessly as her right arm reaches out to him. His expression is wary, and she's hopeful that maybe he realizes this isn't really her, but then her other hand is reaching up, her fingers aligning so that she can twist his neck with a quick snap—

get the fuck out of here Dad grab Iris and get the fuck out

—and thankfully her dad ducks at just the right moment, looking at her with horror. He knows now, knows this isn't his daughter.

"What the hell?" he says, backing out of the room, not taking his eyes off the Mother, who stalks him slowly with her limp, dead leg.

He makes a break for it, running into the nursery and toward the crib. Flora hears that the bathtub is almost full now and is about to start flooding over.

The Mother crosses the hallway to the nursery. Her blood and bodily fluids have oozed from her leg, leaving a slimy trail behind her like a giant snail.

"Flora," her father's voice calls from the nursery. The Mother finally arrives in the doorway. "Flora, if you can hear me in there, this isn't you," her dad says. "Stop this. You can stop this now and we can fix it. We can fix everything." He is crying.

The Mother cringes in disgust at his tears.

you're right Dad it's not me run from here leave

Michael holds Iris, who complains about being pulled from slumber. The crying tugs at Flora, but not just in the typical way. She can feel it tugging at the Mother, too. Literally *pulling* her body toward the baby like a homing device. Flora senses the Mother's deep desire to take her little girl. It is the only thing driving her, like a rat in a cage pressing a button for more food.

Iris still wears her swaddle, wrapped up tightly into Michael's chest. He steps away, walking backward, attempting to bargain with the Mother.

"Flora," he says, "we love you. Iris loves you. Whatever you're thinking of doing, you will regret it. Trust me, please, oh God, please."

Flora wishes he would kick her in the leg or stab her in the neck. But she knows that her father won't hurt her. That's how he ended up in this position, cornered in the nursery, blocked by the crib and rocking chair and Flora's lumbering body. A strength pulses through her veins that frightens her. An inhuman strength.

kill me Dad you have to kill me

The Mother is close to him now, close enough that Flora can smell his oaky aftershave. His cheeks are wet; his hands hold her tiny baby with gentle love. Flora's heart breaks.

But then Michael swiftly turns toward the open window behind him, climbs onto the sill, and holds Iris closer to his chest. A moment later, he jumps and disappears from view.

oh God Dad oh God please be okay please let Iris be okay

Flora's back flares in angry pain as the Mother realizes her plan has been thwarted. She exits the nursery, out through the now-flooding hallway, the slippery wet slowing down her crooked gait. Frustrated by her own slow pace, the Mother drops to all fours, moving more quickly now, dragging her dead leg and using her arm strength to pull her more efficiently through space. She crawls like an injured spider down the stairs and out the front door.

Outside the house, only a faint moonlight illuminates the world. Clouds cover the stars. The Mother stalks the bushes under Iris's window, but she doesn't find Michael there. Instead, she sees a trail of blood.

No. That's not right. She can't see it.

She can *smell* it.

With her nose close to the ground, she follows the trail like a hungry wolf, smelling not only the faint drops of blood but also Iris's soft newborn scent. The one Flora used to drink in while Iris was sleeping on her chest. The Mother licks her cracked, split lips and army-crawls around the side of the house. Thorny bushes poke through her sweatpants and scratch her arms.

The moon is brighter behind the house, and Flora can see the back patio clearly. Connor is there, his face half-illuminated by a fire he has lit in the chiminea. He sits on the ground and moves himself around with his arms, clearly still under the impression that he cannot use his legs. From the shadows behind him appears her father, Iris tight in his arms. The Mother crawls up the stairs of the back deck and stands, regaining her height, but now seeming to grow many inches beyond Flora's actual stature. For the first time in her life, Flora looks from above down to the men below.

And then a voice a few feet behind her and to her left: "Jodi, we demand you *go*!"

The Mother whips around to find Belinda, streaks of dried blood painting one side of her face. And held in front of her, wielded like a weapon—the birth tusk.

Flora's back flares again, and the Mother lets out an inexplicable noise. Something like a freight train in the form of a scream. Again, the house rocks, vibrating from the power of the Mother's anger, but this time it is so forceful that Belinda loses her footing. The birth tusk falls, skidding toward the Mother, landing at her feet. The Mother hisses and recoils from the tusk.

Flora knows this is her chance.

touch it grab it get the birth tusk you can do it

She wills herself to bend down and uses every ounce of energy she has within her to compel her left hand, which is closer to the tusk, to reach out. Her fingers fight against her, like she's pushing through mud, swimming upstream. The Mother resists Flora's efforts, but Connor, understanding what's happening, whistles loudly. The noise distracts the Mother just long enough that Flora is able to grab the birth tusk.

Her hand sizzles like she's touching a hot griddle. Like it did when she was a toddler, curious about the stove. She reacts to the burn instinctively, throwing the tusk away and high into the air behind her. Her hand is now imprinted with the designs from the hippo's tooth: a lion's head and a circle with sprouting long legs mark her palm.

Connor sees the flying tusk and shouts, "Michael, watch out!"

But a moment later, the Mother looks up to find that the birth tusk is traveling back toward her, like a boomerang. It flies through the air efficiently, turning end over end, right toward the Mother's chest. Flora tries to keep her feet planted where they are, willing the tooth to stab her in the heart, but the Mother's downward force is too strong. She falls to all fours again, dodging the flying tusk.

"Belinda!" her father cries out, but it's too late.

The tusk sticks *thwack* into the soft flesh between Belinda's shoulder and chest bone. She looks down, surprised and not comprehending.

Within seconds, the Mother is crawling to Belinda in fast motion. Once there, she uses Belinda's body to pull herself to standing, so that their faces are close. Silence fills the space between them. The only noise is the crackling of the now-roaring fire.

The Mother's spindly fingers wrap themselves around the birth tusk and unceremoniously pull it out. Belinda cries in pain as a steady stream of blood pours from that spot. The Mother holds the tusk even though it burns her skin, and Flora doesn't know why she's not recoiling from the hippo's tooth as she did before. But a moment later, she understands.

The tusk rises and the sharp end finds its way to Belinda's neck. Flora tries to resist as she watches her own hand prepare to slit the woman's throat. It's only a centimeter away now. The Mother wants to do this quickly, because she feels the burning tusk—the only pain she recognizes. But Flora fights her, and the internal struggle is so strong that it puts her body at a momentary standstill. It's just enough time for Belinda to duck out of the way and heave herself toward the others by the back door.

Flora grips the tusk harder, concentrating on nothing else. The Mother, thwarted again and angry, tries to throw the tusk away. But this time, Flora refuses to loosen her fingers. A migraine builds behind her bad eye, a physical manifestation of the inner battle between these women. Flora drops to her knees and drags herself toward the chiminea. The Mother fights her, resisting with every move, but finally, Flora has the advantage. She thinks of her daughter's smile and smell and tiny fingers and chubby cheeks and dark hair and pouty lips. She thinks of her cooing and gurgling and even her crying. She thinks of the rise and fall of her chest, the way she holds tightly onto Flora's index finger when she drinks from a bottle, the way her arms splay above her head when they escape from the swaddle. These images are powerful motivations. More powerful, even, than the Mother's superhuman strength.

Flora drags her body toward the fire, the Mother protesting in her freight-train discord, the deck and house and earth shaking. Flora sees the sound waves of her screams: blurry pulses of air emanate from her body. Like she is a stone in water, her fury rippling through the atmosphere. Flora works against herself. The hardest force she has ever fought is right here, within her own body.

Finally, she makes it to the chiminea. She hears Belinda and her father shouting for her to stop, shouting that there must be another way. But Connor does not protest. There's a reason he started the fire. He understood there was no other way. Just like Zephie understood when she tried to burn down the house.

Flora grabs the hot opening of the chiminea and lifts her broken, battered body onto her knees. The Mother understands now what Flora is trying to do, and she flares her back in protest, but Flora ignores this pain. She knows it is nothing compared to what is coming. With one final push of the only strength she has left, fueled by the images of her baby's perfect lips and hands and smile and sweet eyes and soft belly, Flora heaves the birth tusk into the fire.

The ivory, unable to catch a flame, sits in the center of the angry orange and red, seemingly untouched. And for a moment, nothing happens.

But then—*WHOOSH!*—the flame ignites like lighter fluid, shooting sparks into the sky. Flora's eyes look up, up, up, as the fire gets taller and taller, dwarfing the Mother and the whole group and soon even the house. High above, a form takes shape in the brilliant, blinding light of the flames. Its edges are soft, its lines alive and dancing. But Flora recognizes it at once: the giant hippo head of Taweret.

The fat head curves and gives way to the huge nose, the widening nostrils. Its eyes are small beads trained on the Mother. It sucks air into its huge mouth, like it did in Flora's bedroom, but this time it shoots fire from its nostrils like a braying dragon.

First Flora's feet catch fire, like when Jodi tried to destroy the tusk. Nothing else around her burns, even though she stands on a wooden deck; this fire is meant only for the Mother.

The flames quickly climb up her body, licking her calves, wrapping themselves around her knees and her thighs. As the fire reaches her torso, she smells melting plastic and charcoal and rubber and dirt. Her nostrils are moist with the stench of her own burning flesh.

Flora allows herself to fully sink in now, fully drown within the Mother's consciousness. She disappears from her body as it is completely overtaken by flames.

Beside her, the others scream.

52

Flora slips in and out of consciousness.

She feels bright lights.

Hands on her body.

They are unwrapping her limbs, peeling her skin like tinfoil from a burrito.

53

She is in a hospital room. Every inch of her body is held together with gauze.

Someone is here. A nurse, maybe. Flora senses a woman's presence flitting from one side of the bed to the other. She hears a pen glide on paper and tap a clipboard. The sound is comforting.

The surface beneath her moves. She hears the humming of the motorized bed and feels her body shift in response.

The moment Flora smells the bleach, she slips away again.

54

Connor is here. He touches her hand—or, rather, the spot on the cast that hides her hand. She hears him sniffle and knows he is crying. He must be alone.

"I don't know if you can hear me," he says, "but you're gonna get through this, Flo. You have to. I need you. Iris needs you."

The room feels different with him in it. Full.

55

Flora's father talks to a doctor. Their voices are muted whispers, like they are afraid Flora might hear them.

She imagines her own funeral, imagines her father standing over a deep grave with her coffin at the bottom. He bends over the earth in grief, a man who outlived both of his daughters.

A question haunts her.

where is Zephie buried

56

Everyone is here now. Connor, her father, Esther. Even Iris. Flora cannot see her, but her bones know: they ache and pulse with longing for the tiny baby.

Something is about to happen. There is a sense of ceremony in the room. The mechanical bed buzzes again, and machines beep and whir around her. She feels as if she is at the end of a very long tunnel.

The doctor speaks. Flora hears every few words. *Medically induced coma...respiratory insult...intubation...excision...grafting...*

Flora remembers her childhood, sneaking into her parents' room to watch television. She would situate herself on the pink carpet of their floor and turn the volume down low. One time, her mother found her. Flora thought she'd be mad, but her mom smiled. Then she settled in next to Flora and unwrapped a handful of caramel candies for them to share.

Flora is there, sitting in that room, leaning against her mother's purple bathrobe that smells of sunflowers, feeling the soft carpet on her unburnt skin, when the doctor puts her under.

57

Flora walks in colorful, vibrant woods.

It's warm. The sun streaks through the trees like a painting. In fact, the entire world looks like a work of art. As if she could reach out her hands and touch the paint with her fingertips, mixing its colors and altering the landscape with a simple gesture.

Her body is healthy, her skin radiant. She can see from both eyes and walk with both legs. Her hand is not branded with images from the birth tusk.

Flora comes to a clearing in the trees. The ground is blanketed in grass instead of branching roots, and the open sky above her goes on forever and forever and forever.

"You're here!"

It's Zephie. She wears a dress matching Flora's, a flowing baby-blue cotton piece. Her hair is tied back, and the gold flecks in her eyes are more pronounced here in this half-real world.

"I'm so glad you're here," Zephie says, jumping up and greeting Flora with unbridled enthusiasm. She pulls Flora by the hand toward a fallen log. And that's when Flora realizes why this landscape feels like a painting: it is the creation of a child. She can tell by the too-bright colors, the butterflies that approach rather than fly away, the trees that bend in response to her movements. It's like she has stepped into the illustration of a children's book.

Together, Flora and Zephie forage for candy mushrooms and stuff themselves full of jelly beans. Their bellies never hurt. They climb trees and swing from long vines and never scrape their knees or bump their heads. They giggle and sing and roll down grassy hills and do somersaults under the sun that never feels too hot.

The two of them find a shady spot under the biggest, most majestic tree Flora has ever seen. Each of its leaves is bigger than Flora's head, and they shine with vibrant oranges and reds and yellows even though it's not autumn. Flora imagines this place doesn't have seasons, but rather boasts the best part of each season all the time.

Zephie snuggles in close to Flora. "We'll be safe here," she says.

Flora considers what that would mean. Staying with Zephie in this picture-perfect world, living in a body that works and isn't consumed by pain.

"Zephie," Flora says, feeling the cartoon-soft grass beneath her legs, "I can't stay here."

"What do you mean? Why not?" She looks at Flora with sad, round eyes.

"I have to at least try to go back."

Zephie pulls away. "No! I made this place for us! A place where *she* can't get us!"

Flora pauses, then gently strokes Zephie's hair. "We don't have to worry about that anymore," Flora says. "That version of her is gone."

But Zephie bites her lip and shakes her head. She is still frightened. Flora wonders, then, if Zephie understands who she really is.

Flora takes a breath. "Did you know your real name is Zephyr?"

Zephie frowns and tilts her head to the left. "What do you mean *real* name?"

"You always hated it when I called you imaginary, right? You always felt like you were real, didn't you?" Flora asks, and Zephie nods. "Well, that's because you *were* real. You were a little girl. You were my twin sister. And your name was Zephyr, or 'Zephie' for short."

Flora watches as Zephie takes this in. She pulls the girl into her lap and rubs her back. After a moment, Zephie asks, "So what happened to me?"

"You were hurt," Flora admits. "Very badly. Your body stopped working after only six weeks."

"Who hurt me?" Zephie's eyes lock with Flora's. "Was it *her*?"

"Yes, it was our mother." Flora doesn't know how to articulate such complicated circumstances to a child. "But it also... wasn't her."

Zephie contorts her face as she tries to puzzle together Flora's words.

"Her brain tricked her," Flora explains. "It knew she would never hurt us, never in a million years. And so it made her think she was doing something good. It made her think she was saving us."

"Why would her brain do that?" Zephie asks.

Flora shakes her head slowly, pondering. "You remember the Night Hag?"

Zephie nods, fear lacing the rims of her eyes.

"It haunted me my whole life," Flora says. "And in the end, it looked like Mom, but...I think that's just because it knew that's what would scare me the most." She fiddles Zephie's hair between her fingers. "It wasn't really Mom. It was...something *else*. And it was there that morning, the morning she hurt us...so maybe— well, maybe the Night Hag haunted her, too. Maybe it made her do those terrible things."

Zephie considers this. "What happened when the Night Hag left?"

"I'm not sure she ever did," Flora says. "Mom spent her whole life punishing herself. She never let herself get close to me." Flora realizes that she might not forgive her mother, not yet, but she is at least beginning to understand her. "She was too afraid that if she got close to me, she would hurt me again." Flora tastes the salt of her own tears. "She deprived herself of a lifetime of love in order to keep me safe. At least, that's what she thought she needed to do."

"But she was wrong?" Zephie asks.

Flora thinks about this. "I don't know," she admits. "But I do know that I would have been happier with a mom who loved me fearlessly. And showed it."

They listen to nearby birds chirp a singsong melody nearby.

"So that's why I have to go back," Flora finally says. "I have to be there for my daughter. In a way that Jodi couldn't be there for me. For us."

"And where do I go?" Zephie asks, and Flora's heart breaks.

"You have to leave me," she answers. "You never belonged to me. I've kept you trapped without even knowing it."

"But I don't want to leave you," Zephie says, fat tears rolling down her cheeks.

"I know," Flora says. "And I'll miss you, too."

They hold each other for a long time. It feels familiar, and Flora remembers their time together in the womb, because she can remember such things in this place. The weightless floating of their two bodies, perfectly intertwined, speaking through pulses and hiccups and kicks. Their own shared, sacred space.

Zephie sniffles. "If I leave you, I'll be alone. And I don't want to be alone," she says.

Flora looks at her, and her heart squeezes as she gets an idea.

"You don't have to be," she says.

Zephie looks at her, curious.

"You can go find Mom. Our *real* mom. The *real* Jodi." Flora holds Zephie's gaze intently. "And I promise you—she will keep you safe."

"But how do you know?" Zephie asks.

"Because," Flora says, a deep peace in her bones, "she has waited a lifetime for that."

Epilogue

Today is Iris's third birthday.

Flora has organized a party for her, her first "real" birthday party, and Iris is thrilled. For weeks, she has been telling everyone she meets, "My birthday is coming off!"

And Flora laughs each time. "It's coming *up*," she says, eyes crinkling with joy.

The guests are set to arrive in an hour. It's nothing fancy; Flora has ordered snacks and juice boxes in bulk, and she spent all of yesterday baking cupcakes with Esther. Connor found a piñata at the party store and now attempts to hang it from a tree in the backyard with Flora's father. Flora stands at the back patio door, watching as Connor balances on the ladder. She can't help but laugh at their struggle. How many capable men does it take to hang a rainbow-colored unicorn?

"Ready for the horns!" Esther calls from the kitchen.

The two women have been frosting the cupcakes, which are also unicorn themed. Iris really has a thing for unicorns.

Flora heads back toward the kitchen, wincing slightly at the stiffness in her right leg. For the most part, she has gotten accustomed to the prosthetic, but she sometimes feels residual pain when the weather shifts or the temperature drops.

"These look amazing," she says to Esther, dipping a finger into the bowl of pink frosting. She tastes it just as Iris comes barreling in from upstairs.

"I can't *wait* anymore!" she says. "I wanna *see!*"

Flora knew this would happen. They spent the morning opening family presents, and afterward they challenged Iris to play with her new toys upstairs while they prepped for the party. But she's three years old. Flora looks to the clock and realizes Iris lasted almost an hour. Impressive, actually.

"Come on in," Flora says, smiling and bending down to pick up her daughter. "Wanna taste?" She points to the chocolate cupcakes.

Iris nods enthusiastically, so Flora sets her up at the table with her treat.

Outside, Connor and Michael have finally secured the piñata to a low branch. Connor folds up the ladder and, when he sees Flora watching them through the kitchen window, gives her a big thumbs-up. *We did it!* Flora waves and smiles.

She watches her husband, pausing time as she often does these days to drink in the moments. His skin is tanned, as he spent most of the summer at the swimming pool with Iris. His hair is starting to thin and, though he denies it, gray. Flora loves the salt-and-pepper look, especially in the facial hair he has let grow the last month. She often runs her fingers through it, scratching the stubble playfully, and he pants in return like a happy dog.

Iris finishes her cupcake and smiles, her face smeared with pink frosting. "All done!" she sings. "Again!"

Flora laughs. "You can have another one at the party, okay?"

And though Iris frowns in response, she nods and climbs out of her chair.

"Okay!" she says, then runs out the back door and down the patio steps into Connor's arms. He picks her up and throws her in the air. Iris's laughter bubbles.

Flora's mother is still around, but in the ways one would expect to be haunted by a loved one. She feels her in the simplest of moments: when brushing Iris's teeth and singing Jodi's favorite song; when cooking scrambled eggs with cream cheese like Jodi always loved; when she can't get a stain out of Iris's favorite dress and wishes she could ask her mother how to treat it.

Jodi has also visited Flora in her dreams. Zephie is there, too. Flora doesn't often remember the details of what happened, but she always remembers the feelings. The peace. The love.

On the most recent anniversary of Zephie's death, Flora and her father buried the birth tusk together. Flora found a clearing in the woods of her backyard that was similar to the setting Zephie had created for the two of them. She even found a mossy fallen log, under which she dug a small hole in the soft dirt for the tusk.

"Are you sure?" her father asked before leaving the tusk behind.

Flora nodded. "We don't need it anymore."

As the group sings "Happy Birthday," Flora is hit with a wave of nausea. She instinctively brings her hand to her lower belly, where a new life is growing. They haven't told many people yet since it's still early. She's only eleven weeks. But the spirit in this one is strong: her nausea hasn't let up the last few days, and she swears she can already see a tiny bump.

She has new symptoms this time around. Patches of scaly eczema have appeared between her fingers and are just starting to itch. She also grew a sweet tooth in the last week. But every pregnancy is different; discrepancies are normal.

Iris blows out her candles, and the group claps in celebration. She smiles wide, showing off her front right tooth, which sticks out at a crooked angle thanks to her thumb-sucking habit. Her beautiful hair hangs in waves down below her breastbone because Flora hasn't had the heart to cut it even once since Iris was born.

Flora looks around at the group of people who have shown up for her daughter. She is so grateful for this tribe that has grown over the years. Friends, neighbors—even Wanda is here, whose company Flora has come to enjoy in small doses.

she did save my life after all

A few of Flora's clients are here, too. She has become one of the most sought-after postpartum doulas in the area, working closely with new moms. And she loves it. She has a purpose. She has a village. Turns out it really does exist, after all.

Flora helps Iris unwrap a cupcake and then grabs one for herself. As she takes a bite, she laughs, the intensity of the sugar in the frosting tickling her teeth. Iris laughs, too, and then runs to join her friends. Flora watches them blow bubbles with the long wands she purchased for the party.

"You need anything?" It's Belinda, who has become a strong fixture in their lives and a dear friend to Flora.

"I might sit down for a few," Flora admits. "Feeling a bit tired."

Belinda ensures that Flora is comfortable, then goes to help Connor and the others with the piñata.

Flora watches the festivities as she unwraps a second cupcake, licking stray icing from her fingertips. She takes a huge bite, the strawberry and chocolate and vanilla flavors igniting her taste buds.

And this time, when the frosting squeezes between her teeth, the shock of the sugar makes her right eye twitch.

Acknowledgments

If raising a child in this world takes a village, then so, too, does bringing a novel to readers. In Flora's words, it'd be "fucking impossible to do alone."

First, I must thank my agent, Richard Abate, who loved this story even when it was still a messy, confused draft. Thank you for being my brain twin, forever producing partner, and friend. And thank you to Katie Newman, my manager, for building our team and for believing in me as a writer from my earliest days. (And also for the best, most thoughtful gifts.)

Thank you to Helen O'Hare, my incredible editor. We have a better meet-cute than mine and my husband's, and I wouldn't have it any other way. Our working relationship was fated from the beginning. Special shout-out to Judy Clain for reading the manuscript and immediately sending it to Helen. I am forever grateful.

Thank you to Josh Kendall for your insight and for believing in this novel. Thank you to the marketing guru Anna Brill who so kindly and gently forced me back onto social media. Thank you to Sabrina Callahan and Gabby Leporati for genuinely loving this book and helping to get it out into the world. Liv Ryan, thank you for all your help along the way—and for the brilliant title!! Linda Arends, my production editor, thank you for understanding when I got pink eye twice in the same month and had to push deadlines. Gregg Kulick, thank you for the fantastic and beautifully creepy cover. Eileen Chetti, you are a copyediting genius, and I bow to you. And thank you to Laura Mamelok and Nancy Weiss for handling UK and foreign rights—it is a rare treat to see my work cross the ocean.

Writing a novel can be very solitary work, so I must thank the writers in my life who have not only kept me company on the journey but who have also read pages and lent their brilliant minds to share notes on this project. JoAnneh Nagler, Julia Erwin-Weiner, Katrina Ryan, Marc Morgenstern, and Genio Borghi—thank you for all your wisdom and support week after week. Having a core writers' group has meant so much to me, and you are all so talented. To my Stanford buddies Jessie Weaver and Tracey Lange—you are both not only prolific and, therefore, an inspiration, but you are also so supportive. Thank you, Jessie, for answering my endless, panicked texts about every stage of the process. And Julia Seales—we met more recently, but you have been so kind and generous and the biggest cheerleader.

As this book touches on so many of the difficulties I faced as a new mother, I want to thank my dear friends who have evolved into mom friends over the years—and who held my hand through the hardest days, both before and after kids. Thank you, Rachel Franco, for sharing your story with me and lending an ear. Thank you, Juli Enke, one of my favorite people on this planet, for telling me again and again that exclusively pumping did not make me a failure. Thank you, Laura Scott, for your willingness to always laugh at life and, in turn, brighten the lives of those around you. And thank you, Kitty Keating, for being my

ACKNOWLEDGMENTS

lifelong friend and number one resource for all questions about parenting. Pretty sure the two of us are keeping Marco Polo in business.

I need to also acknowledge those who have been with me through all of life's highs and lows, like Rachel Leeds (the OG and forever BFF), Sara Scott (my second mom), Kaycee Stahl (the coolest person I know), Caroline Ryon (okay, also the coolest person I know), and my ride-or-die LA family: Nina Shamloo, Whitney Fern, and Bianka Cisneros. You three have been by my side for the last decade. We've grown and evolved together in miraculous ways, and what a joy it has been to share the journey with such kind, capable women.

And, of course, my family:

Jimmy, I love that becoming parents has brought us closer than ever. I know that this is a book you would normally never pick up, so thanks in advance for reading and loving it!! Truly, though, thank you for supporting me. There's nothing quite like the approval of your big brother.

And thank you to my sister, Dawn, for loving my children like your own and for your abundant generosity and endless support. You and Jimmy are raising incredible little ones. It is so fun and such a privilege to Mom beside you.

To my dad, Jim Walters: I remember the hours you spent glued to your desk working on your own book. Our projects could not be more different—though perhaps yours was also a horror in its own right—but the work ethic required is the same. I have always admired your passion, curiosity, and persistence. Most of all, I am so impressed by your willingness to dive into new projects and teach yourself new skills. Few people have such an innate drive to learn new things. Thank you for bestowing on me this love of learning. It is one of the greatest gifts of my life.

ACKNOWLEDGMENTS

To my mom, Alana Walters: You have absolutely, without a doubt, been my biggest cheerleader from day one. How does one properly thank another for that kind of support? You have been a constant source of creativity, artistic inspiration, and love. Growing up, you ferried me from piano lessons to singing lessons to play practice to dance…and I truly cannot think of one time that you ever complained. Instead, we laughed and listened to country music in the car and ate veggie roll-ups. Thank you. I love you so much.

A special shout-out to Uncle Josh for gifting me and Marco some date nights—and for being an essential part of our extended family. And Indy, thank you for all the sweet cuddles and for always staring at me intensely enough that I'm forced to get some Vitamin D at the park.

Luna, you are a big ol' bed-hog. But your heart is even bigger. You have a soul sweeter than most humans I've met. We are so lucky that you chose us.

Chiara, my baby girl. You made me a mother and, in turn, a better daughter as well. There's a fire in your soul that will change the world. But for now, I'm more than happy to cuddle up together and watch The Lion King for the seventy-third time.

Francesco, my rambunctious and deliciously sweet boy. You are the center of gravity wherever you go. Your joy is infectious. I will never forget your chubby little fingers always reaching for me to bring you "uppy." I could hug you all day, my little koala.

And Marco. My partner in all things. My best friend. We have built a life that is better than any fantasy. One of the greatest gifts of having children with you has been watching you blossom as a father. You are, by far, the best man for the job. Thank you for loving us fearlessly. We are all so lucky to have you. *Grazie, amore. Sei il mio chiodo fisso.*

About the Author

Jacquie Walters is an Emmy-nominated screenwriter who has sold five pilots in the last three years. In all, she has written and produced over a hundred episodes of television. Jacquie designed her own major as an Echols Scholar at the University of Virginia and later graduated from the novel-writing program at Stanford University. She lives in Los Angeles with her husband, two children, and beloved golden retriever.